REVENGE
of the
PAST

Narielle Living

Cactus Mystery Press
an imprint of Blue Fortune Enterprises, LLC

REVENGE OF THE PAST
Copyright © 2019 by Narielle Living.

All rights reserved. Printed in the United States of America. No part of this book may be used or reproduced in any manner whatsoever without written permission except in the case of brief quotations embodied in critical articles or reviews.

This book is a work of fiction. Names, characters, businesses, organizations, places, events and incidents either are the product of the author's imagination or are used fictitiously. Any resemblance to actual persons, living or dead, events, or locales is entirely coincidental.

For information contact :
Blue Fortune Enterprises, LLC
Cactus Mystery Press
P.O. Box 554
Yorktown, VA 23690
blue-fortune.com

Book and Cover design by Wesley Miller, WAMCreate, wamcreate.co

ISBN: 978-1-948979-06-1

Third Edition: February 2019

Dedication

In memory of
Linda Booth
August 3, 1942 – August 30, 2012
Our friend and neighbor, who was always there with
love, support, and encouragement.
You are greatly missed.

PROLOGUE

May, 1861
Watertown, CT

THWACK.

It's much harder to kill a human than a farm animal. For one thing, this particular human was bigger than the pigs they owned; with the pigs, it was one quick blow to the head, then straight to the butchering.

Thwack.

There was no need for that type of butchering today, nor was there a need to take care of the carcass; there would be no food from this endeavor.

With a sharp axe, anything is possible. She knew enough to aim for the head, making sure the job was done right. She didn't want the unthinkable to happen; she didn't want Titus to survive.

Placing the axe head down on the wide plank floor, she leaned against it as if it were a cane and stared out the window. She didn't see the blood-spattered pane or the tattered gray cotton hanging over the window, focusing instead on the land outside.

The early dawn light had brightened the sky enough for her to see the shine of the dew-soaked yellow chrysanthemums by the barn. The Connecticut countryside rolled out before her, rich in greenery and resources. If rumors were true, though, that could change quickly, and devastation would strike. Everyone was talking about the War, the North against the South. There would be plenty of bloodshed if the Confederate army invaded, that much was certain.

Glancing over at the bed, she noted that it looked like she'd been successful.

Titus' face was barely recognizable, covered in blood with the skull partially caved in and an ear hanging off. His chest had stopped its rise and fall, a sure indication that no air entered his body.

It was done, and nobody knew she'd been here.

She could leave now, secure in the knowledge that the morning's bloodshed in this house of sin would eliminate the stain of evil like a cleanser to the soul. She'd eliminated a very foul beast that reached into every one of them and grabbed hold of their persons, making them commit unspeakable acts. Now this threat was gone, and future generations of her family could live without fearing the wickedness.

She had to do this, not just for herself, but for all of them. She killed so she wouldn't be killed. But may God have mercy on her soul, she couldn't remember the last time she'd had so much fun.

CHAPTER ONE

Present Day

KATIE WONDERED IF THIS WAS the night her life would end—from a heart attack. Her heart pounded in her chest, painful and ready to burst. It was a good thing she didn't have to run right now, or she'd be dead.

"I really don't want to do this."

"C'mon, it'll be good for us," her friend Ella encouraged.

"'Good' as in, 'Vegetables are good for you', or 'good' as in 'My boyfriend is a police officer, and he's making me do this so you should come with me' sort of good for us?" Katie scrunched down in the front seat of Ella's car, hoping a magical traffic jam would appear and make it impossible to get to class.

"Katie Hollister, how can learning self-defense be a bad thing?"

Katie shook her head. "It's not a bad thing, and philosophically I have no objection to this."

Ella continued as if Katie hadn't spoken. "Besides, it's for women only, and it's taught by law enforcement, so it's bound to help keep us safe, right?"

"Says the woman who still doesn't lock her doors," Katie muttered.

It amazed Katie that Ella was so blasé about home security. They lived in a relatively low crime area, but that didn't mean there was none. Crime still happened. This past summer, Ella had dealt with more than a few problems in her new house. First, there was the ghost of a woman murdered there decades before, while at the same time some of the less enlightened locals spray painted nasty messages on the side of the house. Katie closed her eyes, wondering how her friend was able to maintain a positive outlook on life considering the prejudice and horror Ella had faced.

But the real reason Katie didn't want to go had nothing to do with ghosts or local attitudes. Katie wasn't afraid of ghosts. If she had been, she wouldn't have been able to live in the house she'd grown up in. And she wasn't afraid of learning self-defense techniques, either. It might actually be good for her.

If she could get away with only taking the first week of class, that would be perfect. But Ella had asked, cajoled her into it really. Ella's boyfriend, Kevin, suggested the class, saying it was important that they learned the techniques. In order to take this class, though, Katie had to commit to being there for all the nights of instruction.

Which would be fine, except...

...the final night was a test of sorts. It was a simulated attack, performed by the police officers who were teaching it. They would wear protective gear and attack the women, creating real life scenarios. The test would be if the women were able to use what they'd learned and escape.

Being attacked, even for a benign purpose, scared Katie spitless.

She knew she wouldn't be able to handle men coming at her, even if they weren't actually going to hurt her.

She didn't want to do this class, but Ella had talked her into going to the first one. Then, when it was too late and she'd already signed up, she found out how it would end.

Badly, she was sure. What was going to happen when they knocked her down or roughed her up or did whatever they were going to do and Katie couldn't escape? What was going to happen when she ended up lying on the floor in a heap of fear?

But she had promised Ella, and she always kept her promises to her friends.

Katie crossed her long legs at the ankles, jamming her ringless fingers into her fleece jacket pocket. She'd fortified herself for the night, knowing a drink or two would help calm her nerves. Nobody would smell the vodka on her breath, and it would help her get through the ordeal.

Good thing she'd done that because it looked like there wasn't going to be any traffic jam to help her out.

They had arrived.

"Straight kick, go!"

"Straight punch, go!"

Reuben's voice, naturally loud, barked out commands that ripped through

Katie. She was tired, sweaty, and starting to feel more than a little cranky. They'd been practicing kicks, punches, and blocks for a solid thirty minutes.

If she'd known it would be this grueling, Katie might have filled her entire water bottle with vodka.

The overhead fluorescent lights of the school gym made a buzzing noise, an annoying sound that added to Katie's emerging headache. Maybe the school gym smell had triggered it, but memories of physical education classes gone wrong were drifting through her mind. She tried in vain to suppress the particularly distasteful ones that involved rope climbing and gymnastics equipment, unsuccessful activities during her school experience. She didn't want to relive those moments for anything, and she tried not to think about it. Right now, she needed to endure Reuben and his barking commands.

Reuben might be tough, but he wasn't the boss of her. Maybe she'd just stop on the pretext of needing a breath of fresh air; then she could wait out the rest of the class. Or maybe she could twist her ankle, sort of accidentally on purpose.

"Hollister!" Reuben yelled.

Katie sighed. *Now what?*

"How tough are you?"

"Not very," she admitted.

"Yeah, well, that's not going to do you much good when you're being abducted."

Katie shook her head. "Nope, it's not."

"You got a death wish or something? Let's see you put a little more effort into those punches. Nothin' to be afraid of here; this is the place you get to practice this stuff."

She knew he meant well, but Reuben was starting to be a real pain in the ass.

"Katie-love…"

Every muscle hurt; yet another divine benefit from class the night before. And she was dreaming about Hannah again, dreaming that the ghost was right there in the room with her. Not that there was anything wrong with dreaming about a ghost, but a part of Katie's mind wondered if Hannah was real. True, she'd believed in Hannah as a child, the same way she'd believed in fairies and unicorns. But that was a different time, and her childhood was long gone.

"Katie-love, you have to listen to me. There's a danger coming to you…"

Katie could barely hear the lilting Irish voice trying to speak to her. The words sounded like they were far away.

"Really, this is very, very important."

The voice was insistent, which made Katie not want to listen. What kind of dream did this, anyway? It was just her luck to get a hallucination who nagged.

Katie heard a ghostly sigh. "Fine then, have it your way. I'm starting to fade, anyhow. But I'm afraid you're going to have to get up, since your mother is waiting for you downstairs." After a moment's pause, the voice added, "There are pancakes, too. Blueberry."

Katie opened her eyes a little at a time, adjusting to the bright sunlight spilling through the windows. Boxes were stacked in every corner of the room, jewelry spilling all over the lace runner on the bureau, and a hodge-podge of clothing and shoes scattered about.

Although her stomach was queasy, she eased herself out of bed, driven by the thought of pancakes. A good, solid breakfast would probably go a long way toward making her feel better about life in general.

It was moving day for the Hollister family. Not for her, though; she'd already packed everything she owned and trucked it all the mile and a half to her parents' house. All of her things were lying in boxes, waiting to be unpacked. This was her new life—her new life in her old childhood home.

Times are tough for everybody these days, Katie reasoned as she struggled to pull a brush through her long, blonde hair. Katie couldn't help feeling remorse over being forced into this move.

She was broke. Her salary wasn't enough to cover her expenses anymore, and the bills kept piling up. Katie was desperately afraid of losing her house. She was only twenty-eight years old, and she reasoned that ever since the economy had tanked it was difficult for many people to pay their bills. Luck was on her side, however, and within a month of listing her house with a real estate agent, Katie received an offer that was too good to turn down—especially for someone facing bank foreclosure.

Things could be worse. I could be living at home with Mom and Dad. That would truly be a nightmare.

Her father, a retired minister, was looking forward to living in a different part of the country. Her mother, a retired bank manager, seemed equally enthusiastic. Not only were they leaving behind the working life, they were moving to Scottsdale, Arizona, a place they felt most at home.

"Scottsdale, watch out," Katie muttered, throwing on an old sweatshirt.

"Here comes Belinda and Paul."

"I'm leaving behind all the syrups you like, plus a good supply of food in the pantry. You should be set for a week or so with that." Katie's mother hovered, looking uncertain. "Do you want us to leave anything else?"

"Mom, I'm going to be fine. Don't worry, I'll take good care of the place. You and Dad just focus on getting to your new house and loving your retirement. I'll be right as rain."

The creases deepened on her mother's forehead. "Remember, you don't have to worry about a thing. Stay here as long as you need; we don't have to sell this place yet. I don't know if we'll ever want to sell, it's been in our family so long. Do you know your father lasted almost thirty years as minister for Grace Church?"

Katie put her fork down. "Belinda, he's my father. Of course I know that. Don't worry, I'll be fine."

Her mother sniffled. "Sweetheart, that's what mothers do, we worry about our kids. But you're right, I know. I was just packing the last of my things yesterday and thinking about this old house." Belinda took a seat at the kitchen table and continued talking. "Our family has lived here since the late 1800s." Her mother got that far off look Katie knew so well, the look that told everyone she was reliving her heritage. "It's almost as if the Hollister family was meant to be here, ever since Hannah Donovan migrated from Connecticut all the way to Yorktown in 1867. Can you imagine the hardships that poor girl had to endure?"

Katie cleared her throat in an attempt to reel her mother back. "So, Dad showed me where all the shut-off valves are, and I think I know enough about the house to be able to take care of any maintenance issues. I also have the plumber's and electrician's phone numbers in case of an emergency."

Snapping back to the present, Belinda's face was serious as she regarded her daughter. "You know we're going to take care of the taxes for you until you get back on your feet. I don't want you to worry."

Katie's face tightened as she struggled to smile. "Thanks, Mom. I appreciate that. But for now, you can take your bank manager's hat off and relax. Are you sure the car is completely packed?"

Her diversion worked. Belinda launched into a detailed account of everything she packed for their drive west, including emergency supplies.

Katie let the sound of her mother's voice drift over her, loving the cadence yet struggling with feelings of being smothered. Sometimes that's how her mother made her feel. It was all going to be fine, if she could only manage to get her parents out the door and on their way.

Her mother's voice continued. "...and of course, the only thing that really tears me up is leaving you kids behind. My word, especially now, with you coming home and Anna Louise and her health issues, your father and I almost had second thoughts about leaving."

Katie blinked. "Mom, what are you talking about? We're all fine. This is something you and Dad have been wanting to do forever." Her mother's words finally sunk in. "What do you mean, Anna Louise has health problems?"

Anna Louise was her sister-in-law, her brother Beau's lovely wife, an incredible asset to his well-built home. Katie didn't really mind being around Anna Louise, but she and her brother had trouble seeing eye-to-eye on most things. Beau believed in his own point of view being the only point of view, often creating friction between brother and sister. Sometimes Katie wondered if her brother told his wife how she was supposed to view the world as much as he told his sister. It's not like Katie felt sorry for her sister-in-law; the woman had made her choice to marry Beau and seemed happy with it.

I wonder if Anna Louise's health problems are from living with a man as uptight as Beau. That's not fair, I know. I love my brother; I just wish we got along better.

Katie's mother gazed at her, appearing lost in thought.

"Um, hello...? Earth to Mom...? We were talking about Anna Louise, remember? What's going on with her?"

Belinda blinked. "Yes, dear, I do remember. I guess you forgot the conversation we had last week with your brother's wife, where she told you what was happening." There was a slight pause before Belinda added, "Don't worry. It's just female problems. I'm sure they'll work it all out."

Katie had a fleeting memory of listening to Anna Louise talking about something or other, but it had been at a recent dinner at Beau's house, and Katie had had too much wine. The wine drowned out the unnecessary chatter and made her feel less alone. She loved her family, but even in the midst of family gatherings she felt isolated.

Katie wondered with guilt if maybe the chatter wasn't so unnecessary, but there was no point in thinking about it now. Her mother was still talking, and Katie was having trouble keeping up.

"...so we'll check in with you at night by sending an email. I can do that from my phone now, isn't that amazing?"

Katie nodded. "Amazing."

"What will they think of next?"

"Who?"

Katie's mother looked at her, a puzzled frown on her face. "Excuse me, dear? Who are you asking about?"

"What will who think of next? Who are 'they'?"

Belinda sighed in exasperation. "Katie, really, haven't you outgrown saying that to me?"

Smiling, Katie answered, "Nope, I don't think that's going to happen."

Belinda smiled in response, leaning forward to push the hair off her daughter's face. "Darling, promise you'll call if you need anything?"

"Don't worry about me, Mom. Besides, I've got Hannah here with me."

"I haven't seen her around lately."

"That's because Dad's retired. You know he doesn't believe in her, so she probably stays as far away as possible from his scoffing attitude."

Katie wasn't certain she actually believed there was a ghost in the house, either, despite the number of times she heard the voice. It was easier to go along with her mother on this one, yet Katie wondered. Of course, she knew ghosts existed, that much was obvious—but a permanent house ghost? Katie thought maybe she was simply going crazy or sometimes had too much to drink. After all, why would a ghost hang around with her family for well over a century? Wouldn't she at least want to move on, go to Heaven or wherever she was supposed to go?

"He's not the only one with the attitude in this house." Belinda looked at her sternly over the rim of a coffee cup. "I seem to remember that someone else at this table had trouble acknowledging our ancestress from a century and a half ago."

"Mom —" Katie did not want to have this discussion now.

"You know, Katie, if it wasn't for Hannah..."

Katie hated this. She did not want to discuss it with anyone, ever. Unfortunately, her mother didn't realize how much she loathed the subject.

"...you might not be alive today."

CHAPTER TWO

KATIE HATED DREDGING UP THOSE memories, but the feeling of being shackled to her chair crept over her as Belinda told the story... again. She knew exactly what her mother would say, word for word, and as expected, Belinda began by sadly shaking her head.

"That poor girl. I wonder whatever happened to her."

"You mean Liz? She moved."

A door slammed shut in Katie's head. Sometimes she could distract her mind enough not to be swallowed by the memories, but that didn't always work. Sometimes, even the biggest distraction in the world couldn't keep the floodgates closed.

"I'll never forget the look on your face... Hannah brought me straight to that place where he had you. I didn't know she could leave here; up until then, I thought she was stuck wandering this house." Belinda continued, oblivious to her daughter's discomfort. "My God, when I think of how it might have ended..."

The problem was, Katie knew how it ended. Not in the worst possible way, but certainly not in a good way. Eyes shut, the door in her mind creaked open to the time she was ten years old. Back to the time when she thought she knew everything, thought grown up rules were stupid, thought she could take care of herself. Back to the time when she had a best friend named Liz who lived across the street.

That day had been hot, sticking to them like a melted popsicle. They started out with nothing to do, and Katie wished it had stayed that way.

"C'mon, let's go, he needs our help!"

"But, Liz, we don't know him..."

Katie's voice trailed off as she squinted at the man standing in front of them. Her mother and father always told her not to go with strangers, and this man definitely qualified as a stranger.

Liz blew out an exasperated breath, causing her straight brown bangs to rise off her forehead. "For gosh sakes, he lives in the neighborhood! Besides, look how big he is. How's he supposed to get that kitten from that little space in his house? We've gotta help him, or the kitten's gonna die!"

Katie knew her friend had a point, but that was only if there was a kitten. The thing was, Liz couldn't stand any type of cruelty to animals. Katie had seen her friend rescue frogs from deep pails and put earthworms back in the grass. There was no way Liz would walk away from a kitten that needed saving.

But still, Katie had a bad feeling about this man, mostly because she didn't know him—and her mother always said don't trust a stranger. Now he was looking at them funny, his mouth clamped shut like he was trying not to yell at her or something.

"Are you girls gonna help me? Because I have a feeling that little guy's been stuck up there a while now, and we might not have much time left—especially on a hot day like this; his insides will just boil him to death. You don't want him to die, do you?" In Katie's eyes the man was big, really big, and something about him didn't seem right.

"I don't care if you're going or not," Liz announced to her friend. "I'm not going to let a helpless little kitten die."

Katie knew what she had to do: she had to get help from a grown up. The problem was, if she left her friend now, she didn't know where this guy was going to take Liz. It was better for her to stay with them so she could get help later.

Straightening her spine to make herself taller, Katie nodded. "Okay, I'll go with you." But I don't trust him, she added silently.

They walked through the quiet suburban neighborhood, down a maze of streets Katie had never seen before. "Liz," she whispered, "where are we?"

"We're still in our neighborhood, silly." Liz giggled, amused that Katie didn't know her own neighborhood.

Finally, the man stopped in front of a small brick ranch house with overgrown grass in the front yard. One of the shutters hung crooked, giving the house an unkempt appearance.

"Let's go around the back," he said, putting an arm around each girl. Katie didn't like the way his arm felt and tried to wriggle away. The man tightened his grip,

pinching her shoulder and quickening his pace. He let go of Liz to open the back screen door and pushed Katie in behind her friend.

Katie's mind was blank with fear. Part of her wanted to scream, but she knew it wasn't polite to yell. She stumbled slightly upon entering the kitchen, and the man reached out a hand to steady her before smiling. That's when she noticed that his teeth weren't just crooked, but very, very yellow.

"I think we're going to have fun," he told them.

Despite the warmth of the late September morning, Katie was chilled.

"Honey, are you okay?" her mother's voice cast around her like a net, reeling her back to the present. "Did you hear what I said?"

Katie's eyes refocused, taking in the familiar kitchen surroundings. Blue checked curtains hung in the windows, and the light oak cabinets held a soft shine. The brown countertops were wiped clean, gleaming against the butter yellow walls. She heard the soft ticking of the kitchen clock over the sound of her breathing and was able to focus on the rooster painted on the clock face.

"I'm fine, Mom... fine." She managed to keep her hands steady as she brought the coffee cup to her lips.

"I know it's still hard to think about that day. It's hard for all of us. When I think of what that man could have done to you..."

Did. Her mother didn't realize that it was more about what that man did to her, not what could have happened. It was always about that. That was the day she became isolated from the rest of the world.

"Thank God I could see Hannah." Belinda's voice was shaky, as it always was when she spoke of that day.

Katie had no intention of telling her mother anything, but before she knew it, the words were tumbling out of her mouth. "Hannah was in my room this morning."

It wasn't often that Katie got to see her mother caught up short, as there wasn't much that surprised Belinda Hollister. This, however, surprised Belinda Hollister. Her hands fluttered up to her face, as if they were uncertain of what to do with themselves.

"But... you've never seen her before, have you?"

Katie shook her head slowly, surprised that she had told her mother. After all, confessing to hearing a ghost was like telling the world you were crazy. Sort of. Her friend Ella had seen a ghost over the summer in her new house, but that was different. Ella was obviously not crazy, Ella was the dependable, solid type; whereas Katie... well, Katie wasn't always known for making good, solid choices. It was easy to believe Ella, but the thought of Hannah always made Katie uncomfortable.

Maybe because Hannah was, and always would be, tied to the events of that day.

"No, Mom. As far as I know, you're the only one in the family who has seen our house ghost. But I did hear her this morning." She neglected to mention the other times Hannah had appeared. It wasn't significant, and why encourage her mother?

Belinda nodded. "I wonder what she wanted. Usually, she comes to us because she has something to tell us... something—" She paused as if to make sure her words were just right. "Important."

"Hmmm... do you know how she ended up here?"

Belinda shook her head. "No. All I know is that Hannah Donovan is related through my grandmother's side of the family, and she allegedly came here in 1867."

"I wonder what she was running from?"

"What makes you think she was running from something?"

To Katie's relief, the doorbell pealed. She didn't want to tell her mother how she knew anything about Hannah since she didn't know where her information came from. Katie didn't always remember when Hannah spoke to her or the specifics of what she said, but that wasn't a comfortable subject either. But one thing was certain, and that was that Hannah must have shared at least part of her story with Katie because Katie was absolutely certain her ancestress had arrived in Yorktown as a result of running from something.

The voices from the front hallway filtered back to the kitchen. Katie suppressed a groan, knowing it would be in poor manners to act unwelcoming. But, really... first, she was awakened by a supposed ghost, then her mother had to bring up the whole childhood thing, and now this.

"Katie, it's so good to see you! Goodness, you're looking a little like the morning doesn't agree with you." Ella's sister Lisa was not known for her tact. Or subtlety.

Standing behind Lisa, Ella made a 'sorry' face. Katie smiled at her, hoping to convey a sense of understanding. She knew her friend was regretting bringing Lisa but probably had no choice in the matter. Since Lisa had moved to Virginia a few weeks ago, she had been a constant but not always welcome presence in everyone's life.

"So, Belinda, are you packed and ready to go?"

Lisa, not worried about being overly familiar, made her way across the kitchen straight to the cabinet door and got a mug. Katie had a moment's confusion, wondering how Lisa knew where the coffee mugs were kept.

Sharing a look with her mother, Katie shrugged. Who knew how Lisa knew anything? *Must be some sort of animal instinct.* After pouring herself a cup of coffee, Lisa started roaming around the room, absently picking up objects and putting them down.

Belinda cleared her throat. "Yes, we're packed and ready to leave. I expect we'll be getting on the road later this afternoon."

"I just don't know how you did it all by yourself. I absolutely couldn't have packed everything myself. In fact, I insisted to Dan that he had to hire movers who did all the packing. It's such tedious work, don't you think?"

Fortunately, Belinda seemed amused by Lisa. Katie reflected that all her years as a pastor's wife served her mother well in situations like this.

Ella interrupted her sister. "Katie, we came over to see if you needed any help today. You were so helpful this summer when I moved that I hoped to return the favor."

Lisa picked up a plate from a shelf on the baker's rack and turned it over. "Huh. Pfaltzgraff. I didn't think anyone bought that stuff anymore." Once again, Ella shot Katie an apologetic look.

"Thanks, Ella, but I think we're all set. Mom and Dad are packed and ready to go, my furniture is here, and most of my boxes have been unpacked. I only have a few boxes left." Automatically, her thoughts strayed to what was in there. She was saving the last boxes for when she was alone in the house, after her parents left. She really wasn't up for answering questions about the contents or listening to a lecture about it. They were her boxes, her life.

Lisa's attention shifted to Katie. "So, will you be redesigning this kitchen? I don't think this layout really works. It's an interesting house, though. These old Southern homes have a certain charm. Do you have a ghost, too?"

Katie swallowed past the dryness in her throat. She was going to have to unpack those last boxes as soon as possible if she was going to make it through this day.

CHAPTER THREE

SOME DAYS WERE EASIER THAN others for Cleve Yodell, and today qualified as not only easy, but advantageous. There was nothing quite like the feeling of killing someone to make your day brighter.

He had known for almost a year about his wife's lover. She wasn't very good at hiding these things, but he let her believe that she had kept her little secret. As the months went by, her carelessness grew, as did her belief that she wouldn't get caught.

In a way, it was too bad he had to do this to her. He liked her more than he had liked any other woman in his life, which was why he married her. She was certainly beautiful, and the sex was better than average. But it became clear to him in the past twelve months that she was going to hold him back if he stayed married to her. She didn't have the vision he had or the ability to see how much better their life could be.

She actually liked their lives and the drafty old house they lived in. She liked knowing that his family, one of the original New England settlers, had lived there for generations. She was fond of saying how wonderful it was that the house had a "history" and thought it gave them a certain standing in the community.

He could never understand how she equated that drafty old pile of timber with the idea that it made them someone. How could she not see the derisive looks townspeople shot at the house?

Besides, they lived in Watertown, Connecticut; not exactly a location dripping with culture, despite what his wife thought. It was a fairly small town, without much industry or business. Located in the middle of the state, the quiet population usually found work in neighboring cities. His wife thought the town was a great place to live, quaint and cute; he found it stifling.

But your ancestors were among the first settlers in this town, she argued. *Of course your family is important; you should be proud of that fact. We should look into getting you in some of the holiday parades, wouldn't that be great? I'll talk to the people at the Historical Society.*

As if the people at the Historical Society had ever cared about him and his family. He was fond of his wife, but sometimes he wondered why he cared about someone who wasn't very smart.

Maybe he cared because she served a purpose, and her death would help him move on to the next phase of his life, the important phase. And although he always enjoyed killing, it was too bad that she was one of the people who had to die.

It was simple, really. After all, most of his plans had been in place for a while now. The cash was hidden in a lock box in the attic, enough to last him a year if he was careful. The papers forging his new identity were there as well. Untraceable.

If all went as planned, he would be able to implement everything in just a few months. Once the score was settled, he could begin a whole new life, a life in which he took his rightful place in the world, a life filled with the things his family should have had over a century ago.

The life that the voice had told him was his for the taking.

Leaning back against the cheaply made headboard of the bargain motel off the highway, Cleve thought about what had led him to Scranton, Pennsylvania that night. He'd known upon waking that morning that today was the day. It was early September, summer was done, and it was a perfect time for a new beginning.

Also, the voice had whispered to him. It always told the truth. *Our time has come. We must act now, before it's too late.*

He mentioned to his wife that morning that he wouldn't be home until around seven. He even managed to grumble a little about the boss making him work late, how it wasn't fair that everyone else was going to be getting out at five and he had to stay late and work on the presentation.

Pressing against him, she gave him a hug and told him not to worry. "I'll miss you, and I'll be right here waiting for you," she said with a smile, looking sexy in her short nightgown and sleep tousled hair.

He admired the depth of her deception. It was too bad, really. If things were a little bit different, she might have been a good partner for him. But now…

At precisely four p.m., he turned onto the street where he had grown up and lived his entire life. Turning the car engine off before he reached the driveway, he coasted to a stop on the dirt space where he always parked. With the windows down, he could hear periodic birdsong in the air as he assessed the scene in front of him. Nobody was around, which was perfect. There weren't many neighbors anyway, but the last thing he wanted was some nosy little kid walking by the house to sell Girl Scout cookies and ruining everything; then he would have to kill three people, and that just made things more complicated.

He slipped through the back door that he had oiled last weekend, removing his shoes and placing them on the kitchen mat. It was obvious from the upstairs noises what was going on.

It was exactly what he had hoped for.

The tricky part was not leaving any marks. Although the fire would destroy most of the evidence, Cleve was smart enough to know that not even fire could cover up a bullet hole in the skull. Sometimes bullets could be traced, too, especially with all the gun paranoia and anti-terrorist measures government agencies had these days. Sometimes people worried about the darndest things.

The house was old, but he knew to walk on the outer edge of the stairs as he silently made his way toward the people upstairs. His backpack held all the tools he needed for his day's work.

At the top of the stairs, he stopped, careful to look in the hallway before stepping out. After being certain nobody was in the hallway, he turned left and went into the bathroom. The upstairs bathroom had two entrances, one from the hallway and one from the master bedroom.

It was an ideal setup.

Silent, he stepped into the bathtub and stood behind the shower curtain. Opening his backpack, he took out the cloth and zip ties, leaving the backpack sitting in the tub. He was a patient man. His knew his wife always used the toilet after sex. Waiting in the shadows of the bathroom, he found himself oddly aroused by the sounds and smell of copulation, excited by the eroticism of sex mingled with the knowledge of imminent death.

By the time his wife entered the bathroom, he couldn't stop the grin from spreading across his face. Stepping out of the bathtub, he reached out and touched her arm. All it took was one moment, a stunned instant when she couldn't speak, and he was able to shove the cloth gag into her mouth. Working quickly to subdue her, he bound her arms and legs, ensuring that the zip ties were secure and she was unable to move. Unfortunately, she didn't cry. He was expecting tears, had even braced himself for them; instead, she just looked up at him, eyes wide with terror, body trembling.

No remorse must have meant she didn't care about him at all, that Cleve meant nothing to her. Perhaps it was better that she died.

"Don't move, or I'll kill you right now," he whispered.

Leaving her on the bathroom floor, it was time for the next phase. Reaching back into his bag of tools, he removed the items he needed, shoving them into his back pocket. Opening the door a crack, he peered into the bedroom. Her lover lay sprawled across the bed, hairy chest rising and falling with his breath, penis flaccid against his gorilla legs. The man's eyes were closed, and his arms were stretched above his body.

All it took was one well-aimed, powerful blow to the solar plexus, and the man was doubled over in pain, unable to breathe. Cleve quickly pulled more ties from his pocket, wrapping them around the lover's wrists and ankles and shoving a gag in his mouth.

The gags were the most important part of his tool kit. If there was one thing Cleve couldn't stand, it was sniveling and whining, and he didn't want to hear it from either one of them. Besides, it cut down on the chances of anyone hearing shouts from the house.

Then the fun part. Walking back into the bathroom, he dragged his wife by her hair, then lifted and tossed her onto a chair in the bedroom. Both of them were securely tied, unable to move, unable to speak. They were the perfect audience, really.

Locked in the stuffy upstairs master bedroom of the old house, Cleve was able to provide them with the details of what was happening.

It's important to know why you must die, Cleve reasoned. So, he paced back and forth in the room, outlining his plans, his hopes, and his dreams.

"All these years, my family has been in a position of not having anything, of not being anyone. All these years, we've had the misfortune to be who we are, to live here in this cursed house. But I'm the one who will change all that. I'm the one who will see to it that the Yodell family gets what they deserve." He paused for a moment, a high pitched giggle escaping. "Of course, the Yodell family is really only me, but who knows? Maybe someday I'll find... another. And we're about to change, morph into something new. I even have a new name...would you like to know it?"

The tears were finally there. His wife couldn't stop crying, silent sobs of desperation. That was more like it.

"Don't worry, you've played a very important part in all of this. I think you'll like my new name. I kept the same first name, you see," he was pacing, nodding at them as he spoke, "because it's just easier, and I'm less likely to slip up. My new last name is Farrington. Don't you think that's perfect? It makes me sound like an important, rich person, just like you always insisted my family was..." He was trying to be reassuring, but he didn't think his prey was in a mood to be reassured. What a pity.

He briefly debated telling them about the other, then dismissed the idea; they weren't evolved enough to understand.

"Now that you understand the big picture, we come to the entertainment portion of the evening." Cleve pointed at his wife's lover, who was immobilized on the bed. "Let's start with you."

A fire in the middle of the night is truly beautiful, Cleve mused. The image of the flames dancing against the black sky was one he would treasure, especially since he had hated that house for so long. And now it was gone, up in smoke, the ashes mixed with his wife and her lover.

Cleve smiled, reliving the moment when he realized his careful planning had paid off. The money hidden in the lockbox, the new driver's license, the motorcycle he had stolen from the doomed lover—it had all been used that night to make his escape. Of course, he'd had to ditch the motorcycle and use his own later. He wouldn't want to get pulled over for driving stolen property.

Still smiling, he got up from his hotel room bed, noticing the thin, cheap comforter. Soon enough, he wouldn't have to stay in a pit like this. Soon enough, he would have everything he was entitled to, which was a hell of a lot.

But first he had to walk out to the dumpster in the back of the parking lot. He had a plastic baggie filled with teeth that he should probably dispose of. Pulling them from the dead lover's mouth had been difficult, but this would most definitely delay the identification of the corpse.

He had no illusions that it would be overlooked. He gave law enforcement more credit than that—certainly a man missing his teeth would be noted at an autopsy. But for now, at least, he was hopeful they would assume it was Cleve who died with his wife in the fire.

CHAPTER FOUR

HEADLIGHTS SHONE IN HER REARVIEW mirror, momentarily blinding her. Squinting at the scene in front of her, Dani Burgess scowled. It would have to be Jimmy Russo, pulling in too close and too fast behind her at almost the same pre-dawn hour. The September night air in Connecticut was laced with a chill that held the usual foreboding of winter, but Dani barely noticed the temperature; what mattered right then was the mess she was going to have to sort through. The call had come in around 4:30 in the morning, and it had only taken the two detectives a half hour to haul themselves out of their respective beds and get there—but it was twenty-five minutes more than it should have been, and lost time could mean lost evidence.

Dani hoped the exhaustion didn't show on her face. A full day testifying in court, evening classes, and extra studying meant she'd only had a few hours of sleep when the phone rang. If she looked like she felt, Russo was sure to comment.

"You look like shit." He took a moment to hike his pants up over his ever widening waistline. "Those night classes are a bitch, aren't they?"

Taking a deep breath, Dani tried to remain calm. Jimmy wasn't trying to be a jerk, and she had no doubt that he actually thought he was being nice. The fact that he was older played a significant role in his attitude toward women, and the fact that as a friend of her family he had known her as a gawky pre-teen completed the condescending attitude. No matter how hard she worked, Jimmy would always see her as the little kid she used to be. She deliberately ignored his comments and walked over to the fire chief, George Fuller.

"Do we know who called?" she asked, taking out an index card and pen.

George shook his head, soot and sweat mixed with grimness. "Sounded like kids. The call came in around two o'clock this morning on a cell phone; you can check the record later. My guess is teenagers trying to get home before curfew, didn't want to identify themselves and get in trouble for being out late."

He turned and looked at the house. The firefighters were mostly finished, but they couldn't leave yet. The obvious fire was out, but men still worked, swarming the area to ensure complete obliteration of the flames and checking for remaining hot spots that could possibly ignite later if not dealt with now. Voices and muffled laughter drifted toward Dani, a sure sign that none of the men responding to the call had been hurt and gallows humor was in full effect.

The dispatcher had reported casualties, and she felt a moment's distaste for the surge of adrenalin coursing through her. She loved her job but hated that she loved it. After all, somebody died tonight. She shouldn't feel so happy to be there, but she couldn't avoid what she felt.

This was probably something that was best not mentioned in front of the department shrink, Internal Affairs, or her mother. Really, who the hell enjoyed this sort of work unless they had serious problems?

Dani's mind raced at the possibilities as she surveyed the scene in front of her. The smell of smoke was heavy and would probably cling to her clothes and hair for days to come. At first glance, the house was a blackened ruin, but Dani knew from just looking at the scene that the devastation was far from complete. Most people assumed a fire destroyed everything; they would be surprised at how much of the structure and contents actually survived.

Accident or arson, the cause of the fire would eventually be discovered. She wondered if they could go inside, or if it was still unsafe. Dani knew enough to rely on the fire chief's assessment; he wouldn't let anyone in if it wasn't clear.

Her evening instructor's voice echoed in her head: *You've got to work from the outside in, usually. Start where there's the least amount of damage.* At the moment it was hard to tell, but Dani wondered exactly where that might be since everything in front of her looked fairly charred.

The amount of work she had to do to get through Arson Investigation School was staggering, but it gave her insight into potential crime scenes like this. Tonight made the classes worth it, regardless of the sleep deprivation.

The area was lit with floodlights so the firefighters could see better, illuminating pieces of the occupant's lives, everyday things found in everyone's house. The wall to the kitchen had been mostly destroyed, revealing a stove with a tea kettle resting on a burner while the tattered pieces of a white curtain hung from an upstairs window like a dejected surrender flag. Glancing to the left and right, no neighboring houses were in sight, which was both good and bad; good because it meant the fire did not spread and cause damage to other homes, bad because there were no witnesses.

"So what've you got in there?" Jimmy asked the fire chief.

Dani tensed at the question, feeling put out. She knew her response to Jimmy was unreasonable, but she couldn't help being irritated. She liked to take her time, survey the scene in front of her, and make an assessment before she did anything else. It made sense not to rush things. But since Jimmy was the senior officer, he usually took the lead, leaving her with a constant feeling of trying to catch up to him.

George shook his head. "We'll have to check it out more thoroughly, but my first assessment is that point of origin is the basement."

Dani nodded. Point of origin was where the fire started, and she knew the basements in some of these old houses were ready to go up in flames. People didn't always pay attention to the crap they left lying around, and next thing you know, a fire starts and everything's gone.

George was still talking. "Homeowners probably left their junk lying around down there, never really thought much about it until it was too late. We found two bodies in the upstairs bedroom, we're assuming it's the occupants."

"Who lived here?" Dani wondered if anyone made it out alive.

"The house is owned by Cleve Yodell, and Eileen down at the station told us he lived here with his wife."

"Just the two of them?" Jimmy asked.

George nodded. "Yeah, it might be open and shut, but I doubt it. Of course, we can't know anything for sure until the autopsy comes in. The medical examiner should be here soon. They're over there." He pointed with his head to the far corner of the front yard where two bodies lay, covered by white sheets. Of course, the firefighters had dragged the bodies out when they first went in to fight the fire; they had no way of knowing while they were in the house if the inhabitants were already dead, or alive and unconscious. Everybody knew now.

Dani glanced at her cell phone to check the time, wondering how long it would be before the medical examiner got there and if she should start looking around. Since Watertown was so small, funding was nonexistent, and they relied on the medical examiner in the nearby city of Hartford; unfortunately, nearby meant at least forty minutes, probably closer to an hour.

George stopped staring at the remains of the house and turned to Dani. "There's one more thing, though."

Dani's mind focused, losing the last blurry edges of fatigue. She knew that tone, had heard it plenty of times when George taught one of her arson classes. "I'll bet it's a good one."

"Yep, sure is. When we got here, we could see the smoke coming through the screen doors, front and back."

Dani's gaze snapped back to the house. If there was smoke coming through the screen doors... "That means the front and back doors were open." Nobody left their doors open on a September night in Connecticut, not when temperatures were starting to ease much lower and thermostats were being turned up. It would have helped the fire spread, though.

Jimmy let out a long breath. "Damn. Now it's something else."

George shrugged. "We don't have all the facts. But no, it doesn't look good, since nobody leaves their doors open at night. Hell, nobody I know even leaves their doors unlocked anymore, not like when we were kids."

Dani's eyes narrowed. She had a strange feeling as she surveyed the ruins, a feeling that couldn't always be explained but couldn't be ignored, either.

"How badly are the bodies burned? Is visual identification possible?"

"No, the ME is going to have to do the dental records, that kind of thing. I took a quick look at the bodies, didn't see any obvious signs of anything. They were both in the bed when we found them."

Dani knew there were a number of different ways people tried to cover their crimes. Until she had proof one way or another, she wasn't going to assume anything about this case.

George looked at her and nodded toward her car. "You ready to suit up?"

"Of course," she bristled, wondering if the question was meant to be a comment on her readiness as an investigator. The detached, logical portion of her brain knew it was just a question, but the female detective who was hassled daily by her male co-workers couldn't help wondering if they were just waiting for her to mess up. Well, they'd have to wait a long time. She was ready for this case; she would sort through and figure out whatever had happened here.

"Hey, kid," Jimmy called. Dani turned to him, surprised at the note of tenderness in his voice. "Be careful in there, okay?"

She nodded at him. "Always. Why? You know something I don't?"

Jimmy stared at the ruins in front of him. "Naw, nothing like that. It's just this house, that's all. Could still be hot spots in there, places you can fall through the floor or whatever. But I'm tellin' you, with all the weird shit that's happened here over the years, nothing about this place would surprise me."

CHAPTER FIVE

KATIE SAT IN THE SAFETY of her screened porch at the back of the house. While darkness descended, her thoughts returned to the boxes upstairs, the ones she had shoved under her bed in a lame attempt to hide the contents. She lived alone now, but this particular routine was born from shame rather than necessity. Some habits made no sense, yet they were done anyway, a sort of madness surrounding the actions.

It was ironic, really, the two distinctly different sides of Katie. There was the Katie that the world saw, the bright, beautiful woman with a gracious Southern charm. The smart blonde who wore Laura Ashley-type clothes and showed kindness to everyone she met. The Katie who went to church every Sunday and helped her friends without being asked. That was the woman everyone assumed Katie was. Most people would never believe the other side to Katie could exist—or, Katie hoped they wouldn't believe it. As far as she knew, her secret was safe.

The "other" Katie, the woman fueled by darkness, climbed the stairs to her bedroom. Trying not to think about what she was doing, Katie walked to the side of her perfectly made bed and fell to her knees, reaching a shaking hand under the dust ruffle. The box was labeled "office supplies."

Office supplies, indeed.

Fumbling with the cover, she finally managed to open the box and lift the old day planners balanced on top. She'd been careful with her hiding spot, matching the top contents of the box to the label and hoping nobody would dig any deeper to find what was on the bottom.

Katie was good at hiding things.

And there it was, the amber liquid glistening a warm invitation as she grabbed the neck with sweaty hands.

I wonder what everyone would think of me if they could see me now.

Her trembling, scared hands fumbled to unscrew the cap as a desperate need climbed up her spine. Although the shame ran deep, her desire for alcohol outpaced any actions that could change the course of events. Thoughts of stopping, of not taking this step and eliminating the humiliation she always experienced, were buried in the unreachable part of her soul.

Not today.

Not tonight.

I need this for now.

Her disgrace was born from the knowledge that hiding her actions meant they were wrong. And yet, there were times when this was the only way she could get through the night, the only way the nightmares would go away, and the only way she felt reasonably human.

The times Katie decided to stop drinking were always a failure. She would make up her mind, usually based on a previous night's disastrous events and an intention to live a different kind of life. That was her deepest desire, after all: to live a different life, a life in the open, a life of possibility and hope instead of one in the dark. Some days she was so very tired of it all, hiding the bottles, drinking before she went to parties to make it look like she wasn't drinking so much, drinking alone at night, trying to see events through the fog of memory, wondering what she might have done the night before...

Some days she wanted to live her life, her real life, the one she imagined was happening in a parallel universe, the life where she had the peace and happiness she desperately craved.

Once, she was able to last three weeks without touching a drop of alcohol. Usually, it was more like one week. One whole week before she was trying to push thoughts of alcohol away. One whole week before her hands started their non-stop shaking. One whole week until her feelings of worthlessness took over completely. One whole week until she picked up the bottle again.

Tonight, it was her mother's fault. If her mother had not reminded her of that dark, awful period in her life, Katie might have been okay on this first night back in her childhood home. But it was too much, really, to be here, the very place where she first learned she wasn't safe from the monsters of the world, that in fact she'd never been safe.

She didn't want to drink, but she couldn't stop drinking.

Holding the cap in one hand and the bottle in the other as she walked downstairs, Katie went to the kitchen and dumped a generous portion of bourbon into her Mickey Mouse coffee mug. Tonight, she would drink it straight.

Carrying the bottle and the now full mug back to the screened porch, she sat absorbing the still night, trying to obliterate her own darkness within. Squinting her eyes shut didn't stop the images from rolling through her mind. The unkempt yard. The feral glint in the man's eyes.

Katie wound her fingers tightly around the cup as she gulped, wondering if the memories would ever leave her head. Memories of grease on the linoleum that caused her sneakers to make sticking noises every time she took a step or stale air that smelled of part cigarette smoke, part old hamburger, and part unwashed laundry.

If only I had a delete button for the parts of my life I want to erase.

The alcohol had stopped burning her throat, so she was able to take a larger swallow this time. Worst of all was remembering the muffled cries that came from the gag he had put in her friend's mouth, the moans that pleaded with Katie to *do something, help her*, and the image of tears rolling down Liz's face as the man ripped the shorts from her young body.

On the patio chairs, Katie was frozen, reliving the moment. The moment when she knew she was powerless to do anything, the moment she saw the knife held to her friend's throat. The monster was in complete control of the situation.

And somehow, through some miracle of fate...

Hannah saved the day.

Apparently, the ghost had appeared to her mother and warned her, told Belinda she'd better get a move on and go save her daughter. She even led Belinda through the neighborhood, straight to the man's door. The cavalry arrived just in time. In time, at least, to prevent the monster from slicing the girls open or doing any more physical damage.

Not in time to stop the entire nightmare, though. Katie wondered about her friend, Liz, wondered if Liz reached for some kind of comfort the way Katie did. After all, Liz had it worse. It was Liz who had her shorts torn off, Liz who was bound and gagged. Katie had done nothing, she'd been too small to stop it from happening and too young to know what to do in the face of a threat so big. It was no wonder Liz's parents had packed up and moved her away; maybe it would have been better if Katie's parents had done the same.

"Reliving the past, I see."

Katie was finishing her third mug of bourbon when the voice intruded. Refusing to acknowledge the presence of another, Katie reached for the bottle and poured one more drink.

"The drink won't help, you know."

It helped in the moment, which was all Katie really needed.

The voice grew softer, even as it became insistent. "Please, Katie-love, look at me. I need to talk to you, and I don't know how long I'll be able to appear tonight."

"I can't see you." Katie's voice was loud in the quiet of the porch.

Katie was surprised to hear Hannah sigh. Who knew ghosts could do that? Unfortunately, the specter kept talking.

"Yes, dear, you can see me, just like your mother could. Now straighten up and listen, I've got something to tell you."

Katie tried to focus her eyes over the rim of her cup. There it was, plain as day, right in front of her, the opaque image of a woman in late 1800s period clothing. Long, dark skirt, cream colored blouse buttoned up to the neck, hair piled on top of her head, and a very concerned face staring at Katie.

She took another swallow, waiting for the ghostly vision to dissipate. No such luck.

"Whad'ya want, anyway? And how come I always see you when I'm having a little drink?"

"Katie-love, something very bad is coming your way."

Katie half-snickered. "Sumthin' bad this way comes, huh? Hey, how come you look all upset? I didn't think ghosts could get upset."

"I'm upset because you're drunk, and I'm upset because there seems to be a darkness encroaching upon your world even as we speak. A darkness beyond the usual one that you are intent on carrying around. Something must be done."

Katie was silent a moment before making a decision. If her mother could see Hannah and talk about it freely without getting carted off to the loony bin, then dammit, so could she. She might as well give in to this thing, whether it was an apparition born of her own insanity or from being drunk—or maybe, unthinkably, this was the real thing. After all, she knew that there were times when ghosts appeared to people; all she had to do was look to her friend Ella for proof of that. Over the summer, Katie and her friends had all seen the ghost in Ella's house. So why should this situation be any different?

"Why are you here, Hannah? According to family legend, you're only supposed to show up when someone's in trouble."

"That's what I've been trying to tell you. Someone is in trouble. You."

"Hmmm, sure." Katie retreated to her world of inebriation.

Hannah continued, sounding desperate. "You might want to consider moving away from here, or maybe getting a roommate. This is not a good time for you to be alone."

"I've always been alone—everyone's alone, it's how we were born. Into an unfound door..." Staring into the night, she started talking the half truth talk every drunk speaks. "I have a memory, maybe I was five or six years old, of standing by myself on the back porch. The wind was blowing a lonely song, and the feeling of utter isolation filled me. It felt like the backyard stretched for miles, putting everything and everyone further and further away."

Katie stopped, losing track of what she was saying. It didn't matter anyway, since she was only sitting on her back porch, talking to a ghost and getting drunk. Who really cared what a drunk woman had to say? She put her head on the table and closed her eyes. Maybe she would rest out here, just for a minute.

"Katie-love, you're not alone. I understand that it was difficult for you, I really do. The life I lived was very difficult, too. I know what it's like to face evil, to try to find your way in this world. But unlike me, you have friends, people you can count on. You have to know that there are those around you who can help. I'm afraid if you don't realize it now, if you don't see what's going on, that soon it's going to be too late for you."

CHAPTER SIX

THE RINGING IN HER EARS was insistent, pulling Katie out of a dream where she was standing on the ocean floor, looking up and watching her family row a small boat over her. She sat up, startled to realize that the ringing noise was the phone and frantic for another moment before she remembered it was Friday. There were no Friday classes to teach, thank God. It would have been beyond embarrassing to have the college call because she failed to show up at work. She might drink some nights, but she always managed to show up when she was supposed to. Except for that one time—but she was fairly certain nobody at work knew she was drunk.

Katie closed her eyes and pressed the button to answer the call, mostly to stop the phone from its continuous echo through the empty house. Hopefully, she sounded awake and coherent.

"Good morning, this is Katie." Good, she managed to insert just the right amount of chipper in her phone greeting.

"Oh, sweetheart." Belinda sighed through the phone. "I must have woken you. You sound like it was a late night."

Katie tamped down her irritation toward her mother. After all, it wasn't Belinda's fault she possessed strong maternal instincts; it was just annoying to be on the receiving end of them.

"Good morning to you, too, mother. How is your trip so far?"

There was a short silence on the other end of the phone before Belinda let out another sigh, this one soft as a whisper and not meant to harass. "You know I'm praying for you, dear. Always. You're my daughter, and I love you fiercely. You know that, right?"

Katie kept her eyes shut, trying to block her growing irritation. Her mother might send prayers off into the heavens on behalf of her daughter, but in the end, what did that really do? Praying to a God who didn't answer was not only a waste of time but vaguely insulting.

Katie took a breath and sat up straight in bed. She was in control of her life, even if it didn't seem like it, and she really didn't need her mother running spiritual interference for her.

"Mom—"

"I'm sorry," Belinda interrupted. "I didn't call to pester you. I..." Belinda's voice broke as she finished her sentence. "...called because something happened."

Katie came fully awake at the sound of those words. "Is Dad okay? Are you guys all right? Did you have an accident?"

"It's your brother, Beau. He's had a heart attack, and he's in the hospital right now. Apparently, he..." Belinda stopped, obviously trying to compose herself. Katie heard another crack in her mother's voice as she continued. "The doctors have him in a coma, Katie, and we're not sure what's going to happen from here. Your father and I are turning around and coming home."

For a moment, Katie couldn't move. How could her brother—who was definitely not an old man—have had a heart attack? The words didn't make sense to her.

"Mom, are you sure? There's got to be some kind of mistake. Isn't he kind of young for that? How did this happen? Where is he now?"

"Oh, Katie, I wish it was a mistake. Anna Louise called our cell phones last night after they brought him in. I guess she's the one who found him in his office, which must have been terrible for her. Thank God, though, that she went looking for him when she did."

Anger surged through Katie, red hot and indignant. "Why didn't she call me?"

Belinda's voice was gentle. "She did. She said you weren't answering your cell phone or the house phone but that she left messages on both."

Katie closed her eyes, trying to keep the images of last night out of her head. Anna Louise probably had called; her phones probably had messages on them, but Katie was in no condition last night to hear or answer the phone.

She hated to ask her mother this, and she hated the way her voice sounded like a little girl when she asked. "Is he going to be okay?"

"We don't know. The doctors told Anna Louise the only way he could heal was to put him in a medically induced coma. The next twenty-four to forty-eight hours are going to be key to his recovery. If they decide to bring him out of this coma by then, that would be a very good sign."

Katie's head hurt. "I don't understand. What do you mean by medically induced coma? Does that mean the doctors actually put him in a coma?"

"Yes. Apparently, he was so agitated in the hospital that he was trying to pull all the tubes and oxygen out. Your sister-in-law said she'd never seen him like this; he just went crazy in there."

"From having a heart attack? That doesn't make sense. It doesn't sound like Beau at all."

"I know." Belinda sighed. "I don't know what to think, but we're on our way back right now."

"What if he doesn't... I mean, what if he isn't..."

Belinda's voice cracked. "We won't think about that right now. Your father and I should be home within a day."

"Okay. I'll get your room ready." *And put everything else away.*

"No, sweetheart. No offense, but I think we're going to stay with Anna Louise. She's going to need help getting through this, and at least we'll be able to take care of the house or anything else she needs."

Katie nodded, even though her mother couldn't see her. "That sounds like a good idea. What can I do?"

"Go visit Beau, talk to him. They're encouraging us to do that, in case he can hear us. We want him to know we're here for him, that we love him, and that he's going to get better."

"Okay, I'll go this morning. Be careful coming home, Mom."

Whenever sickness, fear, or tragedy fell on her doorstep, it made Katie vulnerable, made her feel as if everything and everyone could be wiped out of her life without a moment's notice.

Like her brother. How could he have had a heart attack? Sure, he probably ate fast food about once a week, but that couldn't possibly be enough to cause this. He was only thirty-two years old; this couldn't be happening.

She wrapped her arms around her middle as a sudden cold surged within her body. Katie knew better, but her mind projected an image of her parents in a twisted car wreck as they raced to get back.

Stop that. It's your fear talking, that's all.

But once her body started shivering, she couldn't stop.

Jumping out of bed, she braced for the moment of nausea, the moment she had to steady herself from the wave of dizziness that swept through her body.

Some nights had a worse effect on her than others. It occurred to her that she should have something to eat before she ran to the hospital.

Maybe she would even have something extra with her breakfast, just this once, just this morning, to fortify herself.

All hospital rooms have a smell that immediately permeates clothes and hair. It's not pleasant, but Katie tried to ignore the odor of sickness overlaid with cleaning fumes as she stared at her brother lying motionless in the bed. She vaguely wondered how anyone could get any rest here, a place of constant noise and interruption. Steady electronic beeps coupled with the general groan of discomfort that could be heard throughout the hallways made hospitals seem as if they weren't a haven of either rest or healing, but rather places of discomfort and agitation.

Katie hated it there. Her first reaction after entering the room was to run away, to just leave her brother lying all by himself in that bed with tubes and monitors hooked into him. Normally a healthy, handsome, and vibrant man, his body lay pale and waxen upon the sheets. She almost couldn't stand it and was grateful for the extra support she'd taken before leaving the house.

She approached the bed with caution. Although the steady beeping noise told her otherwise, she couldn't help wondering if he was already dead. He sure looked it.

"Beau?" Even if he had been awake, he wouldn't have heard her voice, shaky and timid, in that antiseptic-smelling room.

She cleared her throat to try again. Anna Louise and the doctors had told her it was important to talk to him, that in all likelihood he could hear what she had to say. *Be encouraging, tell him you love him, tell him you know he can get better and everyone wants him healthy.*

Katie wondered who was going to be encouraging to her, though. She had trouble having faith that her brother was going to be just fine when, frankly, he looked like death already.

"Beau, it's Katie... I just... I wanted to be here... I wanted to let you know I'm here. And I love you, and you're going to be fine." Her voice gained strength. She could do this, she could be supportive and helpful. "I know you're strong enough to get through this, and when you're feeling better, we're all going to be here to help you and make sure you stay healthy. Mom and Dad are on their way. We all love you so much."

Tears blurred her vision. As adults, they hadn't been particularly close, but that was nobody's fault. On paper, she and Beau were opposites. He was a conservative man, the one who often told Katie she needed to settle down and get married. In his mind, it was almost a sin that she hadn't done so yet. He often told her she would make a fine and proper wife to the right gentleman. When he first started saying those things, she thought he was kidding, but it turned out that he believed everything he said.

Beau thought being married made everyone's life better.

Eventually he stopped saying it, instead telling her to simply settle down and straighten herself out. She was fairly certain he didn't know about her drinking, as she went to great lengths to keep all that a secret, but sometimes she wasn't so sure. It was when he spoke to her as if she were six years old that she got really mad, and those were the times she walked away. There was no reason for her to subject herself to that kind of insult, she reasoned, and she didn't need to be around him when he was like that.

But despite all their differences, despite his push to get her to live a life he thought was better, he was her brother. He was the one who had taught her how to throw a ball, he was the one who stood up for her in school when she was getting picked on by Cathy what's-her-name. He was the one who spent his entire allowance on a huge stuffed bear for her in those awful days after the incident with her and Liz, who would sleep outside her door some nights to guard her and make sure the bad guy wasn't coming back.

He was her brother, and she loved him, no matter what. She couldn't bear to lose him, not yet. This wasn't supposed to happen like this.

The doctors were only allowing visitors in for a limited amount of time, and Katie's time was almost up. She leaned forward and whispered in his ear. "You're my brother, and I love you. I know you're going to get better, and I'm going to be right here for you when you need me." Softly kissing his forehead, she left the room.

At the end of the hallway was a floor-to-ceiling window letting in cascades of morning light. Uncertain, she stood in front of the window. She wasn't ready to leave yet. With nothing else to do, and with Anna Louise possibly avoiding her, Katie rummaged through her purse for her phone. Checking her email, she saw twenty-five new emails, ranging from the benefits of penis enlargement to the benefits of berries to the benefits of buying medicine online. She deleted all those potential benefits and checked her Facebook page instead; that was bound to have something more interesting.

Lots of her friends were talking about upcoming fall events, school dances their kids were going to, baking pies, or sharing soup recipes. It was mostly mundane stuff until she got to Lisa's post. She was only friends with Lisa because Lisa was Ella's sister. She was the kind of friend who comes with your friends. There was no way to avoid her, and Katie didn't want to be rude, but sometimes Lisa was a little difficult. Today's Facebook entry on Lisa's page read: "Of course the furniture delivery was late today. Don't these people understand that I'm on a decorating schedule? Can't wait to see how the animal print fabrics look paired with the florals. Designer said it would be divine!"

It was bizarre reading about someone decorating their house as she stood in the hospital hallway. But the post was pure Lisa, reflecting the woman's obsession with having the best of everything. Always conscious of getting the latest trends in fashion and interiors, Lisa had a tendency to plow into people's lives with a lack of sensitivity and a single-minded determination. Katie suspected she really was a good person but it was hard to get past all the surface stuff with her sometimes.

It wasn't until she'd scrolled through her page for a bit that she noticed she had a friend request. Curious, she clicked on the icon to see who wanted to be her friend.

The request had arrived the night before, and there was no profile picture. Katie's brow wrinkled as she read the name, trying to place how she might know this person. Titus Foote. The message that came with the friend request was simple: "Looking forward to getting to know you."

Katie knew that there were nights when she didn't remember everything. A momentary panic washed through her as she struggled to remember what she had done last night. Thoughts of a blackout scared her more than anything, and she struggled to remember details of her evening on the back porch. She knew she had talked to Hannah—she wasn't going to think about the ghost right now—and she knew she had her Mickey Mouse coffee mug. Beyond that, she wasn't sure.

Damn. A memory blank, more lost time.

Maybe it didn't matter. It was a simple friend request, and the worst thing she could have done was some harmless online flirtation. She was positive her drinking habits would never lead her to do anything rash or dangerous.

Accepting the friend request, Katie checked the time. She wasn't sure when the doctors would let her back in to see her brother or how long Anna Louise would want to spend in there. Maybe it was better if she left. Maybe they would know more by the end of the day.

Suddenly, a wall of grief slammed into Katie, leaving her shattered.

What if he dies?

She felt at that moment like it was a certainty. What was her family going to do without Beau?

She needed to get away from the hospital, away from the smells and the death and the shadow of hopelessness. She needed to get home and fortify herself, maybe call her friends for backup support. There was no way she could get through this alone.

CHAPTER SEVEN

SUNLIGHT AND BIRDSONG DID NOT lessen the impact of seeing a house destroyed by fire. What remained of the structure stood in stark contrast to the blue sky, and the yard was littered with a soft gray carpet of ash debris. Autumn in Connecticut forged a clean sharpness in the air, but even that couldn't dissipate the smell of wet, charred wood.

Dani stood outside and took her time surveying the scene in front of her. As soon as she'd heard the final piece of history of this house, she had come back, determined to walk through the crime scene again.

After what happened Wednesday night, there was no doubt this was a crime scene. Once the medical examiner had shown up and pulled back the sheets, it took about ten seconds for him to notice that one of the bodies was missing his teeth.

As in, there were no teeth in the dead man's head.

None.

If that didn't scream "cover up," Dani didn't know what would. Obviously, they were dealing with a criminal who watched one too many television shows and thought he could get away with it by not leaving evidence.

Dani's stomach tightened. "I'm going to get you, you son of a bitch. You killed two people, and you think you got away with it. But I'm smarter than you, and I'm going to find you."

As of right now, the police had not released any details to the media. As far as the general public knew, the owners of the house were the unfortunate victims of an accidental fire. But Dani had a feeling that this cover up was a lot more involved than anyone suspected.

Jimmy had said the other night that this house had a weird history. That comment stuck in Dani's head, especially after seeing the condition of the male body. She figured if there was already bad mojo in there, maybe learning about it would give her insight into this crime.

So she did what lots of cops in small towns do, she started asking questions of everyone she knew. The great thing about small towns was the same thing that drove people insane: everyone knew everyone else's business. Not only did they know your business, but they also knew all about your family and everything your family had gotten up to in the past eight decades. The oral tradition was alive and kicking in suburban America.

Dani got an earful.

First, she found out that the guy who lived in the house had inherited it; the house had been in his family for generations. Like many others in the area, it was an old house, built in the early 1800s, and the family was one of those old-time New England families who had been around forever.

The people she talked to mostly agreed that the owners, the Yodell family, were a couple of sandwiches short of a picnic. General consensus was that although Cleve Yodell was nice enough, his mother and father had been very strange people. The dad had a reputation for having been a drinker back when he lived here, but in general the family kept to themselves. Most felt sorry for Cleve when he was young, having to grow up with his oddball parents, but nobody saw any reason to do anything about it. After all, it wasn't against the law to be strange. It might be socially unacceptable but not illegal.

Based on something one of her friends had hinted at, she called her nephew Shane at his new college dorm room. Judging from the party sounds in the background, Dani hadn't interrupted his studies. He seemed happy enough to talk with her, but that may have been because he missed being at home.

"Hey, kiddo, how's college going?" It still seemed to her like Shane should be riding his bike through the neighborhood or playing Little League instead of grown up and off at school.

"Everything's groovy, auntie. Of course, I can never get enough good food around here, and I've had to scout out the pizza joints. What's up with you?"

Dani had to suppress a laugh as she imagined her nephew eating nothing but pepperoni pizza for the duration of his college life. There were probably worse habits he could develop, so she wasn't going to worry about it.

"I'm looking for some information, and I think you can help me out."

"Ooooh, cop stuff, right? Are you trying to catch a bad guy?"

Dani smiled. Shane was teasing her. The kid didn't have a mean bone in his body, and he was basically a good person. In fact, from his interest in her work over the years, she wouldn't be surprised if he eventually declared his major to be Criminal Justice.

"Yeah, I'm trying. What can you tell me about the old house on Echo Lake Road?"

"The one the Biellis used to live in?"

"No, the old one on the corner of Buckingham Street that belonged to the Yodells. Did you know them?"

"Oh, man, creepy house. Yeah, I sort of knew them, everyone did. They were doing some weird witchcraft kind of stuff in there, I think. Kids used to go there to learn about that stuff."

"Kids? Did you ever go there?" Dani's radar was on full alert. If anyone had hurt her nephew...

"No, man, I think they ended like a long time ago. Like, maybe they stopped five years ago or something. But I know someone who used to hang out there all the time, I can ask for you if you want. I heard there was some serious sh—uh, stuff happening there."

Dani thanked him for his time and said yes, she would appreciate any information Shane could dig up for her. She rationalized that her brother couldn't be upset with her for asking about this or accuse her of putting his son in any danger. After all, Shane was in a completely different state, probably in more ways than her brother wanted to know.

Standing outside the burnt house, Dani surveyed the wreckage with a critical eye. It was important to go in with an awareness of potential structural damage, as she didn't feel like crashing through the upstairs floor into the basement. From what she could see, most of the destruction had occurred in the basement and attic, which was typical in older homes. The type of construction in New England homes built so long ago sometimes meant there were open walls with nothing between the plaster and outside of the house. Sometimes the walls were stuffed with newspaper instead of insulation, depending on the inhabitants through the years. Because of this, fires starting in the basement generally shot straight through the walls and into the attic, creating a hazard on the top and bottom of the house.

Her cell phone rang, sounding harsh amidst the birdsong.

"Burgess."

"Hey, kid, how's it going out there?"

Kid. Dani closed her eyes, trying to remember that Jimmy meant well, really. "Everything's fine. I haven't gone inside yet. I'm just scouting around out here."

"Yeah, I got your message. Be careful out there, and let me know what you find."

"I will. The Captain said we're meeting tonight at seven to go over everything. Hopefully, we'll have something for him."

"If anyone's gonna find something, I know it's you, kid. Call me and let me know when you're outta there."

"Will do."

Snapping her phone shut, Dani took a deep breath. Jimmy was all right, she supposed, if only he would stop calling her "kid."

It took an hour and a half before Dani struck gold. She knew she smelled bad and was covered in soot and dirt, but she couldn't wait to get back to the station to start working on her find. She would ignore the comments about her appearance because she needed to get in there and log this into the evidence book.

She had suspected most information would come from whatever the victims had left behind. Obviously, mister "I'm-so-clever-I-pulled-teeth-out-of-someone's-head" was going to be careful about leaving evidence, so Dani focused on searching for something belonging to the female victim. After all, with a crime like this, the odds of the perpetrator being male were pretty good.

She found it in the bedroom. Checking under the blackened ruin of the bed, she discerned a twisted metal shape. It was a box, one of those fireproof things homeowners buy to protect important documents. This one had definitely done its job, as not only were all the birth certificates and household documents intact, but also a small notebook. A notebook filled with writing.

It was the wife's journal. Dani couldn't stop the smile that spread across her face when she flipped through the pages and saw what it was. Hopefully, something in there would help them with the investigation. She needed to get back right away so she could sit down and analyze this, page by page.

Caught up in her thoughts of the evidence she had in hand, Dani was at the bottom of the front stairs before she realized someone was in the front yard, watching her. Leaning against her car, he looked to be in his early thirties, unshaven, with a blue bandana tied around his head. His face betrayed no emotion as he watched her, hands in his pockets, obviously waiting for her.

Instinctively, Dani's hand moved to her side, resting on the gun she always carried. "Can I help you?"

With a nod of his head, he answered, "Are you Shane's aunt? Dani?"

"Why?"

Shrugging, he didn't seem offended. "Shane asked me to go talk to his Aunt Dani, the cop. Said you'd probably be out here looking for clues or something."

Cautiously, Dani approached the man. He seemed innocuous enough, but her hand never strayed from her side. "What's your name?"

"So, you're Shane's aunt, right?"

Apparently, Dani wasn't the only one with trust issues.

She nodded. "Yes, I'm his aunt. How do you know Shane?"

Finally, the man smiled at her. He wasn't a bad looking guy, but he had a hard edge to him, not the kind of person she imagined her college-aged nephew would hang out with; he was at least a decade older than Shane.

"Hey, the name's Lee. Shane and I worked together last summer at the gas station."

Dani nodded with sudden realization. This must be the guy Shane told her about on the phone earlier.

"What did you want to talk about?"

Lee looked behind her at the remains of the house. "That place and the family who used to live there. Can't say I'm sorry to hear about it burning down, but I'm sorry people got hurt."

Maybe he wasn't such a bad guy after all, and he was a friend of Shane's. "Have you been here before?"

Lee nodded, lost in thought. "Yeah, we used to hang out here when we were teenagers. I went to school with Cleve, and a bunch of us would come over here at night. Of course, that all ended when Cleve's old man left town."

"Do you know where the father went?" Dani had heard several theories, but she wanted to see if Lee had different information.

The man shrugged, reaching into his front shirt pocket for a cigarette. "Who knows? He was the kind of guy who liked to pretend he was your friend, but underneath he was mean. I always figured he beat his wife and kid."

"Why did you figure that?"

"Because once in a while he'd start drinking, and then you could see this flash of, I don't know, a really bad person. It was like he was someone else when he drank."

Dani nodded. "That happens. Why did you come over at night?" Images of parties with alcohol and drugs flashed through Dani's mind.

"That's when we were told to come. Usually, we'd try to get here around nine or so, but things didn't get started until after midnight."

That fit in with the rumors she'd heard from others. "What things, Lee?"

"Cleve's mother said we couldn't start our rituals until after midnight, so we just sorta hung out until then." Dani could see that Lee was struggling now, unable to suppress a shudder from running through his body. "We were just kids, you know? We didn't know any better—but man, if I ever caught my kid doing that stuff, I don't know what I'd do."

Dani knew the answer even before she asked the question. "What stuff were you doing here?"

"Witchcraft. She was teaching us the dark arts, and we were supposed to share our knowledge with the like-minded ones."

This part was new to Dani. "The like-minded ones? What does that mean?"

Lee sighed. "I don't know. It all sounds crazy now, right? Anyway, Cleve, sometimes he would change, like he'd become someone else and start saying all this weird stuff. Then his mother, she'd be standing right next to him, and they'd be talking about how only certain people were meant to be in charge and it was important to take your power."

These people were definitely off the charts when it came to weirdness. "Take your power?" Dani asked. "Like some sort of personal power, new-agey thing?"

Lee nodded. "Sort of, yeah. Cleve would talk in this odd, deep voice and tell us survival was about power and that power came from within. I don't remember all of it, but I do remember one thing."

"What's that?"

"It might seem small, but it kind of stuck in my mind. It was one of those things that we wanted to make fun of but didn't because those people were a little scary."

Dani wondered why anyone would hang out with people who scared them, but who knew why kids did anything?

"What was it?"

"When Cleve talked, he wouldn't let us call him 'Cleve,' and he got angry if we called him did. He said we had to use his real name."

Dani wondered if this piece of information was really all that important. "What was his real name?"

"Titus."

CHAPTER EIGHT

WHEN COMBINED, INTENSE PAIN AND disappointment create need. Katie felt this on a subconscious level, yet she was unable to articulate it to herself; instead, early in the morning she fed her need with half a bottle of vodka. It was better this way—it stabilized her, helped make her more *here*. Plus, more importantly, nobody could smell it on her breath, and she had it with orange juice, which sort of counted as breakfast.

She'd visited her brother that morning, but there was no change. The doctors were keeping him in an induced coma, and Katie and her family continued to surround him and talk to him, trying to convey messages of hope.

It made her sad in a way she didn't know was possible, this life of hovering.

How the heck Anna Louise is holding it together is beyond me. I could barely last an hour in there with him.

She'd left the room a few times, not wanting to fall apart in front of her family.

It doesn't matter how I feel, I've got to be strong for them. I've got to be strong for Beau.

Katie jerked herself back to the present. It was late afternoon, and she was sitting with her friends on the back porch of her house. For just a moment, everything almost felt normal again, like it had this past summer when she and Roland spent so much time hanging out at Ella's new house. The only difference was that Ella's house was haunted by a ghost that Ella didn't want hanging around. Having the ghost of Hannah wasn't so bad, especially since she didn't rattle chains or wake her up in the middle of the night with ghostly moanings. Katie shivered, remembering the fear when the ghost in Ella's house screamed and made a general mess of things in the kitchen. Of course, that ghost had good reason to try to get their attention. She still couldn't figure out why Hannah stayed.

For right now, though, she was grateful to have the support of her friends. They'd shown up with food and open hearts after learning about Beau.

"What's going on with your brother? Is he out of the coma yet?" Roland asked.

"No, not yet. I don't have much to tell you. He might be okay, he might not." Katie's voice wobbled and she stopped to catch her breath. She couldn't start crying. If that happened, she might never stop. Once she gained control of her emotions, she went on. "Time will tell, really. For now, all we can do is wait and hope for the best."

"Waiting is the hardest," Ella offered.

Katie nodded, not wanting to talk anymore. That feeling of normalcy was starting to slip away, and she wanted to hold on to it for as long as she could.

Looking through the French doors into the kitchen, Katie saw a showdown was taking place in the house. "Ella, I apologize for my roommate's behavior this afternoon."

Everyone turned around to see Daisy, Ella's dog, curled into as tight a ball as possible and trying to be invisible under the kitchen table. Katie's cat, KC, sat atop the table, ears flattened, one paw hanging over the edge in a distinctly threatening manner.

Ella shrugged. "I assumed after that awful hurricane this summer, those two would be friends, but it seems they forgot the bond they shared from natural disaster."

"I don't think KC forgot the bond; I think she's ignoring it," Roland said. "I know Daisy'd be anybody's friend, but that cat of yours seems kind of power hungry. Can't blame her; with a name like KC, she's got to prove herself."

Katie was indignant. "What's wrong with her name?"

Lisa, Ella's sister, chimed in. "I think it's cute. KC stands for 'Katie's cat', right?"

"If only." Roland took a swig of soda and leaned back in his chair.

Katie's eyes ran over Roland's body, noting that despite his manner of dressing in nothing more than T-shirts and jeans, his dark good looks left her feeling weak. He was the epitome of tall, dark, and handsome, with a chiseled face and well-defined body. Not overly muscular, Roland had the easy, natural grace of someone who was used to being physical and was comfortable in his body. She would never admit to him—or anybody else for that matter—that the sight of him sent her hormones into overdrive. She didn't think it would matter much to him anyway. Roland never once made a pass at her or indicated he was interested in her, and she wasn't about to let him know how she felt. She had some pride, after all.

"Kitty cat!" Lisa's voice echoed on the porch, severing Katie's attention. "I knew I would guess it." Lisa reached across the table for a chip. "So, how old is the cat anyway? I've heard they don't live very long, like maybe ten years or so. Is she that old? Because if she's getting up there in age, you may not want to stock up on cat food."

Katie tried not to react. *Does she really think it's okay to ask if my cat is going to die soon?*

Fortunately, Roland changed the subject. "Hey, Katie, do you have any more salsa? This stuff's really good."

"Of course. It's in the garage refrigerator. I'll be right back." Getting up to go to the kitchen, she shot him a grateful look.

"Oh, what a good idea, an extra refrigerator. I think we'll go shopping this weekend and get one for our garage, too." Lisa's face lit up at the thought of shopping.

"Lisa, just because... oh, never mind." Ella closed her eyes briefly and took a deep breath. Katie smiled at her friend, trying to communicate that it didn't matter what her sister said or did. Katie loved Ella, regardless of her relatives. If people were judged by their relatives, not everyone would maintain certain friendships.

"If you'll excuse me, I need to powder my nose. Katie, can you show me where the little girl's room is?" Lisa was making her way toward the kitchen as she spoke.

After showing Lisa the main bathroom upstairs, Katie couldn't help feeling sorry for her. The whole way up the stairs, Lisa chattered excitedly about everything from the move to being near her sister to how glad she was that her sister had such good friends. Walking toward the garage door, Katie shook her head. Who knew she would have sympathy for Lisa? Maybe Lisa was just trying too hard to fit in. Maybe if she loosened up a little, let the real woman shine through, she'd be able to make more friends. It was hard to get a handle on Lisa's personality under all that inane chatter.

Before she reached the garage door, Katie remembered that she had brought the salsa into the kitchen for this very reason. She didn't want to be climbing over things in the garage to get to food that she needed.

Rounding the corner into the dining room, she stopped. The sound of voices carried into the house. Ella and Roland were talking about her.

"Don't worry; you and I both know it'll take her a while to climb over the stuff her parents left in the garage to get to the refrigerator. I know I've been asking you this since I met you guys, so give me an answer, just this once. Why won't you date Katie?"

Katie held her breath. She knew she shouldn't be listening, but she wasn't sure how to let her friends know she was standing right there.

Roland's voice was slow and deliberate. "I can't, Ella. God, I wish things were different, but I don't see myself checking the toilet tank or the boxes in the garage every day. I grew up seeing this kind of thing, and let me tell you, it is one painful ride."

Ella was clearly confused. "What are you talking about? I'm asking you about dating, and you're talking about toilets? Is that some kind of metaphor? I don't get it."

Roland's sigh could probably be heard down the street. "Let's just leave it at 'no' then, okay?"

"I'll leave it alone for now, but don't give up. Whatever's stopping you, I know it can be overcome. You two could work it out."

"Some things can't be worked out until their time. Unfortunately, there's no way of knowing when that time could be."

Katie stood, mortified, in the dining room corner. A wave of embarrassment washed over her as she realized the truth of what Roland said. She'd thought she'd hidden things from everyone, but somehow Roland knew. *Oh God, how could he know?*

She had bottles of vodka stashed in all the toilet tanks in the house.

CHAPTER NINE

KATIE'S HANDS DIDN'T TREMBLE OR betray her as she set the salsa in front of Roland. Nobody in the room could know that she overheard their conversation; it was too humiliating to think about.

Lisa's voice rolled in behind her. "My goodness, I forgot how all that decorating from the 80s used so much *mauve*. Will you be changing the wallpaper in the bathroom this year, Katie?"

"I don't know. What do you think, Lisa? I have no idea where to begin on a project like that."

Katie let Lisa's voice wash over her, the banality of the topic acting as a comfort. Hiding behind words, Katie was able to sustain a conversation that focused on creating a spa-type atmosphere in the bathroom and therefore avoid anything meaningful.

Enough was enough. Images of her brother lying in a hospital bed danced in front of her open eyes. Roland's knowledge of what she had thought was hidden whispered in her head.

Katie stood, knocking over the half full glass of soda on the table in front of her. Moving in slow motion, she reached for the napkins on the table to wipe up the spill.

"I'm so sorry, y'all. I just... I think I may go see my brother again tonight. I'm feeling anxious. I'm not trying to kick you out or anything, but I should get going. Thanks for stopping in to see me."

Roland stood. "We understand. You should be with your family."

Ella's hand closed over Katie's with a warmth that failed to penetrate. "Please call me if you need anything. Even if you don't know what you need, but you know you need something, call me."

Katie nodded as she continued to wipe the spill. "Thank you. I'm sure it will all turn out fine. I'll focus on spending time with him and let the doctors do what they do best."

Ella's face mirrored sympathy as she cleared the remainder of the food from the table. Katie avoided looking at her friend.

It only took her about ten minutes to usher her friends to the front door. The darkness was closing in, and she wasn't sure how she was going to make it through the night, but that wasn't something she'd ever share with them. Ella, Roland, and even Lisa all had typical lives, with no shadows and no despair. They were normal.

Walking to the door, Roland stopped. Even though Ella and Lisa were already getting into their car, he spoke softly. "Are you going to be okay tonight? You're not going to do anything dangerous, are you?"

Katie's laugh sounded more like a bark. "What do you think I'm going to do, bungee jump off the Coleman Bridge?"

"I don't know what you're going to do, that's the problem. But I don't think you're going to visit your brother, are you?"

Katie looked him in the eye. "Roland Lagasse, you've got some nerve. I don't know what you're hinting around at, but if you have something to say, then just say it."

"I don't want you to get hurt."

"It's a little late for that, don't you think?"

The gentle sound of an outside rain shower reached her ears, the rhythmic *tap-tap* on her house a contrast to the turmoil in her head.

"Dammit, Katie. Every time I try to talk to you, I can't get through. You're not listening. You can't keep doing this; you're going to lose everything. I mean, look at you, look at where you are right now. Is this what you want?"

Roland took a step toward her, but Katie didn't want to back down. She glared up at him, wondering how he could be so judgmental. Her cat wound itself around her ankles, distracting her for a moment. Bending to pick up the cat, she focused on petting the animal instead of him.

"Yeah, living at my parents' house while I get back on my feet. There's lots of that going on, you know. Lots of people are moving back home. In case you haven't noticed, this country is in a recession."

"And you, Katie? What are you in? The same depression you've been in since I've known you? You've got to get some help before it's too late."

She tried to calm herself by taking a breath, but it was no use. Her face flushed red, and her voice lowered a notch. The out-of-control feeling pulsed through her body.

"How dare you? Who the hell do you think you are? I don't know what gives you the right to question me or anything I'm doing, like you're some kind of saint. Well, you're not—and don't think I don't know that, too. Maybe instead of spreading rumors about me, you should get yourself back to the reservation and mind your own business. I'm sure there are plenty of people's lives you could interfere with out there."

Putting the cat back on the floor, she held herself very straight, willing herself not to cry.

Roland shook his head. "Christ, I can't even talk to you. I know you're having a hard time right now, but you can't go off like this. I'd really hoped..."

Was he serious? He couldn't talk to her like that, especially after what he just said. This was all too much for her, the mixture of confusion and anger.

"What? Hoped that I would do whatever you told me to do? Hoped I'd become some sort of plastic Southern-style Barbie girl? What the hell do you want from me?"

It was a mess now. Katie's rage took hold, distorting her thoughts. Later, she knew she wouldn't remember what she said, but no doubt she was going to feel like crap about it.

What else is new? I always feel like crap about something.

Roland's face was unreadable. "Try not to hurt yourself or anyone else tonight." He closed the door behind him softly, with a finality that echoed through the house.

Katie took a few steps back and sat at the foot of the stairs. Empty of thought, she was small and alone. Of course Roland knew what she was trying to hide from everyone; he'd hinted at this before. Heck, he'd said it outright to Ella just a little while ago, here in her own house.

Standing, she raced up the steps two at a time, stomping her way upstairs to change out of her floral sundress. A different outfit was definitely in order, something a little sexier. Splashing perfume on her wrists, her anger grew.

He thinks I have a drinking problem but he doesn't understand. I don't have a problem. I don't drink any more than others might take Prozac or some other type of medication. Why is it okay for people to use drugs and call it medicine, but I can't have one little drink?

Who was he to tell her how to live her life? She wasn't hurting anyone.

Grabbing her purse, she didn't even check to make sure the door was locked; she just went straight to her car. Turning the key in the ignition, she backed into the street, not thinking about where she was going.

Katie let out a pent up sigh of relief when she saw the neon lights of the Driftwood Bar and Grill through the blur of the rain-spattered windshield. Maybe it wasn't the cleanest place in town, but she never got hassled by anyone here, and she could always get a drink. Even when other bars stopped serving her, bartenders at this place helped out.

They know what it's like to be on the edge of everything.

In this place, it didn't matter who you were or what you did. Nobody cared about that. Maybe it was the hopeless need living inside her, or maybe after her fight with Roland she wanted to be seen. Whatever the case, this was the place for her to be right now. The nice-girl-Katie receded as she sashayed into the place, knowing she looked good in her tight jeans, sparkly red tank top, and killer heels.

The bar was packed, the usual Saturday night crowd thrown together in the dim lights and musty scents of what passed for a social gathering. Keyboard sounds of jazz music filled the air, and Katie smiled over at the musician. A regular player at the bar, he was known to everyone as "Jazz the Ripper," and his passion for music showed in his performance. He was a sweet man, but Katie didn't know a lot about him. His looks reminded her a little of the actor James Gandolfini. Currently, he was playing "Cast Your Fate to the Wind", a definite echo of what Katie was feeling at the moment.

It's the music from the Peanuts guy, but I know how much he hates it when I tell him that.

With a wave to Jazz, she walked over to the bar, ready for whatever the night would bring. Edging into a space, she barely had time to lean against the counter before a shot glass of something appeared before her.

The bartender cocked his head toward the other end of the bar. "Courtesy of the gentleman down there. Said to give the pretty lady a welcome shot."

Katie smiled. Here was proof that some men found her attractive. Lifting the glass and smiling in the general direction the bartender had indicated, she waited.

She didn't have to wait long. He came up behind her, acting as if he'd known her forever. He smelled of leather and sweat, and he was handsome enough.

It didn't matter anyway. What mattered was her empty glass.

No, what matters is finding my way home.

The small, still voice was an intrusion she didn't want or need—just like she didn't need Roland, didn't care what he thought of her.

That's not true.

Looking into the eyes of her new friend, Katie knocked back another shot. It was going to take some work to drown out that voice in her head. Besides, it didn't matter what Roland thought. He was one of the normal ones, one of those people who lived their lives knowing they fit in, knowing they were part of something bigger.

Katie was not. She was always on the edge, always on the outside, regardless of what she looked like or who her friends were. She was the girl who never quite belonged.

The music changed, and Jazz had started to play a song by Ben Folds Five. His voice reached across the room, and the familiar lyrics made Katie wonder if there was a message in there for her.

"She's a brick and I'm drowning slowly...

Now she's feeling more alone than she ever has before..."

Her new friend leaned in closer to whisper in her ear. "I just got myself a new car, all bright and shiny, parked outside. Wanna see it?"

No.

She smiled up at him. "Sure."

At least the sex had been quick, fast enough that she was able to get out of the parking lot without having to give Romeo her name—if he'd thought to ask, that is. She called them all Romeo, the parade of men who satisfied her hunger for the moment, the men who flirted and bought her drinks.

Just a few minutes of sex, and I can feel beautiful.

She gave a short laugh, glad nobody was around to hear her. She didn't need a reputation as being crazy.

It was a good thing the bar was so close to her house because the drive home was a blur. Before turning the key in the ignition, she swore she heard Roland's words.

Try not to hurt yourself or anyone else tonight.

"Shut up," she muttered, pulling onto the main road.

Of course, she got home just fine. *My car knows the way home. It can probably drive itself.* She laughed out loud again at the thought of her car making sure she got home safely.

Sleep wasn't an option for her, not yet. Her Mickey Mouse coffee cup waited, clean and empty. Pouring from a bottle of bourbon, she sat on the back porch again. Hopefully, she'd remain numb until tiredness set in and she could go to sleep.

"Katie-love, you can't stay here." The voice was intrusive, urgent.

"You're really going to have to stop doing that. You can't bust in on people and tell them what to do."

"Katie-love, really, you've got to move, go inside or something."

Katie refused to look for the apparition. Life was hard enough without the otherworldly showing up.

"Go away, now. I'm sure there's no real emergency."

"But there is, Katie, there is..."

CHAPTER TEN

IT WAS DARK OUTSIDE WHEN Cleve checked into the motel. Certain that enough time had passed, he was anxious to continue on to the next step of the plan.

The campground off Route 17 in Gloucester, Virginia, had been isolated enough that he felt confident nobody would remember him. Arriving two days before, he took care of the important business in Yorktown first and backtracked up to the town of Gloucester. Lonely stretches of the main road peppered with mobile homes and run down churches told him all he needed to know about the place. Following the signs to the campground, he drove to the wooded area to check it out. It was a perfect spot to hide for a couple days.

He paid anonymously, slipping an envelope with cash into the drop box and setting up a small tent on a site as far into the woods as possible. Gloucester was directly north of Yorktown, cut off by the York River yet accessible from Route 17. The birthplace of our nation, Yorktown, Virginia, was only a part of the journey; the Hollister family was the destination.

He almost couldn't wait.

He knew his time was up at the campground when a family with two toddlers set up their tent two sites away from him.

"Hi there!" The woman he assumed was the mother waved at him from her campsite, all friendliness and smiles.

If they become a problem, you can break their neck.

The voice was back, pushy as ever. He knew he could do that, but he preferred to keep a low profile… still, it was something to think about.

A man exited the tent, presumably the father. He gave a smile and a wave as well, turning to talk to the child, who was attempting to drag a fishing pole out of their vehicle. Cleve waved back, wondering what the man would think if Cleve made him watch his wife die.

As full of possibilities as the situation might be, Cleve had to stay focused. He couldn't be diverted from his original goal. Later, maybe, but not now. It was time to change locations and move toward his next primary kill. He was certain that was what the voice wanted him to do.

He left the campground that day without ever speaking to the family. The motel he chose in Yorktown was located on the busy George Washington Highway, a single story, run down place that might have even charged by the hour if a person didn't know better. The room was non-descript; it was the same brown and beige of every motel room in America, with the musty smell to match. But there was a television, clock radio, and wi-fi connection available, which was all he really needed.

He paid for two whole weeks in cash, hoping not to stay beyond four or five days.

It should be finished by then, and I can move on from here.

The person behind the desk barely looked at him during the entire transaction. Certain he was home free, Cleve's heart rate accelerated as the clerk asked for his license.

"I need to make a copy of this. I'll be right back."

As the clerk turned to go, Cleve called after him. "What do you need a copy of my license for?"

The young boy looked nervous. "I'm supposed to do that whenever anyone pays in cash. The boss said so."

Cleve nodded. He was certain his forgery would hold, so it shouldn't be a problem. Besides, the name was different. He'd kept his first name, just for continuity, but had changed his last name to Farrington on all the new paperwork. That sounded better than Yodell, more appropriate to the kind of lifestyle he would soon be living.

Soon the boy was back and gave Cleve his license before handing him an actual key. Trying to be discreet, he looked around the office to note if there were any security systems. He didn't see any keypads or cameras mounted over the desk, but that didn't mean anything; there might be something in the back room. At least the lock looked like something he could easily get past. Cleve would have to come back and destroy that copy of his license, just to make sure. He didn't want to leave anything behind.

"How late are you here?"

The kid looked at Cleve. "Me?"

Oh, the stupidity of youth. "No, I mean how late is someone in the office in case I need something?"

"Someone's supposed to be here until midnight."

Perfect. Later, he'd sit in the parking lot and watch the kid close up. That would tell him everything he needed to know about the security in this place.

His room was on the far end of the motel, number 19. Settling himself on the hard mattress, he thought for a moment of all the people who had been on the bed before him. Sleeping, resting, copulating.

Maybe even dying.

Opening his laptop, Cleve's fingers danced over the keyboard as he typed in his password and connected to the wireless service provided with his room. *This is going to be fun.*

Feeling good about the way the plan was working, his mouth curved into a slight smile. Plus, there was no doubt that the tools of social media made his goal much more attainable.

Facebook had one notification, the only one he wanted. Earlier today, Katie had responded to his friend request.

Leaning forward, he typed a message. *Thanks for accepting my request. Glad to know we can be friends.*

Things would have been very different if Katie Hollister and her family never existed. He knew this because his mother told him so. He knew because the voice had told him, too. They both spoke the truth, but he trusted the voice more. The voice kept him safe.

"Don't ever forget what those people did to us. Some like to think it's all in the past, but unfinished business is what it is."

He closed his eyes, savoring the memories. Casting the circle. The words that sounded like another language as they stood around an upside down cross. The fire, burning wild before being reduced to smoldering ashes. And the smell of it all rose up as if it were with him today, invading his head and drowning him—the smell of burnt flesh.

Overwhelmed by an unnamed desire, Cleve stood. He couldn't sit in this room any longer.

He left his motorcycle helmet on the dresser. Used more for a disguise than safety, he had no need for it tonight. It was time to hunt, to stalk his prey.

The night air pressed heavy against his body like a swell of warm water. The rain showers had passed, leaving behind a clean, earthy scent. The best part of the motel's location was its proximity to Katie.

I'll be seeing you soon, now. He suppressed the giggle before it escaped from his mouth. He mustn't let his emotions carry the moment.

Suburban neighborhoods carry a quiet, peaceful feeling at night. Pulling into the Edgehill subdivision where Katie lived, Cleve slowed the bike. Because some of the houses he drove past had no curtains on the front window, Cleve could see people watching television or eating their dinner. Occasionally, he slowed enough to watch their interactions, but it quickly became boring, as nobody was actually doing anything. Suburbanites lived in a world of routine, unaware of who watched them from right outside their house.

Of course, he knew where she lived. He knew where all of them lived; it was part of his life's work. This was what he was meant to do, restore the family honor and take what was rightfully his.

Easy-peasy.

A dog barked at the edge of one of the yards, a half-bark, half-snarl that let Cleve know the dog didn't trust him. That was fine, since Katie didn't have any dogs. He knew she had a cat that she treasured, though, and he was looking forward to playing with the little kitty.

People need to be more careful about what they post on social media.

This neighborhood was bordered by the Colonial National Forest, hundreds of acres of woodland left undeveloped. Parking his bike at the edge of the woods so it couldn't be seen, Cleve began the rest of his journey on foot. Following the map imprinted in his mind, it wasn't long before Cleve stood in the shadows in front of Katie's house. He couldn't see much in the front windows, but there was a glow of lights in the rear.

Working his way into the backyard, he stepped carefully, trying to avoid any tools or stray items that might have been left outside.

Sure enough, there she was, sitting on the back porch with a coffee cup in hand. Although she sat in a dim light, her blonde hair shone as if from the heavens. She moved her mouth, obviously talking to herself. Craning his head to get a better view of the porch, he could see that nobody was with her.

She looked drunk, sitting there talking to herself. Cleve suspected this was nothing new. He could always spot the people with the real drinking problem, and he was fairly certain she had one.

Plus, the voice had told him, and it never lied.

A recollection of his mother crowded Cleve's mind as he stared at Katie.

Her hair, almost the same shade of blonde as his mother's, combined with the scent of freshly mown grass from a neighbor's lawn, ignited his memory.

"Mama, can I sit with you?"

"Of course you can, baby. Mommy loves you."

"I love you too, Momma. Will you keep Daddy away tonight?"

"Ssshhh, hush now. Everything will be all right. Just hold on to Mommy."

Shifting back to the present, Cleve's chest hurt. Like all children, he'd trusted his mother. Perhaps she'd done the best she could, but he never fully understood why she stayed, why she let his father back night after night.

He could hear his mother crying sometimes, muffled sobs that he knew he wasn't meant to witness. When he thought about it, he realized that the bitter taste of his father's betrayal was with him still.

The voice that first came to six-year-old Cleve was his comfort, encouraging and telling him it wasn't his fault. *"You didn't do anything wrong, boy."*

Cleve kept his eyes screwed shut as he dragged his sleeve across his runny nose. "I must've done something for Daddy to hate me. Why does he hate me?"

"He doesn't hate you, boy. He can't help himself. It's part of the curse of our family."

Cleve's eyes flew open. "What curse?"

"The curse that came back in 1861, way before you were born. But don't worry about it, boy. You're the one who's going to turn that curse around and release us all."

"Me?"

"Yes, you. I'm going to help you."

Cleve's lower lip trembled. "Are you my friend?"

"Yes, boy, I'm your friend. I'm your only friend."

The voice had proved true, staying with him through his childhood and beyond. It had been Cleve's one real friend, helping him through some of the darkest nights imaginable, encouraging him not to give up, not to give in, not to let go of a life he was meant to live. Without that voice, Cleve might have left this world a long time ago.

And it had all been worth it. Here he was, all these years later, no longer a little boy, but a man filled with the knowledge of what must happen. He was meant to do this, he was meant to seek justice and right the wrong that had once occurred. It was his only way to repay the one who had saved him, the voice that had been his salvation and his comfort.

Killing Katie Hollister and her entire family was his only chance at living an authentic life, at giving meaning to his existence.

CHAPTER ELEVEN

THE COFFEE IN FRONT OF her was the worst ever, but it kept Dani from collapsing in an exhausted heap on the police station floor. She'd been working non-stop since the night of the fire, and it showed. Her eyes were gritty with dark circles underneath, and her hair had long since bypassed "good hair day" and progressed to "I can only wear this tied back." She shook her head and took a deep breath, trying to focus as she sat in her usual spot in the briefing room. Every member of the team was gathered with a quiet sense of expectancy. They were getting close, Dani could feel it.

Captain Delyon strode into the room without hesitation. "Let's get started." With a voice that carried, he never needed a microphone. An older man in a crisp uniform, Captain Delyon had a sharpness to his personality that didn't always endear him to those under his command.

The moment of silence had an edge. Everyone in the room knew they were close, but not close enough.

"We've received the autopsy reports on the bodies out at the Yodell house. There's confirmation that the female is Susan Yodell, wife of Cleve Yodell. As we suspected, the male is not Cleve Yodell. Looks like someone thought they could cover this up."

"Or buy some time." Dani realized she'd spoken out loud when others glanced her way.

"Or buy some time," Captain Delyon acknowledged. "Thanks to your work, Dani, we think we know who the victim might be." Holding an 8 x 10 color photo in the air, his voice became even more authoritative. "Harold Johnson, age 32, reported missing the day after the fire. Wife said he didn't come home the night before, not unusual since the two of them weren't getting along so well. However, Harold missed his kid's piano recital the next day, and for him that wasn't normal."

Handing the photo to the officer seated in front, he continued. "I'll pass this around so you can all take a look at it. We're still waiting for confirmation on this, but I have a feeling the coroner's going to tell us this guy's the victim."

"So that leaves the husband," Jimmy Russo's voice held a distinct note of disgust. "Ya know, just once I'd like to see these scumbags do something original."

Dani agreed but kept quiet on the subject. She knew from the look on his face that Captain Delyon had more to tell them, and he'd want to get them out and investigating as soon as possible. This case was strange, but her Captain wouldn't mind that part; what he wanted was the end result, and that meant catching the person who did this.

"From what Detective Burgess found out, this might not be your run-of-the-mill criminal. The husband, Cleve Yodell, has an interesting background. His family engaged in some weird behavior through the years, had people over to practice some kind of black magic and witchcraft. We're looking into it. But first we need to find Cleve."

Dani's mind raced. It sounded like the Captain had something else he wanted to investigate beyond the double homicide. As if reading her mind, his next comment answered her question. "We have reason to suspect there was more going on at these gatherings than a big bonfire. Based on statements from people who knew the family, as well as eyewitness accounts of the rituals that happened out at the house, we're fairly certain we could've at the very least nailed Mr. Yodell's parents on a number of charges, particularly child endangerment. It sounds like the local teens engaged in sexual acts with the adults. Unfortunately, the elder Mr. and Mrs. Yodell are no longer with us."

Dani's mind flashed back to Shane's friend, Lee, the man with the nice smile who worked with her nephew for a summer. Dani's stomach rolled, full of burnt coffee and an emotion she didn't care to name. She tried to focus on the Captain's words instead of thinking about the damage done to those children so many years ago.

"For now, we need to apprehend Mr. Yodell and bring him in. He is, in all probability, a violent and dangerous criminal, and we want him off the streets as soon as possible. I have a photo that I'll pass around as well, but I suspect we won't find him in Connecticut."

A patrol officer in the front row spoke. "Why not?"

"We'll get to that in a minute. First, I want to go over the profile for this guy." At the sound of a groan in the room, Captain Delyon's eyes narrowed. "Don't complain. This stuff works, and you need to hear it."

Dani shifted in her seat, having an idea of what was coming next. Through her exhaustion, she willed herself to listen carefully to what the Captain said.

He cleared his throat. "From what we can tell about this guy's persona, and from what the state psych guy can figure out, we're dealing with a clinical psychopath. These kinds of people can be hard to identify, but we've got enough evidence to back us up on this. According to this report, the behavior of the psychopath is manipulative. We all know that. They lie to everyone about everything, and they're parasites. Usually these guys are egocentric, but the real problem comes in when they get frustrated. Cleve Yodell will have a very low tolerance for the small problems, the everyday stuff we all deal with, and he'll blow up at the smallest provocation."

"Sounds like most of the scumbags we see, Captain. What makes this guy different?" Quite a few men nodded when Jimmy asked his question.

Captain Delyon looked over the top of his glasses at the paper he was holding. "Well, Jimmy, according to the psych guy who gave me all this stuff, the biggest difference is that this type of person has no inner motivation to respond to a moral imperative. Plus, he kills people, unlike most of the other scumbags we see."

"The worst of the worst." Dani said, and the officer next to her nodded.

Captain Delyon handed a photo to the officer in the front row and looked across the room at Dani. "Burgess!"

"Yes, sir?"

"Once this meeting is finished, I want you to go home and pack your bags. The evidence you recovered at the house has pointed us in the right direction. Based on information gathered from the wife's personal effects, we have a pretty good idea of where Mr. Yodell went and why. You're going to Virginia."

Dani hated airplanes. Although it was a logical choice to travel long distances, she would've been happier riding the train. There wasn't enough time, though. She had a scumbag to catch.

Tightening the seat belt so she wouldn't be ejected from her seat if they crashed, she shut her eyes to discourage the person sitting next to her from talking while she tried to sort through the barrage of information the Captain had thrown at her in the meeting. Besides, with her eyes closed she couldn't see out the window, which meant she didn't have to think about the land below her. Far below her.

She thought about pulling out her notes but had a feeling the pictures would be a problem for the person sitting next to her. Besides, the airline food was bad enough without adding crime scene pictures.

I wonder if Captain Delyon's right.

Usually, her Captain was fairly accurate in his assessment of the cases she'd worked. Dani knew that everything she'd discovered pointed to Cleve Yodell being in Virginia, but she hoped they weren't chasing their tails on this one. The story was bizarre. She had trouble believing anyone, psychopath or not, would go to all that trouble trying to kill an entire family in Yorktown.

Because that, in her opinion, was just plain crazy.

CHAPTER TWELVE

THE CHURCH BELLS WERE SILENT when Katie walked down the aisle with nothing to disguise her unsteady gait or hide her wobbly smile. She didn't feel so good, and she wondered if it was an early flu season.

Of course, Anna Louise was sitting all the way at the front, in the same pew her family had claimed for generations. For some reason, the walk was much longer than it had been last week. When Anna Louise looked up at her, Katie pasted a genuine Southern smile on her face and slid across the bench.

"Good morning," she whispered to her sister-in-law. "I'm surprised to see you here. How's Beau doing?"

Anna Louise looked at Katie in silence before answering. "He's still alive, but they haven't taken him out of the coma yet. Your parents are at the hospital right now." There was another pause while Anna Louise fiddled with her pearls. "I didn't want to leave him alone."

Facing front, Katie knew her face was turning red. What was she supposed to do last night, sleep at the hospital?

It would have been nice to give Anna Louise a break. Great, now she was blaming herself, too. Fine, she'd go visit her brother after church.

Leaning toward Anna Louise, she whispered, "I'm going to see Beau after the service. Are you going back to the hospital?"

Spine rigid, Anna Louise wouldn't look at her. Instead, she hissed, "Where were you last night? You told me you'd be at the hospital."

Katie paused, trying to work out where she was supposed to be last night. Obviously, she'd screwed up. Again.

"Did something happen?"

Her sister-in-law's hand rose to her pearls again. "No, but that's not the point. I needed you. I'm exhausted, and now I find out—"

"What?" Katie prodded. "Is there something else going on?" Wouldn't that be typical? Something else happened to her brother and she missed it because she was... busy. Some days it was harder to keep up with life than others.

"Will you be at dinner today?"

The abrupt change gave Katie pause. Something was going on, and as usual, Katie was completely in the dark. Anna Louise wouldn't deliberately hold back information, but she might be reluctant to tell Katie if Beau's condition worsened.

"I didn't think you'd be cooking today."

Anna Louise finally looked at her. "Your parents are in town and need to eat, as do I. Some things are too important to ignore. Pull yourself together this afternoon. Dinner will be at three."

"What's wrong with you?"

"There's nothing wrong with me, Katie, except my husband is lying in a hospital bed, possibly dying, and the people I'm supposed to be able to count on aren't always there."

"What are you talking about?"

The smell of wax from the candles burning on the altar reached her, and Katie took a deep breath. The familiarity of Sunday morning in church soothed her, helping her feel like she hadn't completely lost her mind. Because frankly, her sister-in-law was starting to act just a little bit looney.

The angrier Anna Louise got, the softer her voice became. At this point, Katie could hardly hear her. "Where were you last night? You said you'd be there, and you never showed up. I tried calling you, I left messages, and you never called me back."

Katie flashed on a memory of her cell phone ringing last night, and when she'd seen that it was her sister-in-law, she turned the ringer off. A guilty flush crept up her cheeks. She should have been at the hospital for a longer period of time to support Anna Louise, to check on her brother, but she couldn't. She couldn't face those machines or his mortality. She couldn't face her own mortality.

Katie tried to focus as Anna Louise was still talking. "It's bad enough we have to deal with this—don't make it worse. You know, your brother would tell you to..." The sound of her voice was drowned out by the choir singing. Katie never thought she'd be so relieved to have a church service begin.

As they stood to sing the entry hymn, she glanced around to see who else was there. The usual families that she knew from years of attending Grace Church were seated in the pews around her. As part of the minister's family, Katie and Beau had always sat up front with her mother for Sunday services. They were the only ones who had the same seats week after week.

Grace Church, located in the center of Yorktown, was beautiful. Besides being a church, the building was a historic landmark, the first to be built by settlers in 1697. Situated near the shores of the York River, the cemetery just outside the church windows contained some of America's founding fathers, including a signer of the Declaration of Independence.

This was probably the reason Lisa attended. Katie spotted her in one of the middle rows, standing with an arm around one daughter and the other looking on as she held the hymnal. Both Lisa and her husband were dressed meticulously, and the little girls wore matching flowered dresses.

I'm surprised she didn't make them wear little white gloves.

Katie immediately felt bad for thinking this about her friend's sister, but she knew the only reason Lisa had chosen this church was that she thought it would improve her social standing.

She tried to focus her attention on the service, but it was hard to do so while her head was hurting. Preferably, she'd still be home, burrowed under the bed covers, but after the reception she'd gotten from Anna Louise, it was probably a good thing she'd shown up this morning.

"Let us pray for the sick and infirm..." The minister's voice droned on, mentioning a good number of names, including Beau. A sharp pain cut into Katie's chest when she heard her brother's name.

The minister was chatty that morning, referencing scripture and mentioning a book he'd recently read, giving a sermon that reached out to the multi-generational crowd present. Katie didn't hear a word of it, but she made certain to look appropriately interested. Her gaze wandered over the centuries old building, absently noting the old wooden beams in the ceiling and the wavy glass panes that probably let most of the heat and air conditioning out of the building. The York River sparkled in the distance, a calming sight that always helped balance Katie's inner world.

Finally, everyone stood for the recessional hymn, signaling the end of the service. As people began to file out, Katie's only thought was of escape. A change into comfy clothes and some time alone before she had to be at Anna Louise's for Sunday dinner would do her a world of good.

"Kay-tee, it's so lovely to see you this morning. Are you feeling okay? You don't look so good." As usual, Lisa's voice jarred Katie back to reality. "How's Beau? Is he going to die?"

To her credit, Anna Louise, standing next to Katie, didn't bat an eye. Shaking her head, she said, "Time will tell, Lisa, but we're hopeful he'll recover." Katie looked at her sister-in-law in surprise, noting that the woman may have more class than Katie ever gave her credit for.

Lisa leaned close to Katie. "Don't look now, but there's Mr. Creepy heading toward us."

"What? Who are you talking about?"

"I don't want to point him out and be obvious, but I watched him study you throughout the entire service. There's something wrong with that man, and I don't like him."

"What do you mean, 'study me'?"

"He couldn't take his eyes off you the whole time," Lisa said, "and not in a good way. He was like a butcher checking out a slab of meat."

That's a little dramatic.

Katie wondered how Lisa could have decided she didn't like somebody she'd never spoken to. That was Lisa, though: quick to judge, and probably quicker to condemn.

Turning her head, Katie saw a man approach. It looked like Lisa was right, but Katie didn't see any problem. This man was extraordinarily handsome, with jet black hair and deep blue eyes that were looking right into her. She didn't recognize him, but that didn't mean much in a town of over sixty thousand people. Obviously, she didn't know everyone.

Stopping in front of her, he reached out and grasped Katie's hand in his own. His good looks made it hard for her to breathe.

He's almost as handsome as Roland.

"Hello. How do you do? I'm Cleve Farrington."

CHAPTER THIRTEEN

"CHARMING" DIDN'T EVEN BEGIN TO describe Cleve Farrington, and Katie knew she was a goner when she offered to give him a tour of the church and grounds. She hadn't offered to give tours in almost a decade. She could have done without having Lisa by her side the whole time, though.

"Grace Church is a unique part of Yorktown's history." Katie knew the spiel by heart; she'd been giving tours of the building and cemetery since she was a teen.

"Where did you say you were from?" Lisa wasn't leaving, that was obvious.

One corner of Cleve's mouth turned up slightly, making him appear rakish and amused. "I didn't. I've been doing some traveling this month and just came down from the Northeast. And you? Do I detect a Northern accent?"

"We're from Connecticut," Lisa answered. "Where in the Northeast were you?"

Katie tossed him a shy smile, assuming he recognized her Southern drawl and knew Katie wasn't a Northerner, despite Lisa's use of the pronoun "we."

"Let's step outside, and I can show you the grave markers of a couple of the signers of the Declaration of Independence," Katie said. Her goal was to maneuver Cleve away from Lisa in order to spend time alone with the man. "Lisa, where's your husband and kids? Aren't they waiting for you?"

Lisa shook her head. "No. I told them to go ahead, I'd catch up with them later. I have a committee meeting in the hall this morning for the upcoming Fall Festival. So, Cleve, tell me how you ended up here."

Cleve didn't seem in the least bit perturbed by Lisa. If anything, his demeanor suggested nothing more than an affable manner.

"This is where the road took me. I've been scouting around the country for a new place to call home, and this looked like a nice area."

Katie looked down, frowning. Hadn't this guy just finished saying he was spending time traveling around? Who travels around to find a place to live? Most people she knew either had their hearts set on a particular location, followed family, or used the internet to find a place to live. Didn't he have a job?

Oh Lord, don't let him be one of those "I don't need money, I can survive in my car on a can of beans" kind of guys. Let him be at least a little normal.

"Why didn't you just look things up on the internet instead of traveling all over?" Lisa could always be counted on to get to the heart of the matter.

"The internet really only gives us such a small picture, don't you think? There's so much to learn about a place, and," he looked at Katie and winked, "it's so much more interesting to meet new people."

As Katie smiled up at him, she wondered about the serendipity of this meeting. Maybe her luck was changing, maybe she'd just met Mr. Right instead of finding Mr. Right Now. Hopefully, he was normal.

Lisa didn't let go of things so easily. "What do you do for a living?"

"Computer programming, which means I can work from anywhere in the world. And what about you lovely ladies? What do you both do?"

Yay, he has a job!

Katie answered before Lisa could continue probing. "I teach at the local college, and Lisa recently moved to the area with her family. I think the move has kept her rather busy." Katie gave the other woman a pointed look, hoping Lisa got the message. Couldn't she go home to pick a new paint color or organize her closets or something?

"Wonderful." Cleve beamed. "Now, show me those headstones. There's nothing more fascinating than dead people, don't you think?"

Behind his back, Lisa gave Katie a piercing look. "He's weird." She didn't say the words out loud but mouthed them instead. Katie knew exactly what she was saying but chose to ignore her. Katie wanted to get to know this guy, and she'd probably have a good time doing it. He was handsome, employed, and standing right in front of her, looking interested in what she said. Lisa was a screwball who enjoyed looking for the worst in anyone.

"Lisa, if you'll excuse us, I think I'll show Cleve the cemetery myself. I'm sure you have lots to do before the meeting."

Lisa looked at Katie for a moment, as if deciding what to say. "Okay, fine, whatever. Are you going to see your brother later? If they'll let him have visitors,

I'll come with you."

Katie nodded. "Yes, I'll have dinner with Anna Louise and head over to the hospital after that." Feeling somewhat contrite for her uncharitable thoughts about Lisa, she added, "I'll give you a call."

"How many brothers do you have?" Cleve asked, looking puzzled.

"Just one. He had a heart attack the other day and is in the hospital. He's in a coma now, but we're hoping he'll pull through."

"He's alive?"

Katie forgave him the peculiarity of the question. Some people were better at this sort of thing than others. She told him a little about her brother's condition as they walked outside.

"Yes, he'd been very agitated when they brought him in, so they put him in what they call an induced coma. Anyway, as you can see, some of these graves date back to the 1600s, and some of them are from this century. Over here, you'll see the graves of the Nelson family. Thomas Nelson was best known for being a signer of the Declaration of Independence, and there are a number of early founding families here."

As they wandered past the gravestones, Cleve took Katie's hand in a casual gesture. "Is your family here amongst the non-living?"

Katie nodded. "Yes, but we weren't a founding family. Until very recently, some member or another of my family was the parish minister here."

"Sounds almost like an old New England family type of thing." The sun washed over the two of them as they stood talking. Cleve smiled at her again, a flash of a dimple showing up on his amused expression.

This guy could make headlines in Hollywood. Besides his good looks, Cleve Farrington's charm was mesmerizing. His voice was deep, and he was skillful at drawing her into conversation. Before she knew what was happening, she'd told him all about herself and her family.

Katie stopped, realizing she'd just spent the last ten minutes talking about nothing but herself. She should know better than to allow the conversation to stay focused on her. Men got bored with that quickly.

"What about you? Will you be in this area for a while?"

"Why don't I tell you all about it at dinner?" he answered.

Katie froze, wondering if she heard him correctly. "Dinner?"

"Yes, as in a dinner date. Unless you're seeing someone right now, I'd like to take you out, get to know you better."

Katie hesitated. Yes, she was attracted to this man, but was now really a good time to start dating someone? She'd just moved back into her parents' house, her brother was comatose in a hospital bed. She wasn't sure how to answer.

What was that saying, beware what you wish for? Hadn't she just wished for this very thing?

Cleve leaned in close to her and whispered, "I promise I won't propose marriage or anything. It's just dinner."

Katie breathed in his cologne, reminded of the scent worn by the man in the bar last night. But this was different. This man standing in front of her wasn't like the others. For one thing, his sincerity appealed to her. It had been a while since she met a man who came across as honest and charming... not since Roland.

Roland. There he was, standing in the parking lot of the church, arms crossed and watching her. The shadow of yesterday's argument stole across her mind.

What does he want from me?

Turning her back on Roland, Katie looked up at Cleve, who was patiently waiting for her answer. "I'd be delighted to have dinner with you tomorrow night."

A smile crept across Cleve's face. "I am honored. If you give me your address, I'll pick you up at six. Be sure to wear something casual so you'll be comfortable riding my motorcycle."

Just like Roland.

Before she could stop herself, the thought was there. It didn't matter. She wasn't meant to be with Roland, that much was clear to her now.

Feeling Roland's stare despite having her back turned to him, Katie took a breath, trying to dislodge thoughts of anyone except Cleve.

"I'm looking forward to dinner."

"So am I, Miss Hollister. So am I."

CHAPTER FOURTEEN

WALKING AWAY FROM KATIE, CLEVE whistled a soft tune. He knew the picture he presented to the world was one of a man intent on his upcoming date with a woman he'd just met, a pleasant sort of guy looking to settle down with the right woman. He also knew how far that was from the truth. If anyone in that stinkhole church had any idea of the pain he was about to inflict upon the Hollister family, they'd be shocked right down to their early-settler underwear.

Cleve was careful on the motorcycle ride back to the hotel room. It wouldn't help right now to be given a speeding ticket or have law enforcement ask too many questions about the bike's registration. Way better to stay under the radar and be the nice guy that people like.

Driving back to the motel, he focused on his most immediate problem. According to Katie, her brother was in the hospital. He didn't think the man was doing well, but still, he was alive. That should not have happened. Cleve was positive the brother had been dead when he saw him last. That mistake could cost him his whole plan if he didn't fix it soon.

Cleve had to find a way to get into the hospital room to finish what he started. Beau Hollister could not be allowed to live, not now. He could ruin everything Cleve worked for if he came out of his coma.

It's okay. Everything's still in place, ready to go. The brother is merely a setback. In fact, it makes things more interesting, heightens the hunt.

Pulling into the parking lot, Cleve noted only one other car parked in front of the office. The motel was old and not really targeted to the tourist crowd, which suited him perfectly. Reaching into his backpack, he pulled out the door key, which was attached to a ring with a cheap, diamond-shaped green plastic piece that had the room number written in faded gold letters. The door swung open easily, and the lights were already on in his room. Someone was in there—he could hear movement in the bathroom.

Stepping into the room without a sound, he kicked the door shut behind him. Who would dare break into his room? Didn't they know they were as good as dead?

"Hel-lo?" The tentative female voice called from the bathroom, followed by the woman herself. Holding a toilet brush in one hand and cleaner in the other, the young woman offered Cleve a hesitant smile. "I'm sorry, I'll be finished in a few minutes..."

Cleve looked her over, assessing the situation. It would be easy enough to rape and kill her, and he most likely would enjoy doing so. However, that might draw unwanted attention to him, and it wasn't a risk he was willing to take at the moment.

But he did hate to pass up an opportunity like this. Maybe he could get her to go out to the woods with him, where he could have a little fun.

He realized they'd been standing there for a minute, staring at each other. It was obvious the woman was starting to get a little uncomfortable, maybe even sensing the danger in front of her.

"Unless, maybe, I should finish your room later?" He relished the quaver in her voice.

"Why are you in here?" he demanded. "Didn't you see the 'Do Not Disturb' sign on the door?"

"N-no, sir. There was no sign on the door."

"Are you calling me a liar? I put that sign on my door before I left this morning specifically because I didn't want you in this room. So tell me, what are you doing in here?"

The woman took a step backward, but Cleve wasn't sure where she thought she could run to. Escape to the bathroom? Not a good option, but then again, not his problem. His problem was what to do with her. He wasn't entirely without a heart. He'd let her live.

Smiling a bit to put her at ease, he said, "Maybe it blew off the door handle. They're not all that heavy."

The maid still looked trapped. Cleve softened his voice a little more. "Why don't you forget about cleaning anything else and leave now? Maybe you can leave a note with the head of housekeeping that I'll take care of this room. I don't want anyone coming in here." He thought about what she would look like naked, of the sharp taste of her blood, and inhaled.

Nodding mutely, the woman started toward the door. Cleve took a step toward her, blocking her path. "Aren't you forgetting something?"

Without a sound, she shook her head. Cleve looked pointedly at her hands. "Didn't you want to get your cleaning supplies?"

"No, thank you." Her voice was almost a whisper. "I'll leave them here for you, in case you need them." Quicker than he would've thought possible, she scurried around him and left.

That should take care of that. He doubted she'd be back, given how nervous she looked. It was funny, really, how some women thought they were likely to be raped or murdered in any given circumstance. Cleve smiled, considering the fact that this was indeed the very circumstance women had to worry about.

She was gone, now, so there was no sense in thinking about her. There were other things to consider, like what he was going to do about the Hollister family.

Walking to the old dresser, he dropped his watch onto the scratched surface and started undressing. Church clothes always made him uncomfortable, probably because they were part of a costume he hated to wear. Alone, he had no need for subterfuge as he did in his daily life.

There was one other problem he had noted at the church earlier. Cleve expected that Katie would have some kind of boyfriend or love interest and was surprised when she accepted his offer of a date the following night. But a man had been standing and watching the entire exchange, as if he knew Katie was about to get into some sort of trouble.

Too bad you're in love with a dead woman.

At the thought, Cleve realized it was true. The man watching Katie and Cleve earlier was in love with her—he had it written all over his face. Throwing himself on the saggy mattress, Cleve stared at the ceiling. If lover boy became a real problem, Cleve could kill him, too. Might as well take everyone out.

Reaching a hand under the pillow next to him, Cleve pulled out the old scrapbook. Everything was in there, the entire history that documented the problems Katie Hollister and her ancestors had caused his family. It was all in black and white, part of the damn news, so there was no denying anything. It was time for them to pay for their sins and for Cleve to attain everything that should have been rightfully his in the first place.

His family had saved all the newspapers ever since good old Uncle Jedidiah came back from his trip south in the early 1900s. His great Uncle Jed was a bit of a wanderer and traveled all over, collecting items that were mostly useless but sometimes amusing. He always brought things home for people to see and later tried to sell them and make a profit. One time he came home bearing the newspaper *Cavalier*. This was Williamsburg, Virginia's newspaper, and legend has it that his family gathered round to read all about it. That's when they saw the news.

She was in the paper, on page six, pictured with her husband and family, the woman who brought his family to ruin.

Hannah Donovan had gone south and built a whole new life for herself. A comfortable one, at that.

Through the years, his family had one of the Yorktown or Williamsburg area newspapers mailed to the house to keep up with the news. Births, marriages, deaths… these were carefully clipped, documented, and stored in the scrapbook that was handed down from one generation to the next.

They always knew where Hannah Donovan was and what her descendants were doing. They had a meticulous list of the names of everyone in the Donovan/Hollister family—even before the internet.

As much as he would have liked to go through the scrapbook one more time, he couldn't. Not tonight. It was time to power up his laptop and check the news in Connecticut. Cleve needed to see what, if anything, was being said about his death.

CHAPTER FIFTEEN

"NO NEWS IS GOOD NEWS, right?"

Anna Louise pulled a perfectly roasted chicken out of the oven with gaily decorated pot holders. Next, baby red potatoes emerged. Surely, there was pie in the future as well.

Katie wasn't sure she agreed with the "no news" sentiment but decided to be upbeat. There was no point in cynicism yet. Maybe later there would be time for wailing and crying, but not at the moment. Now, she would show strength for her sister-in-law.

"True, nobody's called, so everything must be okay. I'm sure they'll take him out of the coma soon. He's a strong guy so of course his body will heal quickly."

"Just think, Katie, someday it'll be your house we'll all be gathering at, and you'll be cooking for your husband and family, and Beau and I..."

Anna Louise's voice trailed off as Katie reached out to take control of a casserole dish. Feeling a dash of sympathy for her sister-in-law, Katie decided to be as agreeable as possible. Right now, Anna Louise needed all the positive thoughts and kind words she could get.

"Someday, when I find the right man and get married, we'll absolutely celebrate holidays and have Sunday dinners between your house and mine. It'll be wonderful knowing we share these things. You can do Thanksgiving dinner, and I'll do Christmas."

Katie stopped talking when Anna Louise's eyes filled with tears. Nothing she could say right now would make it better, so she kept her mouth shut.

But keeping her mouth shut didn't deter Anna Louise from voicing an opinion. "You know, Katie, I have to tell you that I am hoping and praying you will settle down and get married soon."

"I have to meet someone first."

Katie didn't think she should mention Cleve, not yet, because that would only drive Anna Louise to new heights of questioning. Besides, for all Katie knew, this wasn't going to be a long-term relationship. So far, it was only going to be one dinner.

"There's plenty of suitable men out there for you. You have to put a little effort in, that's all. You're going to make a wonderful wife to somebody, and then you won't have to worry about all that teaching stuff you have to do now."

Katie didn't think Anna Louise even noticed the silence that lay between them.

"I like teaching."

Anna Louise sighed as she put the vegetables with the rest of the food on the table. "I'm sure you think you do, but as your brother has often told you, there comes a point in life when it's time to settle down and do what is proper."

Katie struggled to control her temper. Anna Louise only mimicked what her brother said, voicing Beau's opinions. Katie had never agreed with her brother and his patriarchal view of family, but now might not be the time to talk about all that. Anna Louise didn't look like she was holding up very well, and Katie didn't want to discuss anything that might upset her.

Best to let sleeping dogs lie. Not upset the apple cart. Not count any chickens. I'll let Anna Louise vent, she's a little stressed right now. Understandably.

"Lemonade or iced tea?" Anna Louise smiled, holding up a crystal goblet.

"Wine?" Katie could only hope.

"Sweet tea it is, then."

Okay, so maybe Anna Louise had a little backbone to her. Enough of a backbone to refuse Katie a drink. It was going to be a long dinner.

Katie started to let her guard down after the salad, thinking that maybe, just maybe, they could pretend everything was normal—as normal as could be expected with her parents sitting at the hospital next to her brother, waiting for doctors to take him out of a coma. They'd made it through the requisite hand holding for the before-dinner grace prayer and the salad and had just begun the chicken and potato course when it got worse.

"If you let me, I can introduce you to some highly respectable men who are suitable for you."

Katie tried not to gag at the thought of what a suitable man might be like.

"No, thanks, Anna Louise. I think I'll stay single for a while."

"Your eggs are getting old, you know. You can't wait too much longer."

Katie paused, fork in mid-air. For a moment, she'd thought Anna Louise had said her eggs were getting *cold*, but that didn't make any sense since there were no eggs with dinner. When she realized her sister in law had said *old*, she felt the familiar indignation that accompanied most family dinners.

"Don't worry about my eggs, Anna Louise. Concentrate on your own."

Katie knew the words were a mistake even before Anna Louise's eyes filled with tears. *Damn.* Family dinners sucked, especially the ones where a member of the family was hovering between life and death.

"I'm sorry, Anna Louise. I shouldn't have said that—"

Her sister in law straightened in her chair and attempted to put on a brave face. Katie knew better, though, and she could see that she'd hurt her hostess.

"Katie, I think I'm pregnant." Anna Louise leaned back in her chair, face paled and meal forgotten.

Katie didn't know what to say. Somehow, congratulations seemed out of place, although she couldn't explain why. Instead, she asked the only logical question.

"You think you're pregnant? Have you taken a test?"

Anna Louise's voice was small. "No. I'm afraid to do that."

"What are you afraid of? Isn't this what you and Beau wanted?"

Anna Louise looked directly at Katie with eyes so full of pain, it made Katie want to retreat. "What if I'm not pregnant? What if I'm just late? That means it didn't happen again, and it might never happen, and now Beau might die, which means I'll never have his baby." She shook her head. "It's better not to know."

Katie might not be very good at dealing with her own life crisis, but she knew what to do for others. Putting her napkin next to her plate, she spoke with authority.

"That's nonsense. We need to know if you're pregnant or not, and if you are with child then we need to get you to a doctor right away. This isn't about you, Anna Louise; this is about the possibility of another life, and I know my brother would insist that you take care of yourself and the baby as best you can. If you're not, then it sounds like you've already prepared yourself for that eventuality. But this time, not knowing can do a world of harm, and you would never forgive yourself if something happened to this baby."

"Do you think I'm pregnant?" It didn't seem possible, but Anna Louise's voice got even softer. "Do you think it's possible, or do you think I'm just late from the stress?"

It was unsettling to see her normally competent, take-charge sister-in-law timid and unsure of herself. Since Katie was the only person at the table, it looked like it was up to her to fix it.

"How late are you?"

"Three weeks."

Katie was glad her sister-in-law confided in her. Obviously, the woman had too much on her plate, and maybe Katie could help with this one thing.

"Three weeks ago, you didn't have a sick husband in the hospital. Do you have one of those 'at-home pregnancy test' things?"

Anna Louise nodded. "I've had one in the upstairs bathroom for two years now. Not the same one, but we kept hoping..."

As she trailed off, Katie remembered something her mother had mentioned before leaving. "You were having health issues?"

"Yes, the doctor said that with my history of endometriosis, it's unlikely that I can conceive."

"What the hell does she know?"

"Well, she did go to eight years of medical school."

Anna Louise sounded vaguely amused, making Katie feel better. The Anna Louise she knew did not fall apart easily, and Katie hoped she'd be able to pull herself together. She didn't like it when seemingly stable people fell apart, making her feel like the world was made of quicksand.

"Have you had enough lemonade?" Katie asked.

Anna Louise knew exactly what she was talking about. "I have, and you're right. I guess it's time to use the bathroom."

They sat at the table for another minute until Katie cleared her throat. In silence, Anna Louise rose and went upstairs. Katie followed.

Less than five minutes later, they had the answer.

"The instructions say we have to wait seven minutes," Anna Louise read from the paper that came with the pregnancy test.

"Yeah, well, your kid says you better figure this out quick because there's a big plus sign on the stick."

"Oh..."

Katie was glad she'd insisted on being in the bathroom with Anna Louise, despite her sister-in-law's protests about privacy. She knew if the test was positive, it was better to be standing right there to steady Anna Louise, as she was doing now.

"Why don't we go into the other room and sit down?"

"I'm okay. I just…oh my God, I'm pregnant."

Katie couldn't stop the smile from spreading across her face.

"Yep. Preggers."

"I'm going to have a baby."

"You're going to get fat."

Anna Louise giggled and swatted lightly at Katie. "Stop that. Of course I'm going to get fat, silly. I've wanted this for so long…"

Katie hugged her. "Congratulations, sis. I'm really happy for you both, and I can't help but think this is the kind of news you need to tell your husband. He'd want to know, coma or not."

Anna Louise hugged her back. "Of course, you're right. I'll go right now so I can tell your parents, too. Katie, thank you so much. If you hadn't forced me to do this, I'd still be wondering and stressed and all sorts of silly things."

Katie couldn't help feeling relieved. Being pregnant always made people act strange, so this had to be the reason Anna Louise was so uptight in church. There was no way Anna Louise had any idea of the real reason Katie didn't answer her phone last night.

Katie shrugged. "I had a feeling as soon as you said it that you were pregnant. No offense, but your hormones have been acting up a little."

Anna Louise laughed. "Do you mind if I go right now?"

"Of course not. I'll take care of cleaning everything here. Go. Don't worry about a thing except calling your doctor tomorrow."

Anna Louise was already up and fixing her hair. "Thanks. Will you visit tonight?" Grabbing her purse, she spoke over her shoulder as she headed down the hallway.

Katie followed Anna Louise down the stairs. "Probably, but I'm not sure what time I'll get there."

"Take your time. Oh, by the way, I met Roland's new girlfriend."

A hollow space yawned inside Katie, and she grabbed the railing so she wouldn't fall down the stairs.

"New girlfriend? Roland doesn't have a girlfriend."

Looking over her shoulder at Katie, Anna Louise stopped. A look of sadness crossed her face, and her voice held a trace of pity. "I'm sorry, I must've been mistaken. She's probably just a friend."

Katie smiled, covering her thoughts. "Yes, I'm sure she's just a friend."

It didn't take long to clear the table and put all the leftover food in containers in the refrigerator, but by the time she got back to her house, Katie felt like she'd run a marathon. Once she let herself in, she tossed her purse on the front table and threw herself into the softness of the living room couch. Closing her eyes, she tried to keep all thoughts out of her head. It had been a day of extreme ups and downs, and she didn't want to begin to sort through her feelings. Anna Louise must've been wrong. Katie would have known if Roland was dating someone. Wouldn't she?

"I'm so glad you're home. We need to talk."

Katie's eyes flew open at the sound of the lilting Irish voice. There she stood, close enough to touch.

Damn ghost.

Could her life get any worse? She didn't have a house, she didn't have a boyfriend, there was no wine with lunch—and now this.

"You. Do. Not. Exist."

Maybe it was all a hallucination, and Hannah would go away. Hannah was allegedly the harbinger of bad things, and Katie wasn't sure how much more bad news she could take. She turned her back on Hannah, hoping sheer willpower would make the apparition disappear.

"I'm sorry to tell you this, but I do exist, and you appear to be stuck with me for the time being. But right now, there's something I have to tell you."

"I'm busy."

The ghost of Katie's great-great-great grandmother shifted so she stood in front of Katie. "No, you're sitting on the couch, feeling sorry for yourself. Please, Katie-love, you have to listen to me—since this is all my fault anyway."

CHAPTER SIXTEEN

"WHAT'S ALL YOUR FAULT?" KATIE was confused. What did Hannah have to do with anything that was going on in her life right now?

"I'm not sure how this happened, but there's a dead man out there, and he's coming here. He's coming for you, and we may already be too late to stop him."

"A dead man?" Sometimes ghosts made no sense at all.

"I know it sounds strange, but this person died many years ago. I knew him."

Katie sighed. Oddly, her desire for a drink was held at bay, another fact that made no sense to her. She assumed that ghosts and dead men in her neighborhood would have the opposite effect and make her want to run screaming for the bottle. Maybe she'd had enough last night to tide her over for at least a day or two.

"All right, Hannah, tell me: how does a dead man come get me? Will he come into my dreams like a B-grade horror movie, or will he show up like a Halloween specter?"

"I don't know."

The silence stretched between them as Katie studied the ghost, who now looked uncomfortable. Besides the discomfort apparent on her face, Hannah appeared the same as always: long, dark skirt, cream colored blouse buttoned up to her neck, hair piled on top of her head. Katie had the crazy thought that Hannah might be doomed to some sort of fashion hell, which would explain the clothes.

"Elaborate, please. If I'm going to gain anything from having you hang around as my otherworldly companion, at least you should be able to give me some good information."

"I believe I need to start at the beginning of the story. I thought it started with his daughter, Jenny."

"Whose daughter?" Katie was impatient. What was Hannah going on about? She had enough on her mind, and she needed a more direct approach right now.

"When I was a young girl, I came to America to work as a maid for a man in Connecticut. It was a time of fascination and fear for me, living in this land of plenty. Remember, at that time it hadn't been that long ago we were all starving in Ireland."

Katie had a vague memory of this period in history from a book she'd read a long time ago. "The famine, 1840-something, wasn't it? The potatoes stopped growing or something?"

Hannah grew slightly taller and became more solid. Katie wondered if emotions fueled a ghost. Her Irish accent grew stronger as Hannah answered.

"Yes, the Great Hunger stretched from 1845 through the end of the decade, but the consequences were far reaching and devastating. Many of us left our country, as we were unable to survive, thanks to the politics of Great Britain."

"I'm sorry you had to endure that." Katie wasn't certain what else to say to this woman who had lived through such a cruel time. The fact that she was a ghost made it even more difficult to know what to say. After all, there was no rule book for this kind of conversation.

Hannah shook her head. "That's not what I need to talk about. Katie-love, I don't know why I'm here, why I've stayed behind amongst the living when all of my family has moved on in their journey. It's only recently, though, that I've begun to think that I've been left here to fight the evil that I once confronted as a girl."

"I never thought about that. You must miss your family very much." Katie realized that if she accepted Hannah as being real, a ghost in her very own house, it meant this woman—or spirit—had been alone for a long time. Decades with nobody's company except a family who only half-believed you existed had to be depressing.

Maybe Hannah needs a drink.

"It's kind of hard to accept that you're real, you know." Katie said. "Even though I talk to you, most of the time I assume you're nothing more than a product of my subconscious mind that allows me to work things out."

Hannah's smile was warm. "Some days it's hard for me to accept that I'm still here, so not to worry, love. I understand."

"What do you do when..." Katie hesitated, uncertain if the question she was about to ask was rude or not.

"Go ahead, ask what you want. But remember, I don't know how much time I have here tonight."

KC the cat sauntered into the room and leapt up on a side table. With round yellow eyes, he stared at Hannah and meowed. Katie shook her head. That cat probably knew more about ghosts than anyone who had lived in the house, but cats don't talk.

"Where do you go when we can't see you?"

It was one of the reasons Katie hadn't believed Hannah was real. Despite her experiences of the summer with a ghost in her friend's house, it didn't make sense to her that Hannah would appear once in a while, then fade away into nothingness. Why didn't she move on? Most ghosts had a score to settle or didn't realize they were dead.

"I don't know exactly where I go, but it's as if I'm resting. The problem is, I don't have a lot of control over how long I can stay with you. Maybe I never tried hard enough, or there's a trick to it that I just don't know."

"So what are you trying to tell me? Something about your life as a girl?"

Hannah moved around the room as if she had a restless energy to work off. "Yes. I used to think that the problem came from Jenny, the daughter of the man I worked for. Jenny was, to put it kindly, off her head. She would regularly refuse her supper because she'd been out in the barnyard hunting small animals and eating them."

"What?" Katie was incredulous. "That's insane."

Hannah nodded. "Exactly. With her father's death, it only got worse. I didn't kill him, but she blamed me anyway. Her family fell into extreme poverty, and Jenny told her child that their life situation was my fault. Her story of how I ruined the family got passed from one generation to the next."

"How did her father die? Why did you get blamed for the death?" Katie was wondering if she should start looking into this story, especially if it was going to affect her life right now.

Hannah stared at Katie for a moment before answering. "Murder. He was killed in his own bed while he slept."

Katie shuddered before realization hit her. "If his daughter blamed you, did others blame you as well?"

"Yes. I went to jail for six years before receiving a pardon."

"What? You were in jail?"

This was definitely not part of the family history that Katie knew. She wondered if her parents had ever known. Her father probably didn't have any idea, since he'd never believed in Hannah's existence anyway. But surely her mother had some indication of this tragedy. It might be a tricky thing to ask, though. She'd have to give this some thought before she started blabbing to her family.

"I don't believe anyone beyond my husband knew of the story in this area. I left Connecticut and came south, trying to find work in a more gentle climate. Northern winters are formidable."

Katie's thoughts were spinning. She was going to have to try to piece the entire story together at some point, but right now her life felt as if it were starting to slip a little bit more out of her control. "So, this Jenny person... she blamed you for the murder, which you didn't commit, right?"

To her relief, Hannah smiled at her. "No, Katie-love. I never killed anyone. I would not take a life so easily."

That was certainly good to know. Katie stared out the window into the late afternoon, trying to fit the pieces together in her head. Sundays in Virginia had a tendency to move like slow, thick molasses, and right now she felt the full effects of that. She wished she'd been able to get that nap in before Hannah had shown up.

"Okay, just checking. So this crazy lady tells her family it's all your fault, and then what?"

"Her anger was pure, that much I know. Anger that is carried through generations sometimes has a chance to get diluted with forgiveness, but that's not the case when it's mixed with madness." Hannah's figure started to lighten.

"Hannah, stay with me so I can get this story straight. You started to tell me that somehow what happened to you is affecting me here and now, right? How does it all tie in together?"

"It was the madness that was passed from one generation to the next that I thought was hunting you. But I've felt him, here, watching you... the man I killed is here..."

Hannah was barely visible, frustrating Katie. She hated it when the ghost disappeared.

"Be careful, Katie-love. I don't know how he's done it, but I believe he's coming for you."

Katie had to strain to hear the last words, as both Hannah and her voice faded. Then she was gone... if a ghost can ever really be gone.

Grabbing the phone in the front hall, Katie dialed the number she knew by heart. When he answered, she had trouble speaking.

"Katie? Is that you?" Stupid caller ID. Everybody always knew who you were.

"Yes, Roland, it's me. I need to talk to you."

The silence stretched between them for a moment as Katie wondered if she'd interrupted anything. Maybe Roland had a date right now, maybe another woman was sitting next to him. Maybe she was twirling her hair around her finger, gazing at him with big blue eyes and a pouty smile. Maybe Katie never had a chance anyway.

"What did you need?"

There couldn't have been another woman, as Katie didn't hear anything in the background. Surely, if someone else had been there, she'd have heard her, some protestation at being interrupted, something.

"I need your help. Can you come over? I've got to talk to you." Katie could hear his sigh. "Please, Roland, it's important."

"Can't we just talk about it on the phone?"

"No, I need to explain this to you face-to-face."

Roland's voice grew soft. "Are you okay?"

Katie nodded, even though he couldn't see her. "I think so, but something's happened I need your help with."

"I'll be there in a little while. Are you in trouble right now?"

"No. I'll be fine until you get here, just hurry. I'm not sure what to do."

"Okay. I'm coming Katie, but this had better be important."

Holding the phone, Katie was about to comment when she realized there was no point in doing so. Roland had already hung up.

CHAPTER SEVENTEEN

SHOWING UP AT ANOTHER POLICE department was always tricky, even when you were there on official business. It didn't help that this town wasn't patrolled by police but by deputies, something that didn't really exist back in Connecticut. Dani flashed her badge at the front window of the York Poquoson Sheriff's Department, smiling with what she hoped was warmth and sincerity but was probably nothing more than a muscle twitch.

"Detective Dani Burgess, Watertown, Connecticut Police Department. I'm here to see Detective Nick Winters."

Buzzing her through the door, the capable front desk woman led Dani through a maze of hallways. The building was typical, squat administrative style, efficient and sterile. The cement walls in the lobby were the same off-white color as the inside walls surrounding the cubicles. Dani figured there must've been a discount sale on off-white paint at the local hardware store.

"They all look alike," Dani said.

"What, dear?"

Crap, she'd done it again. She really had to stop talking out loud to herself. "Just noticing your building looks like the one I work in," Dani said, crossing the fingers of her left hand behind her back.

Following through the maze of hallways, Dani couldn't help marveling at the woman's instant friendly chatter. "We're so happy for Nick," she was saying over her shoulder. Dani nodded, uncertain how to respond. Who treats complete strangers as if they were old friends? This must be one of the things that made a sheriff's department different from a police department. Back home, visitors from out of state would've been lucky to get a surly "Hello," much less the latest gossip or football scores.

"He's wanted this for so long, and he's really very good at his job, you know. Okay then, here we are. You can go right on in—oh, hello Nick, your guest is here. I'll leave y'all to it, then."

The capable woman bustled back down the hallway in the direction they'd come from, leaving Dani staring at a man sitting in a small office behind a desk. There were no blinds on the window, allowing late afternoon sunlight to slant in and brighten the tiny space.

The man behind the desk looked up at her, eyes unfocused.

He's new to the job. Dani knew this even before the guy opened his mouth, which was fine with her. Hopefully, she'd be able to take charge a little more easily. She had less than a second to appraise him, easy enough: not too young, a little bit of experience, light brown hair, height advantage, handsome, nice.

It was probably hard to be him in a job like this.

"Detective Winters?" She held out her hand, certain from reading the nameplate that she had the correct office. "I'm Detective Dani Burgess, Watertown PD. Thanks for meeting with me."

He rose halfway out of his seat to take her hand and waved at the chair on the other side of his desk. "My pleasure. Please, have a seat. Call me Nick, it's easier. Sounds like we've got quite the case here. Hard to believe all this, you know?"

Dani picked up a stack of folders from the chair and set them on the credenza against the wall before sinking into the seat. Her body held the fatigue and stress from the day's flight, as well as the lack of sleep she'd had since the night of the fire. She wondered if she'd get any rest tonight.

Nick leaned forward, hands clasped in front of him on the desk. "I'm the newest detective here. Worked over a decade on patrol, and I'm about all they can spare right now. We've been putting together surveillance for a couple of drug busts in the upper part of the county, but the Sheriff told me to put all that aside to help you."

"Yeah, the lady who walked me in told me they're all very proud of you." Dani realized she'd obviously been referring to Nick's promotion to detective.

Nick blushed at the comment, a trait that struck Dani as endearing. *He's kind of cute.* But cute wasn't the reason she was there, so instead she launched into recent developments.

"As you know, last Wednesday evening we had a house fire, where we recovered two corpses. Turns out one of them was the wife who lived in the house, and we think the other was her boyfriend. It was set up to look like she'd died with her husband, but since we're smarter than the average bear, we figured that out pretty quick. The husband, Cleve Yodell, is missing. During the course of our investigation, I paid another visit to the burnt out house and searched the premises. During that search, I discovered a lock box, the kind of fireproof thing where people keep important papers."

"I read all the reports. This is the part that's almost unbelievable," Nick said.

"I know. It's like something out of a movie. There it was, the big clue we were all hoping for: the wife's diary."

Nick's brow creased. "So our perp kills his wife and her lover, then tries to cover that up with a fire. That's no big stretch, right? We see this sort of thing happen: the spouse loses it, thinks he's smarter than us—bang! We catch him anyway because he's not really all that smart. But this other part, the whole reason you think he's here, that's weird."

Dani agreed. "I know, but our profiler insists that with this kind of sociopath, it's hard to understand what'll really set him off. Apparently, this guy is just looking for a reason to kill, and anything might do it. From what the diary said, he's held a grudge against this family for a long time already."

"I checked the family out before you got here, got some information on them." Nick was silent for a moment, shuffling through his papers. "Wait, I think it's in that stack over there." Getting out of his chair, he walked to the credenza and flipped through the folders Dani had placed there. "Here it is."

Sitting down again, Nick put a pair of half glasses on before he began to read. It made him look a little sexy, sort of like a tough scholar, something Dani didn't think he'd appreciate knowing.

She kept her mouth shut while he read and took the opportunity to study his office. There weren't any family pictures, which was kind of odd. Although, if he'd just gotten the job, he might not have had time to put anything personal out yet. A print advertising the movie *Clerks* hung on the wall behind his desk, but that was the only piece of art adorning the walls. Papers and folders were stacked on every available surface, as well as parts of the floor.

Obviously, a secretary wasn't in the budget for him.

"The summary your captain sent says that the wife kept a sort of journal, with poetry and pieces of her life. From what she wrote, it sounds like she was a little afraid of her husband—with good reason, too. Okay, here's the weird part." Pointing to the page, Nick continued reading. "She mentions in there that her husband was obsessed with his family's lost wealth and blamed a woman by the name of Hannah Donovan for their problems."

"Yeah, but Hannah Donovan no longer exists," Dani said. "She died in 1920-something, right here in Yorktown. From what the wife wrote, looks like our perp kept track of Ms. Donovan and traced her ancestry to the present day."

"And that brings us to the Hollister family," Nick finished. Putting the paper down, he took his glasses off. He was a good looking man, and Dani was startled to realize that she was paying attention to his looks. This wasn't her usual way of doing things; she must be more tired than she thought.

"What do you know about these people?" Dani asked. She didn't expect much since there hadn't been time for him to do any digging.

"I talked to some of the guys who know them. Old family, they've been around for a while. Since the time of Hannah Donovan, in fact. Looks like our Hannah came to town in the late 1800s and married the local minister, and for several generations there's been a member of the Hollister family working at Grace Church, one of the original buildings in the Yorktown Village. Until now, that is."

Dani's interest peaked. "What changed?" Maybe this was the reason Cleve lost his marbles and killed his wife.

"The last Hollister to be minister there has just retired, and neither of his children are following in his footsteps. First time in over a century there hasn't been someone in that family doing something at Grace Church. According to my sister, it was big news around here."

Dani thought for a moment. On the surface, this piece of information didn't seem like much. A retirement? On the other hand, who knew with a crazy like Yodell? Lunatics never made much sense.

"Do you think that's what made our guy lose it?" she asked.

Nick shook his head. "I don't know. You wouldn't think something that simple would do it, but this guy's insane. Maybe?"

"That's what I was thinking. It could be something else, too, something we don't know about yet."

"Hmm. Maybe the sun was too bright in his eyes that day. Or his panties were too tight."

Dani smiled. This partnership was going to work out well.

"There's one more thing you should know about the Hollister family, and this might or might not be important."

"Everything's important." Dani didn't want Nick holding back any information, whether he thought it was irrelevant or not. Ultimately, the investigation was her responsibility, and she took that personally. She didn't want anyone else to die on her watch.

Nick smiled a slow, lazy smile that somehow reminded Dani of a cobra about to strike. "One of the Hollister family's in the hospital."

Dani sat up straight in her chair. "What happened?"

"The official report is that he's had a heart attack," Nick said, "but as we all know—"

"That could've been the result of something else," Dani finished. She reached down to pick up her briefcase before standing. "C'mon, then."

"Are we going to see the Hollister family, Detective Burgess?" Nick was smiling, already out of his own chair.

"Show me where they live, we'll see if anyone's home. I have a feeling we'd better get in touch with the rest of the family members soon. I'd like to prevent any more unfortunate incidents if we can."

CHAPTER EIGHTEEN

"WHY SHOULD I CARE?"

It was the last thing Katie expected to hear Roland say. Standing in front of her with his hair messed from running his hands through it, he looked as if he were struggling to contain his temper. Shocked, Katie had no answer.

"Really, Katie, why are you doing this?"

"Doing what?" Katie hated the meek quality to her voice but couldn't seem to stop herself. Numbness invaded her body as she struggled with conflicting thoughts. Did she do something to offend Roland, maybe something she couldn't remember?

"I haven't even told you the whole story."

"Okay, fine. Tell me the whole story, but you're going to have to make it quick because Kevin's on his way over," Roland said. "We're going out later."

"You don't have to justify Kevin coming over here, you know. He's my friend, too." Actually, he was Ella's boyfriend, but Katie and Roland treated him like one of their old friends.

Roland shifted in his chair, obviously uncomfortable, and looked at his watch. Katie hated the awkwardness that pushed its way between them. Their friendship was about sharing, fun, and laughter, but now all she felt when she was with Roland was loneliness.

"What's wrong?" Katie asked.

"Nothing. It's just that Kevin might want to talk to you for a few minutes."

Katie was silent, thinking about that. Kevin was a police officer in Paterson, the next town over. Ella and Kevin had met this summer while Ella was being harassed by some of the locals. Could Kevin know that Katie had driven home the other night after drinking?

There's no way he would know that. I wasn't stopped. Besides, what I do on my own time is my own business.

"What does he want to talk about?" She might as well ask, especially since it was making Roland so uncomfortable.

"Why don't we talk about the reason you dragged me over here?"

Obviously, Roland wasn't going to tell her. *Fine, I'll find out soon enough anyway.* And even though Roland wasn't going to make this easy, she really did need his help. She needed somebody's help, at least, and he was the only person she could turn to with this.

Taking a deep breath, she started talking before she lost courage. "I don't think I've ever told you this before, but my family has been haunted by a ghost since I was a kid. Not haunted; maybe protected is a better word. I know it sounds strange, and I guess I should've said something sooner, especially after what happened this summer, but even I didn't think it was real."

That much was true, at least. Oddly, when she was helping her friend figure out what to do about living in a haunted house this past summer, it never occurred to her to talk about Hannah. It was a private family sort of thing, and it would've been like telling the world your family's secrets. She couldn't bring herself to mention it, but maybe she should have. It sure would make this moment a whole lot easier.

"Anyway, this ghost, her name is Hannah, and usually she only appears when one of us is in trouble. She saved me when I was a kid." Katie stopped talking, realizing she didn't want to get into that whole thing. The past had nothing to do with the present, and there was no reason for Roland to know about the perv who used to live in the neighborhood.

"So, you have a ghost in the house," Roland said. He didn't sound all that encouraging, but then again, maybe Katie was nervous and reading too much into his tone of voice.

"Yes, and she's been showing up a lot lately." Although she hadn't been around when Beau had his heart attack, which was strange.

Katie stopped talking for a moment, thinking. Had Hannah been with her the night Beau was taken to the hospital? It was hard to remember the details of that night. She knew she'd been hanging out on her back porch, and maybe Hannah had been there. She had a vague memory of talking out loud about her childhood, but who would she have been talking to? Katie closed her eyes for a moment, shutting everything out. It wasn't important whether Hannah was with her that night or what she'd been doing; she just needed to get through this moment with Roland.

Opening her eyes, she continued talking. "She's been telling me that there's some sort of danger around and I need to be careful. When I called you, she had just left, and she told me the story of her life. She said that—"

"Katie, stop," Roland said.

Katie stopped talking, not sure why Roland interrupted her.

"How are you feeling?" he asked.

"What? I'm fine, why?" Katie was confused. Why would he ask her a question like that right in the middle of her description of Hannah?

"Last week, you were sick. I'm just wondering if you've recovered, that's all."

"That was last week. I told you, I'm fine. Besides, you've seen me since then. Why are you doing this? I'm trying to tell you something."

"I know you are, but there's more to this story than just some ghost thing. Were you really sick last week? Or were you hung over? If I look in your bathroom, what am I going to find? Katie, don't you see what you're doing to yourself?" Roland's voice was ragged, and he looked tired.

"I don't want to fight about this again," Katie said. She'd called him for help, not a therapy session. "Are you going to listen to me or not?"

"Are you ready to stop drinking? Because frankly, when you start drinking all the time, I don't know what's the truth and what isn't. Alcohol doesn't exactly make you reliable."

Katie clenched her hands to stop herself from slapping Roland. How dare he? Who did he think he was to treat her like this?

He might have a point, you know. You don't remember most of what happens when you're drunk. That small voice of reason could just shut the heck up right now. The last thing she needed was some weird attack of conscience. She was trying to make a point here.

So is he. Maybe you should listen.

Or maybe she should have a nice big cup of something to steady her nerves as soon as Roland left. God, what was happening to her?

"Is there more to the story that you want to tell me about?" Roland asked. "Because Kevin's going to be here soon."

On cue, the doorbell rang. With a sigh, Katie got up to answer the door. Screw it. She had to tell them what happened, and she didn't care if Kevin was there or not.

Flinging the door open, the out of uniform Kevin stood with a bemused expression on his face.

"You didn't ask who it was," he said.

"My knight in shining armor would've saved me if you were a bad guy." Sarcasm wasn't natural to Katie, but at that moment her frustration operated her mouth.

"Did I interrupt something? I could come back later."

"No, c'mon in," she told him. "We were just talking, that's all."

Katie stalked her way through the front rooms into the back kitchen with Kevin trailing behind.

Roland sat in the kitchen, arms folded over his chest. He nodded at Kevin. Sensing the charged atmosphere, Kevin stood in the doorway, not moving into the kitchen.

"Hey, do you guys need some more time?"

"No, I think we're finished here." Katie's words were clipped, her anger evident.

"Yeah, we're done." Roland's gaze never left Katie's face, but she couldn't tell what he was thinking.

"Kevin, I'm sorry, can I get you anything? Coffee or water or something?" Katie said, embarrassed to almost forget her manners.

"No, I'm fine. Roland and I were going out, anyway. Thanks, though."

There was a moment of awkward silence, something Katie hadn't experienced with Roland before. The whole situation was miserable, but she needed to put on a bright face and hope they would leave soon.

"So, Katie, what are your plans for tonight? Any big dates?" Kevin asked.

"That was smooth, Kevin," Roland said.

"What? I was just asking."

Katie wondered if this was what Kevin wanted to talk to her about. "Not tonight, but I'm going out to dinner tomorrow night."

Kevin nodded. "I heard you had a date with someone new in town."

Katie wasn't surprised. After all, Lisa had been there when she met Cleve, and she'd probably gone and told her sister, Ella, who went and told Kevin. Small towns were great when you needed information, but not so much when you wanted things kept private.

"Yes, I met him at church. He's really nice." Darting a look at Roland, Katie saw that he didn't look like he cared one way or another who she dated. Well, that was just fine with her.

"Where's he from? Is he visiting someone around here?" Kevin slipped automatically into cop mode, interrogating Katie.

"He's sort of traveling around, that's all. He said he was a computer programmer, that he could work from anywhere."

"How much do you know about him?"

Katie couldn't help laughing. "Kevin, that's the point of a date: to get to know someone. I'll tell you all about him on Tuesday, once I find out the details of his life. Don't worry, I know he's a good person."

"Ted Bundy seemed like a nice guy," Roland said.

"I'll be fine," Katie repeated.

"I'm sure you will, but I'd feel a whole lot better if you let us know where you were going and when you were coming home." Kevin's serious manner stopped Katie from making a wisecrack about him being her mother.

She nodded. "Fair enough. You can't be too safe, right? I'll call Ella with the details."

Kevin shook his head. "I'm sorry. I know I'm being overprotective, but seriously, Katie, you have no idea what's out there."

There was a moment of silence as Katie contemplated those words. Unfortunately, she had a pretty good idea of what was out there.

CHAPTER NINETEEN

KATIE JUMPED WHEN THE DOORBELL rang.

"Maybe it's your date," Roland said.

"Maybe it's my friend," Katie retorted. Shaking her head, she went to the door and yanked it open, half-hoping it was a salesperson just so she could slam it shut.

Ella stood on the doorstep wearing a T-shirt that said *The trouble with life is there's no background music.* Her sister Lisa stood next to her.

"I think I've got the wrong house. I'm looking for my sweet friend Katie," Ella said.

"Come in, but fair warning, my sweetness is taking a break right now."

Ella and Lisa followed Katie into the house and back toward the kitchen. In the hallway, Katie heard Lisa's not-so-subtle voice.

"I told you she knew about Roland's date."

Katie stopped short, causing Ella to bump into her.

"Yes, I heard about it from my sister-in-law, who is pregnant by the way and visiting her comatose husband in the hospital. I don't care if he's going on a date; I have a date, too. What I do care about is his attitude, which frankly sucks right now."

She was upset to feel tears pricking at her eyes and tried to comfort herself with the thought that at least she wasn't breaking down in front of the guys. Ella was her friend, so that made it okay. And Lisa... well, Lisa was Lisa, but that would have to be okay for now.

Taking a deep breath, Katie vowed to pull herself together. She could fall apart later, when she was alone. For now, she needed to act like nothing was wrong, her brother was fine, and a ghost wasn't bothering her.

I can always tell Ella. I helped her with the ghost in her house this summer.

She knew as soon as the thought crept into her head that it wasn't possible. After the way Roland had talked to her, Katie didn't think she could handle any more rejection. Besides, how would she start that conversation with Ella? It wasn't like she could simply say, *"Yes, there's this ghost who's been hanging around my family for years now, and she's given me a very unsettling message."* That was too weird. And it wasn't as if Katie wanted Hannah to go away, she simply wanted to understand what the heck was going on.

Maybe she should send the ghost on her way, send her to the next dimension or wherever ghosts went. Life was getting a little too complicated. With Hannah gone, she could shut the door on everything and everyone.

Ella walked over to Kevin and gave him a light kiss on the cheek. "Hey, I missed you," she said, playfully poking him in the chest.

"If you want to get over that sort of feeling, you should marry the guy," Lisa commented. Katie stifled a laugh, knowing her friend wouldn't find that funny.

"That's not funny." Ella was indignant. "I happen to know for a fact that your husband—"

"Blah blah blah. I was kidding, all right? Geez." Lisa shook her head, causing Katie to wonder how many times the sisters fought like this over the years. Little fights, things that siblings always do, things that she and Beau used to do.

She needed to stop thinking like this or she'd start crying again. It was easier to focus on being a good hostess.

"Can I get you ladies something to drink?"

"No, thanks. We can't stay long. We've got reservations for later," Ella said. "I've got to take advantage of the rare bits of time off Kevin gets. It seems like lately he's been working constantly."

"You'd have more time together if you simply planned it all out and didn't spend extra nights taking those self-defense classes," Lisa said. "Why don't you do something else, something normal, like yoga?"

"What's a 'normal' kind of yoga?" Katie asked.

"Pilates," Lisa said.

"That reminds me." Ella turned to Katie, ignoring her sister. "Don't forget, we've got another class this week. I know how much you're enjoying Reuben."

"Um, yeah, about that..." Katie stopped, unsure of herself. "You know, Reuben, he really pushes us kind of hard." This was something Katie needed to talk to Ella about, and now was the perfect time. With Kevin standing right there, maybe she could make them both understand.

Ella nodded as she rummaged through her purse. "Yeah, he does. I think I forgot my phone. That's not going to matter, Kev, is it? You've got yours, right?"

It was obvious Kevin was trying not to smile. "You're fine. I've got a phone. I've got yours, too."

Katie cleared her throat, trying to come up with the right words. "So the thing is, Reuben's a little intense, don't you think?"

"If it's a good workout, maybe I'll join you," Lisa said.

"I didn't say it was a good workout," Katie said. "But Reuben is definitely all about keeping us safe. Actually," she added, hoping to discourage Lisa, "sometimes he's a little mean."

"He cares, and that's what makes him such a good teacher," Ella said. Without missing a beat, Ella turned to Kevin. "How did you get my phone?"

"You left it in my kitchen," he answered, throwing an arm around Ella.

Never mind. She's my friend, so I'll just put on my big girl pants and deal with it.

"Maybe it's a good thing you're taking that class, Katie. You never know who's out there, especially with you going on that date," Lisa said.

"We're not taking the class because of her date. We'd planned on taking the class before she made the date." Ella glared at her sister. "The next class is on Tuesday if you want to drive over with me, Katie."

Maybe the class would be better this time, or maybe it would give her a much needed distraction from her life. There was always the possibility that she could work out some of her frustrations by kicking and punching the bags and shields they used.

"Sure, I'll go with you."

"Great. I'll pick you up Tuesday morning, and we can drive to work together. That way, we can leave from the campus and go straight to the gym."

Katie hesitated. "The only thing is that I'd like to go to the hospital and see my brother after the class."

Ella nodded. "Of course, maybe I can go, too. Hopefully, he'll be better by then, and I can stick my head in and say hi to him."

Katie faked a smile, hoping nobody noticed. "Yes, maybe."

"It's getting kind of late," Roland said. "I've gotta go." Nodding at his friends, he stood to leave.

"I'll talk to you later," Kevin called after him.

"Do you have another date tonight?" Lisa asked. Katie's stomach clenched as she waited for the answer. She tried to assume a look of nonchalance.

"I've got some stuff to do," Roland told them. "Have fun tonight, Ella."

The minute he was gone, Ella turned to Katie and fixed her with a look. "I've got something in the car for you. Why don't you walk outside with me?"

"What is it?" Katie asked, puzzled.

"Some papers from the school. Come on, let's go get them." Without waiting for an answer, Ella turned and walked out of the kitchen, just as Roland had moments before.

Walking fast to keep up with her friend, Katie didn't say anything when she joined Ella outside. After a moment of standing in silence, Ella finally spoke.

"What's going on with you two?"

"What do you mean?" Katie knew what her friend meant but had no idea how she could answer her. What was she supposed to say? *Roland's mad at me because I drink... Roland thinks I'm lying about a ghost that I haven't told you about... Roland doesn't like me anymore.* Any of those statements were true, but none of them were things she could say out loud.

"C'mon, you guys are acting like you've been fighting. Roland barely spoke to us in there, and it's weird. Does this have something to do with the fact that both of you are going on dates?"

Katie tried to laugh in a way that sounded authentic. "No, we're fine. I don't know about Roland. I'm a little tired these days, still getting used to the fall schedule, I guess. Don't worry about us. Hey, let's get back inside before Lisa decides to see what we're doing. You don't want to leave her alone with Kevin for too long, do you?"

Katie could tell that her friend didn't believe her, but there was nothing Ella could say without directly accusing Katie of being a liar.

On the way back to the house, both of them were silent. The familiar thirst was back, the agitation in her soul that only a drink could settle.

As soon as they leave, I can pour one. It's been a long day, and I deserve this. Just one, it'll take the edge off.

Something was different tonight, though. Usually, Katie took comfort in the knowledge that although she might have a drink now and then, she didn't need it. She wasn't like everyone else who drank too much—she simply drank because she wanted to.

It wasn't until everyone left and she flipped the lock on the front door that Katie realized what was different: for the first time in her life, she didn't believe herself.

CHAPTER TWENTY

DANI HAD PULLED HER STILL damp long hair into a ponytail for the sake of speed. Who had time to blow dry their hair when someone was out there killing people? She had felt much better after checking into her room and having a brief chance to rest and shower. There was something about planes and trains that always made her feel grimy, even on short trips.

At the Connecticut airport earlier, she'd checked possible accommodations for the Yorktown area. Her captain had said to stay at a local hotel, but she didn't want to check into one of those chain hotels. They were all the same, and to her, uncomfortable in their uniformity.

She wanted something different.

Besides, it'd been years since she'd had a vacation, and who knew when the opportunity to leave town would come up again?

She found a local bed and breakfast as an answer. It was a gorgeous, stately house that offered all the comforts she was looking for. From the online pictures, the interior of the house boasted warm, rich wall colors hung with elegant paintings and antique furniture in all the rooms. The department wouldn't pay for the entire thing, of course, but she'd get some of her money back. Enough to make it more than worth it.

She needed a place she could retreat to even if it was only for a few hours. The anonymous interiors of large chain hotels depressed her, with their excess of beige and swirly patterned hallway carpets.

She'd never admit it to her fellow officers, but Dani needed something pretty, something that could for at least one brief moment lift her spirits. In her line of work, she, too, often saw the ravages of desperation, and she needed to bring balance to her world.

She could only imagine what her co-workers would have to say about that.

"Checking your Facebook account, detective?" Nick glanced at her from the driver's seat.

"Very funny," she answered. "No, I'm checking the obituaries."

She'd been against getting a smart phone until she realized how helpful it could be during investigations. Dani no longer waited to check information, she did it from the comfort of wherever she was, which was Nick's car at the moment.

"How far is the hospital?" Dani said.

"It's in Newport News, the next town over. We should be there in about twenty minutes, twenty-five if the traffic's bad."

To his credit, Nick didn't ask why she was checking the obituaries. Dani liked that he wasn't harassing her about the small stuff. Because of that, she decided to share her information with him.

"Looks like our boy is listed in today's obits," she said.

"The press hasn't gotten wind of who really died in the house?"

Dani shook her head. "No. So far, we've been able to keep a pretty tight lid on that."

Nick nodded. "Good. We don't want to give him a heads up that we're coming to get him."

Dani smiled. "I like the way you think." *And lots of other things about you, too.* But she was a woman whose work always came first, so whatever feelings might come up for the good looking detective next to her got stuffed in the back of her mind... for now.

With a lane closed for construction on Route 17, it was closer to forty minutes by the time they got to the hospital. Dani was focused on reading everything after the obituary, seeing if anyone had left any comments or notes of sympathy in the online guest book. There were plenty of comments left in the newspaper about the wife, but she didn't see anybody that had anything to say about Cleve.

So he's a loner. What a surprise.

Dani searched the web to find out more about Cleve's family, accessing online birth records through a genealogical database the police often used.

"Doesn't that bother you?" Nick interrupted.

"Doesn't what bother me?"

"Reading in the car. Doesn't it make you nauseous?"

"Nope. It relaxes me."

"Huh." Nick shifted in his seat and turned the air conditioner up. "Makes most people sick."

"I'm a little different than most people."

Nick smiled at her, throwing the car into park. "I noticed. C'mon, let's go harass some doctors."

Of course, Dr. Haverty didn't want to tell them anything. There was patient confidentiality to take into consideration, HIPAA laws and all that.

"You sure, Doc? Isn't there something you can help us out with?" Nick's voice held the easygoing Southern twang that Dani often associated with the good ol' boy network.

She narrowed her eyes at both of them, wondering if they were going to circle around the subject in a way that eventually led to the doctor telling them what they needed to know or if the doctor really wasn't going to talk.

Dr. Haverty leaned back in his chair and looked at them across the cavernous expanse of his mahogany desk. His silver hair and perfectly starched white coat lent him an air of authority.

"Now, Nick, I've known you for a right good time, haven't I? How would you feel if I went around telling everyone your business?"

Nick nodded, appearing relaxed and unconcerned. "I can see you've got a point, there, Doc, but you know—"

"This has turned into a possible assault situation," Dani interrupted. She didn't have time for these two to circle the wagons in their male-bonding game. Nick shot her a look that clearly told her he wanted her to stop talking, but Dani plunged ahead. "We have reason to believe that Beau Hollister may have ended up hospitalized due to an attack, and we need your help in figuring this out. It's very possible that whoever did this might try to come back and finish the job."

Without waiting for an answer, Dani plowed into her first question. "I know that Mr. Hollister had a heart attack, and I'm not asking for confirmation of that. I need to know if you noticed any evidence of a struggle or attack, any bruising or other injuries consistent with that sort of thing."

The doctor sat absolutely still in his chair, appraising Dani. Finally, he sighed, and his shoulders dropped.

"I'll tell you what I can without breaking confidentiality, how's that?"

"That sounds great. Thanks, Doc," Nick rushed in to say.

Dani checked her instinct to give Nick an *I told you so* look. Sometimes people needed to be pushed, and the doctor was one of those people. Besides, she could almost hear the clock ticking. They didn't have time to dance around and play games. They needed information now.

"Okay then. First, in cases such as heart attacks where there are no witnesses, we sometimes have no real way of knowing exactly what happened. If there were bruises, say, in the kidney area, we couldn't say with certainty whether they were sustained from an outside force or from a trauma such as falling into another object or convulsing."

Dani muttered as she wrote in her notebook. "Did Mr. Hollister have any bruising anywhere besides the kidney area?"

"I did not say Mr. Hollister had bruising in his kidney area," Dr. Haverty said.

"Right, you said, 'in cases such as this.' Okay, in 'cases such as this,' would there be any bruising in any other parts of the body?" Dani looked directly at the doctor.

Steepling his hands, Doctor Haverty's face was grave. "In cases such as this, there would likely be head injuries, creating a profuse amount of bleeding. Again, it would be assumed the injury was from a fall or some such incident."

A moment's silence filled the room. Dani's mind raced, trying to put it together.

"Okay, so you've got a person who's bruised—maybe he's been kicked, punched, whatever, but he's obviously been beaten. He's also got a head wound, and we all know how much blood comes spurting out of one of those. How do we get to have a heart attack from that? Did he ingest something?"

Nick cleared his throat. "Here's a thought, and it might be kind of out there, but—"

Dani nodded at him. "Go ahead and say it."

"What if it was plain old fear?" Nick looked at the doctor, who was leaning forward as if to catch every word they said. "Is it possible Beau or somebody could have a heart attack while they were being attacked because they were just plain scared?"

Doctor Haverty nodded, straightening already neat stacks of papers on his desk. "It's more than possible. Fright and a predisposed health risk for myocardial infarction can certainly lead to such an event. So, now it's my turn to ask you some questions. Is my patient in danger?"

Nick pulled out his cell phone. "Not if we can help it. I'm going to call the sheriff and see if we can assign some deputies to sit outside his room."

"Will this be a twenty-four-hour type of thing?" Dr. Haverty asked.

"We'll do our best," Nick reassured him.

"We're going to want to talk to the family," Dani told the doctor. "They need to be made aware of the possibility that this happened, and they may want to take further steps to protect him."

Dr. Haverty's face grayed, and he sagged in his chair. "Is this an isolated incident related only to Mr. Hollister, or do other family members need to take precautions?"

Dani hesitated, choosing her words carefully. She needed to keep people safe, but she had to walk a fine line in doing so. If too much information got out, Cleve Yodell would bolt.

"We should all take precautions, Dr. Haverty, but the Hollister family may need to watch themselves more than usual."

"What does this mean? What do I tell them? The mother and wife are always visiting, we can go talk to them right now if you'd like. I assume this piece of information should come from you, but as his doctor, I'd like to be there."

Nick ended his phone call and nodded at them. "Let's go to Mr. Hollister's room and see if his family's there. We need to tell them that someone very bad may be trying to get at their family, and they need to be prepared for the worst."

CHAPTER TWENTY-ONE

VODKA WORKED WELL BECAUSE MOST people couldn't smell it on your breath, but Katie didn't have to worry about that tonight.

The soft evening air from the open windows wrapped around her like a warm cloak. Fall in Virginia was generally mild, but it wouldn't be long before cooler temperatures settled in the region.

Alone, she raised the coffee cup to her lips and drank. In a little while, she'd pull herself together and go to the hospital to be with her family. It was important to stand by them right now, despite her personal fears.

Pushing a strand of hair behind her ear, she stared at the calendar on the refrigerator, not really seeing it.

The only thing I can do right now is be there for everyone. I can't control whether or not Beau recovers, but I can be a good sister and daughter.

Reaching for the bottle to pour more into her cup, she hesitated. Maybe this was getting to be too much, maybe Roland was right—maybe she shouldn't drink.

The problem, as usual, was that Katie had messed up. She wanted to do the right thing, but sometimes she didn't know what that was. Should she have told others about Hannah before? Probably. That's something friends shared with each other, but then she would've had to get into the explanation of Hannah's role during her childhood and everything else she'd hidden for so long.

Did everyone struggle with friendship as much as she did, or was she an anomaly? Never certain how much to divulge about herself, Katie tried to stay a little outside of things. She was always there for others, loyal and willing to help, but she had a hard time accepting the same.

Her fight with Roland highlighted that. Of course he didn't believe her now, why should he? It probably looked like she was making this up, fabricating a story to get his attention.

He knows how much I care about him.

Now that he was dating someone, she'd have to be careful not to show how much that hurt. After all, how many times had she told people they were more like brother and sister? How many times had she told people they were just friends, nothing more? Too many to count.

The truth settled in her stomach like a sharp ball of ice. Her life was built on lies, all of her own making. She was afraid to admit to anyone that yes, she had feelings for Roland, and yes, she loved him. She'd loved him for so long now, it was as much a part of her as her right arm.

Why did she find it so hard to open up to people? Her past was just that: past. Whatever happened to her all those years ago shouldn't matter now. It was time to let go.

Katie shifted uncomfortably in her chair, staring down at her drink. *Letting go means more than just releasing the past.* The thought was uncomfortable, but for the first time, she didn't back away from it.

The truth was difficult to face, but it was time. Katie was drowning and needed to climb out of the pool of emotion that held her down.

I don't know who I am without a drink. Sometimes I build my entire day around drinking. For God's sake, I live alone, and I still hide my alcohol.

Apparently not well enough, though, if Roland knew where to find it. How many other people knew?

Nobody. If anyone else knew, they'd act like Roland and start harassing her about drinking too much, telling her she needed to stop.

The fact was, she'd stopped drinking before, so she knew she'd be able to stop again. It had never lasted, of course, she'd always picked up another drink—but she should be able to stop whenever she wanted. How hard could it be? It wasn't like she was an alcoholic.

Really?

Alcoholics were losers, people who ended up on the street because they couldn't stop drinking. Or people who almost lost their house to foreclosure because they needed money for their habit. A minimum of six hundred dollars a month worth of money.

Katie avoided thinking about how much money she spent on booze. If she thought about the money, she wouldn't buy the alcohol. Perhaps that wasn't entirely true, but she wouldn't buy so much. Losing track of her finances was ultimately what led to the move back into her childhood home.

And face it, drinking is what made you lose track of your money.

Dropping her head into her hands, visions of her life swam through Katie's mind: the overdue bills that got stuffed, unseen, into a drawer; the hidden bottles throughout the house; the lies that she regularly told to cover her habit; and the coffee cup, always the coffee cup that never held any real coffee.

Lifting her head, Katie regarded the Mickey Mouse cup with sadness and spoke aloud in a voice with regret. "I can't believe it's come to this."

She had no real home—not one of her own, anyway—and her job was stable for now, but if they found out about her problem, that would disappear, too. Then she'd be left with nothing, just like the drunks she'd tried to distance herself from.

That's when it struck her: she didn't have to quit drinking, she just had to learn to drink socially. If all she did was have a drink now and then with her friends, it wouldn't be a problem. Maybe if she started a spreadsheet and tracked when she had a drink, only allowing herself a certain number of drinks per week—

You've tried that already, remember?

Damn that voice of conscience. Yes, she'd tried that before, and it didn't work. But maybe this time it would be different—

What's changed? Nothing. Things have actually gotten worse in your life, not better.

That was true, her downward spiral did seem to be accelerating.

Reaching for the mug in front of her, Katie vowed this would be her last cup. With her sister-in-law pregnant and her brother still in a coma, her family needed her right now. She had to stay sober to be useful.

She could sober up later, before she got to the hospital to see her brother. She still had a few hours before visiting hours ended.

Maybe Roland can help me.

It took a moment for the thought to sink in, but when it did, it made perfect sense. Katie's spirits lifted. It was the perfect solution—she would find Roland and talk to him, really talk to him about all this. He already knew she had a problem, so asking him for help or advice would only bring them closer.

He's probably been waiting for me to tell him how I feel.

Her mind made up, Katie stood and got her purse and car keys from the front hall table. It felt good to be taking action, to get something done. Tired of sitting back while things happened all around her, she would finally take control of her life.

Rushing outside, Katie got to the car, opened the door, and threw her purse in. Her excitement grew as she considered what might happen. Tonight could be a whole new night for the two of them.

Throwing the car into reverse, Katie hit the accelerator and started to back out of the driveway. She felt the bump before she heard it.

A shrill, piercing scream cut through the night air. Slamming the brakes, Katie sat in the driver's seat, trembling, wondering what the hell she was going to do now.

CHAPTER TWENTY-TWO

LATE AFTERNOON SUNBEAMS WASHED INTO the parsonage
living room while the ticking of the clock echoed throughout the house. Lisa
settled deeper into her chair, gripping her mug of tea and looking all around.

"My goodness, you certainly do have a good number of antiques in here.
How long did you say your family has lived in this house?"

Katie tried not to squirm in her chair. Lisa's curiosity was natural, but today
it annoyed her more than usual. She fought hard not to let her feelings show,
though, and maintained a friendly tone. After the near miss of last night, she
hadn't gotten much sleep, but she didn't want to take that out on Lisa.

It wasn't Lisa's fault she'd backed over KC. She knew better than to drive
drunk, but she did it anyway—and this wasn't the first time. Although the
night had been horrific, Katie knew it could have been worse, much worse.

But now wasn't the time to think about all that. Lisa was waiting for an
answer.

"I believe my father told me someone in the Hollister family has lived here
since the late 1800s."

Lisa nodded. "I guess that's more than enough time to collect all this stuff."

Silence sat between them for a moment as Katie wondered, not for the first
time, exactly what Lisa wanted. She'd shown up unannounced not long after
Katie got home from work and had yet to state the purpose of her visit.

Not that she needed a reason to be there, but Katie had things to do.

"So, what brings you to this neighborhood today?" Katie asked, trying the
direct approach.

Lisa shrugged, the picture of feigned innocence. "Nothing much, I thought

I'd stop by and see how you were doing, see if you or your family needed anything."

A pang of guilt shot through Katie as she briefly considered that maybe Lisa's reasons for visiting were altruistic. That thought proved false, though, with Lisa's next statement.

"Plus I wanted to talk to you about my sister."

"Is something wrong with Ella?" Katie asked. She'd never forgive herself if something happened to Ella and Katie had been too drunk or self-absorbed to notice.

"No, nothing's wrong. It's just..."

Katie waited a moment, wondering what this could possibly be about. Lisa wasn't exactly known to sidestep an issue, but it was taking her longer than normal today. After another long moment, Lisa sighed. "I don't think that house she's living in is safe," Lisa said.

"Safe? I would think that it would have to pass a town inspection before the owner could rent it to her," Katie said. "What makes you think it's not safe?"

"Not that it's not safe, exactly, but I was wondering if there's anything... weird in there. Didn't she have some kind of trouble when she moved in this summer?"

Obviously, this was more of an information-gathering visit than an actual social call. Katie didn't even bother to wonder why Ella hadn't told Lisa about their summer experience. Katie wouldn't have said anything to Lisa either.

A couple months ago, Ella had moved from Connecticut to her little house in Virginia. Strange events occurred in the house, and Katie and Roland helped Ella find the truth about what had happened in there. The house was definitely haunted, and they had worked together to help the ghost find her way home. The situation was somewhat bizarre, though, and Ella hadn't wanted to tell her family about any of it, especially since some of the vandalism was created by live people, not just a ghost.

Now, Lisa wanted answers about what happened this summer. Well, she was going to have to get her answers somewhere else.

"I don't know, I think it's a lovely house. Whatever trouble she had was related to the hurricane, wasn't it? Everything's fine over there. Where will your family be having Thanksgiving this year, your house or Ella's?" Katie knew that changing the subject was a sure way to bring the conversation around to something more suitable.

"We'll have to have the holidays at my house, or there won't be any room.

My father's coming down this November, and we're hoping to convince him to stay once he's here."

Katie wondered if Ella knew about this plan but wisely kept her mouth shut. She had enough of her own family issues, she didn't need other families' issues, too.

"How long will your parents stay, and why aren't they staying here?" Lisa asked.

"Until Beau makes a recovery, then they'll probably drive out to Arizona as originally planned," Katie said. She knew her brother would be okay, he had to. She refused to believe he would stay in a coma… or worse, die.

"Why aren't they staying in their own house?" Lisa was nothing if not persistent.

"They thought they could be more of a help to Anna Louise by staying with her." Katie wondered if her sister-in-law had mentioned the pregnancy to anyone else yet, but she kept her mouth shut on the topic, not wanting to hear Lisa's views on motherhood, pregnancy, or anything else for that matter.

"So, are you going to redecorate this place?"

"I haven't had much time to think about it."

"If you want, I can help. This is a gorgeous house, and we can make it really elegant—"

"Um, thanks, but I think I'll wait until things calm down before I make any changes." Katie wondered if Lisa was going to get to her real purpose for visiting or if they were going to continue this awkward conversation much longer. Surely, there was something else Lisa wanted to discuss.

"So, I understand you have a date tonight."

Finally, the true reason they were sitting there.

"Yes, you met him at church yesterday morning."

Katie's mind flashed on an image of Cleve, handsome and sophisticated. It was probably too soon to start thinking of a long-term relationship, but he would be the perfect type of man for her. Good looking, intelligent, and gainfully employed. Besides, as her brother had pointed out recently, she wasn't getting any younger.

"I can't believe you agreed to go out with him. You don't even know him."

Katie smiled through her weariness. "That's the point of a date, Lisa: to get to know someone."

"At the very least, I hope you didn't tell him where you live. That would be a huge mistake."

From the shrill tone in Lisa's voice, Katie knew better than to say anything. What Lisa didn't know couldn't hurt her.

He's picking me up here in about an hour.

"Why would it be a mistake?"

"Are you kidding?" Lisa said. "Tell a complete stranger how to get to your house? You live alone, you can't have unknown men wandering in and out of here."

Katie felt sorry for Lisa's daughters. They were not going to have easy lives as teenagers. She wondered if Lisa would follow them when they went out or just settle for being the parent who drove them everywhere, even on dates.

She tried to placate Lisa. "I don't know, I think—"

"Men like him only want one thing, you know. I heard him talking to you... he is way too smooth."

"Smooth?"

"Yeah, a real Casanova sort of guy. Do you realize he never actually answered any of your questions? He just gave you generalities instead of specifics?"

"No, but I—"

"And he's probably married or worse. You really cannot be too careful, Katie, living all by yourself and going out with strangers."

"Worse?"

Lisa's brow crinkled in confusion. "Yes, worse. What don't you understand about worse?"

Katie couldn't hold back the sigh. "What could be worse than my date being married?"

"What do you think?" Lisa's voice was shrill again. "I have a feeling he's some kind of psycho who's going to do very bad things to you. For the love of God, do *not* leave your drink unattended tonight. Don't let it out of your sight for one second, or he'll probably drop a roofie in it. Psycho freak." Lisa muttered the last two words, but Katie still heard them loud and clear.

Katie didn't know what to say. Manners dictated politeness, though, so she decided to go with that. "Thank you for your—"

"Oh my God!" Lisa interrupted, staring at the living room doorway. "I... oh, Lord, what is that thing?"

CHAPTER TWENTY-THREE

HE ALMOST GIGGLED, WHICH WOULD have been a costly mistake. But really, roofies? Cleve figured out that the supreme pain-in-the-ass woman was Lisa, whom he'd already met, but he dismissed her as an idiot. Annoying? Yes. In the way? Most certainly. But smart? No, he didn't think so. Smart was for people like... well, like him. This Lisa woman was definitely not of a higher intelligence.

Pressed against the outside brick wall of the house, Cleve knew he couldn't be seen. He'd been careful coming here, making sure nobody saw him. He was good at being invisible, able to blend in when necessary. Plus, he'd ducked behind an overgrown shrub against the front brick wall, certain that nobody could see him behind the greenery. He'd previously scoped out the yard and knew all the perfect hiding spots.

People had no idea what could be waiting for them, choosing to live in a world of denial instead. Cleve smiled. It was better that way, really. Other people's carelessness made things much easier for him in the end.

Of course, he'd been extra careful not to be seen planting evidence in Katie's yard. That would've been difficult to explain. Obviously, Cleve was doing important work, work that made the world a better place.

Lucky for him, it was still warm enough that Katie kept the house windows open. Trusting of her, really. Hopefully, she was always lax about security. His plan was coming together so nicely, once he was finished here he could move on to the next phase of his life. But, there was no doubt about it: the Hollister family needed to pay for their sins, a wrong needed to be made right, and Cleve needed to take his rightful place in the order of the universe.

His plan was simple, really. Once the ancestors of Hannah Donovan were eliminated, his duty was done. After all, it was their fault that his family had fallen on hard times, and it was their fault he hadn't grown up with the best of everything, as he so rightly deserved.

They'd started it centuries ago by killing him.

Cleve shook his head, trying to think clearly. The static was back... nobody had killed *him*—it was Titus who'd been killed. His ancestor.

They'll pay for what they did to me. Ignoring the thought in his head, Cleve reviewed his plan.

Cleve still had to eliminate two people: Katie and her mother. The father didn't count since he wasn't a direct descendant.

He frowned and rubbed his forehead, the beginnings of a headache settling behind his eyes. That was wrong... there were three people left to kill. Apparently, his efforts with the brother hadn't been successful, and it looked like he was going to have to go back and finish the job. That would be easy, though. All he had to do was get into the hospital room and put a little something extra into the IV line. Nobody would know, and Cleve would be safe.

He'd better do it soon, though. The arrogant bastard might wake up and tell everyone what happened, which would be a problem. A big problem. One that Cleve could overcome, sure, but he'd rather avoid any major problems at this stage. Things were going so nicely.

And maybe, just for fun, he'd get rid of that Lisa woman, too. Somebody had to shut her up, if only as a favor to her husband.

He heard Lisa screeching the question. He couldn't stop a grin from spreading across his face. Katie must be struggling to answer that one.

Cleve checked to see if anyone was on the street before stepping out from behind the bush. He dashed to the front door, straightened his shirt, and ran a hand through his hair. Raising his arm to knock, he took a breath.

I'm ready.

CHAPTER TWENTY-FOUR

"HE HURT HIS TAIL."

Katie stopped talking. She didn't want to explain this, and the area above her right eye throbbed as a headache worked its way through her brain.

"Sweet Jesus, who ran him over?"

"What makes you say that?" Katie snapped.

The pain spread over her left eye, making Katie wonder for a brief moment if she was having some sort of attack. Maybe this was what an aneurysm felt like, since she was too young to be having a stroke. Or maybe the guilt of what she'd done was catching up to her.

"It sure looks like someone ran the damn thing over. What happened?"

Katie hesitated, unsure. She didn't want to tell Lisa the truth, but the woman was so darn pushy, there might be no way to avoid it. What could she say? *Gee, Lisa, I was drunk again and not paying attention.* That'd open up a whole world of questions, and she wasn't ready to share the answers with anyone, least of all this woman.

But lies had a way of coming back to haunt you. Whatever she told Lisa would have to be what she told everyone else, word for word. If anyone was going to pick up on an untruth, it was Ella's sister.

"Cats don't just break their tails. That's weird." Lisa was still talking. "They use them for balance, but they don't land on them. What happened?"

There was no way out. Katie had to lie.

"There was—"

A sudden, sharp rapping made both women jump.

Lisa's eyes grew wide. "Who the heck is that?"

Katie shrugged. "I'll go see."

Walking toward the front door, Katie smiled. She could see Cleve through the side window panel.

Saved by her date.

Flinging the door open with more enthusiasm than normal, Katie beamed at him.

"I know I'm early, but I was hoping to take you down to the beach while it's still light. Does that sound okay?"

His charm would've worked on her anyway, but right then Katie was simply glad to have an excuse to get rid of Lisa.

"Of course. Please, come in." Leading him into the hallway, she called over her shoulder, "My friend Lisa's here. You might remember her from church."

Cleve didn't respond, and when Katie turned to look at him, he gave her a small smile. She thought she knew how he felt.

"Lisa, you remember Cleve?" Katie announced, walking into the living room. "Lisa was just leaving," she said to Cleve.

Lisa straightened and shot Katie's date a venomous look. "Actually, Katie, I don't think we were finished. Aren't you a little early, Cleve?"

His stare was direct. "I packed a picnic dinner and took a chance Katie was free."

"What if she'd been busy?" Lisa's tone bordered on belligerent.

"Doesn't matter now, does it?"

Lisa and Cleve stared at each other for a moment before Katie stepped in between them. "Lisa, it's fine, really. I think it's a lovely idea. Why don't I walk you to the door?"

With her hand firmly on Lisa's arm, Katie guided her to the door. It was obvious she didn't want to leave, but Katie wasn't giving her any choice in the matter. She had a date tonight, and Lisa was *not* going to ruin it.

The exchange between Lisa and Cleve, though, made her uneasy. What if Lisa was right? *No, it's just him reacting to Lisa being annoying. I can certainly relate to that.*

Ushering Lisa out the door, Katie shut it and sagged against the wood for a moment. Thank God she was gone. Katie didn't know how much more of Lisa's haranguing she could take. Honestly, Ella was a saint for the simple fact of never punching her sister in the throat.

"I'm just going to run upstairs and freshen up a bit," she called into the living room on her way past. "Make yourself comfortable. Can I get you something to drink while you wait?"

Cleve shook his head. "No. I'll just look through your bookshelves here," he said, nodding at the antique walnut shelves stacked with classics. "Take your time."

Running up the stairs, she couldn't stop the smile from spreading across her face. Her headache was sliding away as anticipation for the night began to build. There was something about Cleve, something so instantly likeable, that Katie knew she was going to have fun with him. It was more than his personality, charming as it was. He had a way of looking at Katie, a way that made her feel special, as if he really heard her. It was as if she were the most important person in the world to him...

...that's not always a good thing, a voice whispered. Katie pressed her palm against her forehead, trying not to hear the words.

"Not now, not now, not now... I don't need you right now. Cleve is a good person, I have nothing to worry about," she whispered, shutting the bedroom door.

"Actually, you do."

"Hannah, go away."

"This is exactly what I've—"

"I'm kind of busy right now. Can we do this later, Miss Fig?"

Katie walked around her bed and into her master bathroom. After rummaging through the medicine cabinet, she pulled a bottle out from behind an old prescription for swimmers ear. Shaking a couple ibuprofen tablets into her hand, she popped them in her mouth, turned on the faucet, and stuck her face under the running water to swallow the pills. Straightening, she wiped her face with the back of her hand, noting Hannah's ghostly image reflected in the mirror.

"Very lady-like."

"Thanks, Mom," Katie retorted.

"Why did you call me Miss Fig?"

Katie ran a brush through her hair and spritzed herself with a light perfume. "Fig: figment. Right now, I'm thinking you're a figment of my imagination."

"Katie-love, we've been through this—"

A wave of unreasonable frustration surged through Katie. *It's her fault Roland and I are fighting.* The small, rational part of her mind tried to insert a denial, but Katie shoved those thoughts away.

Katie spoke directly to Hannah. "And yet you remain. I know: odd, isn't it? I haven't been very nice to you, I don't pay attention to you, I don't actually believe in you, yet you keep coming back. Therefore, you can't be real."

"That's your criteria for reality?"

"That's it." Katie knotted a turquoise scarf around her neck and added silver dangly earrings. "And now I'm leaving. Thanks for stopping by. Say hello to Puff for me."

"Puff?"

"The magic dragon."

Katie headed for the door. She looked good in her black pencil skirt, sparkly top, and scarf. She smelled good, too.

"Is this because of Roland?" Hannah's voice was gentle. "I know how much you care about him, and the fact that—"

"The fact that you made me look like an idiot in front of him made me realize how not real you are. Or aren't, or whatever."

Hannah's voice sounded desperate. "It's not my fault you never told him about me. You've got to take this seriously. Everything I've been telling you—"

"Is a product of my own fears I've dragged from childhood into my adult life. Goodbye, Hannah."

Katie closed her bedroom door.

Cleve was still in the living room, examining her bookshelf and waiting patiently with his hands behind his back. He smiled when he saw her.

"My, you look lovely. I can hardly wait." Staring into her eyes, his gaze locked with hers. "This is certainly going to be a night I will always remember."

Katie shifted on her feet, suddenly uncomfortable. The look on his face was almost disturbing. After a moment, her manners took over. "Thank you. So, you wanted to have a picnic?"

Belatedly, she realized that wearing a skirt might not be appropriate for a beach picnic, but it was too late now. She couldn't run back upstairs and change, again. She'd have to act as if she dressed like this for picnics all the time.

"Yes, but first we need to talk." His demeanor became serious, a disorienting switch.

Katie felt the first stirrings of unease. "Okay. What did you want to talk about?"

Cleve took a step closer to her. "What happened here last night?"

Katie froze. "What do you mean?"

"I think there's something you need to see."

CHAPTER TWENTY-FIVE

KATIE COULDN'T IMAGINE WHAT CLEVE was talking about, but she let him propel her out the front door. Whatever it was, it couldn't be worse than running over her cat's tail.

"I don't know what to make of this, but it was in your yard, sort of at the end of the driveway when I got here. I moved it out of the way."

Cleve gestured at a tangled heap of metal lying in her side yard. The frame was twisted, bent beyond repair, and parts of the red paint looked as if it had been scraped off. Katie couldn't even tell what brand of bike it had been, but based on the size, it looked like it belonged to a child.

This was so much worse than running over her cat.

Much, much worse.

A desperate cry rose in her throat, and she raised her fist to her mouth to keep it from escaping.

"Is it yours?" Cleve was solicitous, hovering over her as if she were a delicate piece of crystal.

"N-no... I've never seen it before." Katie's voice was barely audible, but Cleve seemed to have no trouble hearing her.

"Was it here earlier?"

Katie looked at him. "Does it matter?"

"It might. Was it here earlier?"

Katie shook her head, not wanting to answer. She didn't trust her voice, not with what she was feeling. The pile of metal sat in front of her, accusing. Where did it come from, and could she have had something to do with this? She shivered, despite the relative warmth of the day. Bad things were not supposed to happen on bright, sunny days when you could hear birdsong and laughter in the neighborhood. And yet, there was the twisted bicycle in front of her, proving that thought to be untrue.

"Does that mean no, or you don't know?"

"I don't think so." Staring at the mangled heap, something occurred to Katie. "Wait, Lisa didn't say anything about this."

"Maybe she didn't see it," Cleve suggested.

Katie shook her head. "No, Lisa sees everything. I kid you not, she'll pick up on every little thing, things most people wouldn't notice. Then she'll tell you all about it in excruciating detail."

Cleve gave her a small smile. "Really, Katie, she seemed fairly intent on spending time with you. Isn't it possible she pulled into the driveway and simply marched up to your front door without looking at the yard?"

Of course it was possible. Anything was possible. Along with that thought, the prospect of what this bike meant after her drunken night last night was almost too frightening to consider.

Please, don't let me hurt anyone. Especially a child.

It was one thing to drink and screw around; those were things she kept fairly under control. It was one thing to not even know the names of the men she slept with—that wasn't really doing anyone any harm.

But to hurt someone? That was unthinkable.

Katie cleared her throat. "Did you say it was toward the end of the driveway? It was probably left there by someone wanting to get rid of it. They must've assumed it would get picked up on garbage day."

Cleve looked down at her. "Maybe we should go inside. You don't look so good."

She attempted a flirtatious smile but was certain she only managed a movement of the lips. "Just a few minutes ago, you couldn't wait for this date. It was going to be a night to remember."

"Oh, it'll be a night to remember, of that I have no doubt."

Katie let him steer her back into the house, all the while trying to think of what this meant.

Maybe it was just a mangled bike left in her yard.

Maybe she ran someone over last night.

But if that were the case, wouldn't she have heard about it? Wouldn't it have been on the news or something? Her neighborhood was the kind of place where everyone knew each other and looked out for each other. Surely, if a child had been hurt, one of her neighbors would've mentioned it to her?

Maybe not. Everything from last night was still a blur, so she couldn't be certain of what had really happened. The beginnings of another headache started to creep over her.

Katie marched straight to the kitchen. Taking a seat at the old table, she watched wordlessly as Cleve got a glass from the cabinet and poured her some water from the pitcher in the refrigerator.

He's being so nice to me.

Placing the glass of water in front of her, he folded his arms across his chest. "You seem a little disconcerted. Is everything okay?"

Katie nodded and took a sip of the water. There was no way she was going to tell him about her fears. That would be a date stopper for sure.

But he was persistent. "Where were you last night? Is it possible that something happened in front of your house and you were unaware of it?"

Katie's voice sounded far away to her own ears. "No, nothing happened out there last night."

Cleve was persistent. "Are you sure? Sometimes people drive drunk, accidents happen."

Katie's body tingled with a feeling of dread. She didn't know what to say, didn't know how to make this all go away. "My neighbors would have said something to me," she told him.

"Maybe your neighbors don't know everything," he said in a soft voice. "Sometimes people drink, and they do things that their neighbors never suspect. Maybe this is one of those types of things."

Katie couldn't stop the shiver from running through her body. What she really wanted in that exact moment was to call Roland and beg him to come over. She really needed him right now, but that wasn't going to happen. He wouldn't be driving up, or coming to help her. He was still mad at her, and this time it might be a permanent sort of thing.

The thought of not having Roland in her life was too much to bear, so Katie pushed it away. She could only deal with one thing at a time, and right now the dark emptiness gnawing at her center was more than enough to handle.

If ever there was a time to start making life changes, this would be it. She had no choice, not if something truly terrible happened because of her drinking.

Looking up at Cleve, she felt her eyes fill with tears. "I think we need to call the police. Right now."

CHAPTER TWENTY-SIX

"WHY?"

Cleve's question was reasonable, all things considered. But Katie didn't feel like being reasonable, not right now. Right now she felt like tearing things apart, like crying until she couldn't see and begging for forgiveness from whichever God would listen.

"Because." She knew it was a petulant thing to say, but she couldn't stop it. Lord, her mother would be mortified at her manners right then. What on Earth was wrong with her?

"I don't think calling the police right now would be such a good idea." Cleve looked distinctly uncomfortable and reached for her water glass. "How about I put something a little stronger in this, just to help you. Obviously, the bike thing upset you, but I'm sure it's nothing, really. Besides, what would you tell the police?"

He was right. What could she say to the police? *Hi, officer, last night I got drunk and drove somewhere, and since I hurt my cat so badly, it's possible I ran over a child on a bike, too.*

No, there was nothing she could say that wouldn't sound suspicious. "Maybe you're right," she admitted.

Cleve looked relieved, and who could blame him, really? He'd shown up slightly early, prepared for an incredibly romantic picnic-on-the-beach sort of date, and she became semi-comatose at the sight of a bike.

He must think I'm an idiot, or at the very least, crazy.

"Here, drink this. You'll feel better." He'd replaced her water with white wine he'd gotten out of the refrigerator. "It'll put you in a better mood for our date."

Katie laughed. "I'm surprised you still want to go out."

Cleve's stare was as direct as his tone. "I wouldn't trade this for anything right now."

Hmmm…okay, he's a little blunt, but maybe that's just the Yankee in him.

He kept talking. "I've got a picnic basket outside on the bike, and I'm ready to go whenever you are."

"On the bike?" Katie must have misheard him. Why would he put a picnic basket on that scrap heap of metal out there, especially since they didn't know where it came from?

"Not the bicycle, silly." He smiled at her, a benign and knowing smile. "I have a motorcycle."

Katie picked up her glass and took a large sip of the wine. "You told me that on Sunday. I can't believe I forgot. Just give me one quick moment, and I'll run upstairs and put on a pair of jeans."

Smiling at him, she stood, finished the wine, and dashed upstairs.

The Yorktown beach was far from isolated, but Katie felt like she and Cleve were the only ones there. The warm September sun made this an ideal time to relax outside, and Cleve was so attentive and sweet, she couldn't help being enchanted by him. Truly, the man thought of everything. For their picnic, he'd brought crusty French bread, stuffed olives, a wedge of brie, grapes, and fried chicken. And wine.

Katie was surprised that he'd brought not just one bottle, but two. That was fine with her, especially after the scare she'd just had. Besides, it wasn't like she had to drive. She was allowed to have some fun, right?

For a while, they discussed the history of the area. Downtown Yorktown has a distinctive style, built to reflect the area's colonial history. Katie loved talking about the little town, from its early beginnings in 1691 through the surrender of Lord Cornwallis ending the Revolutionary War. Surrounded by battlefields and historic monuments, it was easy to imagine the hardships of the early settlers as they tried to cope with a new land, as well as the struggles of the native peoples as they tried to cope with the new inhabitants and the slaves as they were brought to this new land. Some of those struggles continued today, and as Katie spoke she felt a passion for the injustices she'd seen and read about, a kinship with the people who worked so hard to overcome poverty and racism.

She knew what it was like to be on the outside of things.

Of course, Roland was descended from the Mattaponi, a fact that occurred to her as Cleve asked more questions.

Darn, she was just going to have to square her shoulders and face up to the fact that it was time to move on. Obviously, Roland had, as evidenced by the fact that he was dating someone. Not that she'd ever given him a reason to stick around and wait for her.

"So what do you think, Katie? What would they say about it all?"

Too late, Katie realized that her mind had wandered, and she hadn't heard a thing Cleve said. She was, however, the queen of covering up her mistakes.

"I'm not sure," she told him. "What do you think?"

Cleve laughed, and she was fairly certain he knew she was bluffing. But she didn't care because when he looked at her, she felt like an absolute princess. Nobody had made her feel that way in a very long time. He was charming, educated, polite, and interested in her, so what more could she want?

Everything. I want everything. A home, a husband, a life...

They continued talking until the sun set, at which point Cleve pulled candles out of his backpack, stuck them in the sand, and lit them. Surrounded by a warm glow, Katie was surprised to see him pull a third bottle of wine from his pack. Without asking, he expertly uncorked the wine and proceeded to pour her another glass. Katie marveled at his manners, at the smoothness with which he did everything.

The evening ended all too soon, but Katie knew when enough was enough. She liked this guy, and she didn't want to blow it with him.

Struggling to her feet from the blanket on the sand, she took his outstretched hand and let him pull her up. They packed everything into his backpack and were on their way back to her house.

I can't invite him in... not yet... he's not one of those guys from the bar... I don't want him to think I'm some kind of slut.

Pulling into her driveway, Cleve shut off the bike, removed his helmet, and helped Katie off the seat. Offering his arm, he walked her to the door. The evening had been perfect, and now it was time to decide how she wanted it to end.

Hit by a wave of panic, she didn't know what to do. What if he asked to come in? What if he didn't? Which would be worse?

Taking a breath to clear her thoughts, she decided it didn't matter. She could deal with whatever happened on her front porch.

As they faced each other, Cleve smiled down at her. "I had a wonderful time tonight, Katie. I hope we can do this again soon."

Katie blushed, hoping he couldn't read her thoughts about wanting him to come inside. "Of course, I'd like that."

"Try not to worry about the bike, okay?"

Well, shoot. She hadn't been thinking about it at all. It had gotten pushed to the back of her mind in the midst of her hormone rush, but now she was thinking about it again. *I am truly a bad person.*

"I mean, I'm sure whatever it was," Cleve continued, "however it got there, it probably wasn't anything to do with you. You'd have noticed something like that, right? People don't just run over a bike and not notice, right?" His smile held the same warmth, but a cold chill ran down Katie's spine.

"Right. Anyone would notice a thing like that. Thanks again for a lovely evening. Let's talk soon, okay?"

"Goodnight, Katie. Sleep well," he whispered into her ear. Without further comment, he turned and walked down to his bike, put the helmet back on, and started the engine. With a final wave, he turned in the driveway and drove off.

Waving back, she unlocked her front door and hurried inside. Closing the door, she leaned against it, trying not to imagine why that bike had ended up in her yard.

"It doesn't matter," she said out loud. "I didn't do anything, and like Cleve said, I would know if I had."

All the same, she couldn't shake the uneasy feeling creeping through her body.

CHAPTER TWENTY-SEVEN

THERE WAS SOMETHING ABOUT THIS area that put Dani at ease. Flatter than Connecticut, with no hills except the battlefield redoubts, Yorktown was a pretty little suburban town that hadn't grown as large as its urban counterparts. The bed and breakfast she'd chosen was a place of charm and good food. People were nice, the pace was a little slower, and September in these parts still felt like summer. She smiled a few times to see people wearing sweaters—back home it would've been bathing suit season with temperatures like this. *Fer cryin' out loud, the outside temperature is still in the low 70s.*

Sitting in Nick's office, they finished their sandwiches while going over the case. She felt like they were making some progress and started to get that feeling in her gut. It wouldn't be long, but that didn't mean she could relax. Until this guy was behind bars, she'd focus all her energy on making the arrest. This scumbag needed to be locked up.

"I hope he makes it," Nick said, interrupting Dani's thoughts.

She couldn't stop the frown that spread across her face. "What are you talking about?"

"Beau," he answered. "I hope the Hollister guy makes it, that's all. Geez, his wife just found out she's pregnant. He's got a lot to live for." Nick shrugged, popping a French fry in his mouth. "Seems to me the good guys gotta get a break sooner or later."

Dani agreed. "Hopefully sooner."

A quiet knock at the door interrupted them, and Nick called out a loud, "Enter." Dani turned in her seat to see a patrol officer standing in the doorway.

He nodded at her. "Hello, ma'am. Sorry to interrupt. Detective Winters, I was told you wanted to see me."

Dani's first thought when she saw the deputy was *military*. Good looking, with the type of hair and stance that screamed of service in the armed forces, his manner was guarded. Deputies weren't often called into an investigator's office, so he had to be wondering what was going on.

Nick nodded at the man. "Yeah, Kevin, take a seat. This is Watertown, Connecticut PD Detective Dani Burgess. We're assisting on a homicide that happened up there. We've received information that you may be connected to this case."

Kevin looked from Nick to Dani and extended his hand to her, giving it a brief shake before he sat down. "Pleased to meet you. Okay. I don't know how I could be connected, but tell me what this is about."

Nick pushed his sandwich to the edge of his desk and rifled through the papers in front of him. "Let me find my notes before we start…"

As he did so, Dani reached into her computer case on the floor next to her, pulled out a folder, and handed it to Nick.

"We don't think it's a direct connection, but it's enough that we think you may be able to help us."

Nick smiled over his handful of papers at Dani. "Thank you. You're a very organized woman."

Dani smiled back, determined not to be affected by him despite the way her stomach occasionally dropped when he smiled at her.

"I have to be. Time's running out. Anyway, Kevin, can you tell me a little about your girlfriend?"

She knew she sounded bitchy, but that was the only way she knew to talk to her male associates. If she didn't assert herself, she'd drown in their chauvinistic comments. Although Nick hadn't shown any tendency toward that kind of thinking, she wasn't letting him get away with any sort of patronizing attitude. Plus, it helped combat her growing attraction to him.

Kevin looked stunned for a moment. "Ella, she's a great woman. We met this summer… um… it was… let's see…"

"While you were working on her case, right?" Dani asked.

Kevin blushed. "It's not what you think…"

Dani leaned forward in her chair. "Listen, I don't give a rat's ass about your relationship with this woman. I don't care if you responded to a call and screwed her that same night—we've got bigger problems than that. That's your department's issue, not mine, got it?"

Kevin looked at her for a full moment before responding. "What did you want to know?"

Hell, it looked like she'd pissed this guy off. Too bad, she had to stay focused. This wasn't the time to worry about hurt feelings.

"I heard she's got a friend, someone in the Hollister family. Is that true?" Dani said.

Kevin nodded. "Yeah, Katie. What about her?"

"Tell us everything you know about her."

"Whoa... okay... wait a minute here," Nick interrupted. "Kev, see, the thing is, we think Katie might be in some sort of danger. Neither Ella nor Katie are in trouble with us, but we do think they're connected to this case."

"The homicide?" The tone in Kevin's voice was disbelieving. "Who got killed? Didn't you just say it happened in Connecticut?"

Dani sighed, running a hand through her hair. "Yeah, but it looks like my guy came all the way down here to good ol' Virginia just to inflict revenge upon the Hollister family, one by one. So, start talking. What do you know about Katie?"

Nick leaned back in his chair, folding his arms in front of his body. "It's a good thing you're both Northerners. Kevin, I assume you're used to this kind of attitude, right?"

Dani shot a withering look at Nick. "We don't have time to play nice here, okay? It's not about my attitude, it's about catching someone who may be ready to kill again. Whatever it takes to get the job done, I'm going to do. I'm not here to make friends."

If she were here to make friends, she wouldn't spend so much damn time in this closet-turned-office, instead she'd be out having a glass of wine, maybe with a man who had just been promoted to detective. But for now, that wasn't going to happen since they had a killer to track down.

"Good thing," Nick said quietly. He smiled at her again and turned to Kevin. "Go ahead and tell us about Katie."

Dani knew Kevin was weighing his options and trying to figure out how to get more information from them. She didn't blame him, she would've done the same thing.

He looked from Nick to Dani before he started talking. "Katie was one of the first friends Ella made when she moved down here, mostly because they work together at the college. From what I know, Katie teaches computer and IT stuff, and she's been there for a while. She just moved back into her parents' house, but her parents aren't there anymore, so she lives alone. She seems nice, always friendly and bubbly, one of those blonde Southern belle kind of women."

Dani frowned. "I'm not sure what you mean by 'blonde Southern belle.' Does that mean she's pretty?"

Kevin smiled. "It's a kind of stereotype, I guess. Yeah, she's sort of pretty. Got blonde hair and pretty eyes—"

"What color?" Dani interrupted.

Kevin thought for a minute. "Light? Maybe blue, maybe green... I don't spend a lot of time looking into her eyes. My girlfriend probably wouldn't appreciate that, you know?"

Nick smiled. "I know what you mean. She's bubbly and fun, gracious and charming, always well-mannered, right?"

Sounded like the kind of woman Dani wasn't. "Bubbly" and "fun" were definitely not words used to describe her, but she was okay with that. She preferred to remain more of a mystery to others instead of coming across as an empty-headed Barbie doll.

Kevin nodded. "Right. I noticed Southern women seem to be like that, always polite and pretending they're happy."

"Pretending?" Dani's voice was sharp. "Do you have reason to think she's unhappy?"

Maybe people in the Hollister family knew more than they were saying. You never knew what people hid from the world, and their ability to inflict pain on each other was astounding. *We're going to have to take a closer look at the family to make sure we don't miss anything. I don't want to waste my time here.*

"No. I just don't think anyone can always be happy all the time. It's not natural."

Dani nodded. "You're right about that. Have you noticed anything out of the ordinary about Katie Hollister lately?"

Kevin's hesitation was slight, but enough to make Dani pounce. "Listen, Deputy, lives are at stake. I don't care if you know some little piece of gossip that your girlfriend warned you not to repeat. Whatever it is, just tell us. We'll decide what's important."

Nick agreed. "She's right. As much as I hate to say it, this isn't the time to keep your private life private."

Kevin blew out a breath. "Since you asked, I've noticed that Katie's been having a hard time lately. Love triangle sort of stuff, where the guy she didn't know she was in love with gave up on her and started dating someone else. I've tried to stay out of the whole thing, it can only lead to problems later if I stick my nose in this."

"True enough," Nick agreed.

"She's been pretty upset about her brother, too, with him being in the hospital and all, but she hasn't talked much about it. At least that's what Ella said. Katie knows some of the other folks in the sheriff's department, mostly Reuben. She's going to that self-defense class he's teaching at night. You might want to check with him to see if he's noticed anything."

"Have you noticed anyone new hanging around her? Has she said anything about strange men or cars or anything?" Dani asked.

It was a long shot, but they'd have to ask Katie the same question. Beau's mother and wife already denied seeing anyone or anything out of the ordinary, but they'd been so stunned at the news that Dani wasn't certain they were thinking clearly.

"I know she started dating someone she met at church, but I don't know anything about him."

"Whaddya mean you don't know anything about him? Hasn't your girlfriend filled you in on the details of this new guy?" Dani demanded.

If there was one thing she knew, it was that women liked to talk to the people they were close to, especially when it came to dating. This was important information, and most women shared it with each other. Even Dani was guilty of gossiping with her friends. It couldn't be helped.

"Well, yeah, she's been talking about it some, but you know..." Kevin shrugged, seeming embarrassed.

"You weren't listening," Nick finished.

Kevin shook his head. "As soon as Ella started talking about the new guy, something about how her sister didn't like him, I sort of tuned it out. You know how it is."

No, Dani didn't know how it was, but she wasn't going to labor the point. "Do you at least know a name?" Dani asked.

Kevin shrugged. "I really wasn't listening. But I'll call Ella and find out. She should be finished teaching soon."

"Thanks. We'd appreciate that," Nick told him. "We're not sure if this guy has made contact with her or not, but we're pretty certain he's got Katie in his sights. And we're not sure how he did it, but we suspect he had something to do with her brother being in the hospital."

"I thought Beau had a heart attack?"

Nick nodded. "Lots of ways to make that happen. For now, focus on finding out that name for us. We're going to have to interview Katie ourselves. We don't want to tip this guy off too soon that we're onto him. He doesn't know that we know he's alive, and we'd like to keep him in the dark as long as possible."

"We had a picture of him in here somewhere, but it seems to have disappeared," Dani told them, rifling through yet another stack of papers on the back credenza.

"I think Jimmy took it to show to some of the others," Nick answered.

Dani's breath came out in a huff. "Well, Jeezus, can we maybe get some copies made?"

Nick smiled a slow, lazy smile at her. "Sure thing, ma'am. We're here for you, and we aim to please."

Dani shot him a look of venom. "I'm not trying to be a bitch, but c'mon, this is basic police work, you know?"

Okay, maybe she was trying to be a bitch, but she was tired and frustrated. If she'd ever done this sort of thing at home, she never would've heard the end of it. She had to make it clear that sloppiness at work had no place in any case she was handling. Besides that, Nick's smile put her on edge.

Dani didn't want to lose her temper, but the combination of being around Nick too much and the stress of finding this guy was starting to get to her. She knew she was barking out commands, but she wanted this finished. So did the chief of police back home, who called her every two hours for an update. Maybe after it was finished, she could start something new.

"Are we doing anything to protect Katie?" Kevin asked.

"We've got extra patrols covering her house," Nick said, "but right now we're sort of short staffed. We had to pull a couple of guys for duty at the hospital to watch her brother."

"Should I spend more time with Katie, make sure she's okay?"

"I can't authorize you to do that on department time," Nick said.

Dani had been amazed that they'd been able to spare a deputy for hospital security. She knew money was tight in every community, and usually getting extra manpower took an act of God. Maybe she could push for a little more help so they could get to this guy quicker.

"She's in very real danger," Dani said. "Maybe it wouldn't be a bad idea."

Nick sighed. "I hear you, but like everyone else, we've got budget issues. Honestly, we can't afford to have Kevin on this, too."

"We probably can't afford for him *not* to be on this," Dani argued.

"There's one thing I've gotta ask you," Kevin interrupted, looking at Dani. "Is Ella in danger?"

"Whenever Ella spends time with Katie, she may be putting herself in this guy's sites, but we can't be positive of that. I'd be very careful, and maybe see if you can get your girlfriend to back off the friendship for a few days." Even as she said it, Dani knew that was unreasonable. If her own friends were in danger, there's no way she'd leave them alone.

"How am I supposed to do that? If I say anything, it will only make Ella determined to protect Katie."

Dani shrugged. "I don't know, but I'm sure you'll think of something."

"Is Ella taking Reuben's class, too?" Nick asked.

Kevin nodded. "Yeah. There's Katie, Ella, and Ella's sister Lisa decided to join them."

"I'll make sure Reuben spends extra time with them this week," Nick said. "It's not a guarantee of safety, but at least they'll be taught about being aware of their surroundings and how to defend themselves."

Kevin's face was creased with worry. "That's really nice, Nick, but if everything you say about this guy is true, I'm not sure one little self-defense class is really going to be able to protect them."

"Probably not," Nick admitted, "but right now, it's all they've got."

CHAPTER TWENTY-EIGHT

THREE A.M. WAS A GOOD time for him. It was a time of darkness and secrecy. There was a cloak of silence everywhere, an impenetrable shroud that allowed him to remain invisible. Nosy neighbors were asleep, and the only thing to worry about was a dog alerting others to his presence. Not that there was anything to worry about here, there was only a cat, and an injured one at that.

Cleve stood for a moment outside Katie's house, looking at the darkened windows. A dim glow came from the upstairs windows, probably a hall light kept on at night. He wondered if she slept with night lights on because she was afraid of the dark or because she was afraid of tripping and falling. Based on what he knew about her, it could be either.

Tonight he'd learned even more during their date. She'd unknowingly made everything easy for him and given him plenty to work with, so what he was about to do might be fun. Not his usual kind of fun, but that was fine. It was good to have variety in life.

There was a twisting inside him as he thought about it all, thought about Katie's reaction. She had a problem, that much was certain, and she really should get some help to stop drinking.

Her problem is not your problem. Your problem is her. The voice was back, insistent and harsh.

But she'd seemed so nice.

They always do.

She hasn't really done anything wrong.

Yes, she has. She's one of them. She's responsible for the ruination of us all.

It was possible that not all women were detestable, but the voice Cleve listened to was adamant that a good many of them were worthless. A momentary vision of his wife flashed through Cleve's mind, followed by the sound of guttural laughter ringing in his head.

That one was so nice, and look what she turned out to be: nothing but a cheap whore, like all of them. They'll ruin you, kill you, take what they can. You can't rest until this work is done.

Cleve shook his head, feeling dizzy. Taking some deep breaths, he focused on the outline of the tree branches silhouetted against the half moon. Focusing on one object and breathing slowly usually made the dizziness pass. The voice, however, never really went away. It was a part of him now.

After a moment, his head cleared, and he walked into Katie's back yard. Removing the shears from his jacket pocket, Cleve got to work. As he clipped the heads off the roses, he mused about the trusting nature of people. Really, Katie hadn't known him all that long, yet she was telling him all sorts of information he was able to use against her. She needed to learn to be more careful about that sort of thing, or she was going to get hurt.

He almost laughed out loud at the irony of it all.

I wish we could see her reaction.

He knew things about her now, things she told him and things he observed. *She is struggling with her garden efforts yet is proud of what she's accomplished so far. She loves animals, and I believe she's tormented by what she's done to her cat.* But most importantly, he knew how much she drank and that she usually passed out at night after getting drunk. That would be the most important information of all.

For some reason, she wasn't like her brother. She wasn't to be taken care of so quickly—she was to be savored, played with, and maybe even tortured just a little bit.

The men, they just get in the way. The women are the real problem, causing the most destruction. It's the women who deserve the punishment.

Cleve moved on, anxious to finish the job. So much to do, it all had to be orchestrated so carefully. It was a wonder he was able to balance it all. The grass underfoot was soft, a cushion to any noise he might have made walking through the yard. He'd worn sneakers for the event, but still, you couldn't be too careful.

There was movement in the house. Cleve froze, knowing he couldn't be seen, yet feeling caught. A pair of eyes watched him, surveilling his every move.

Staring at the upstairs window, he saw the barest hint of an outline. Someone was there, watching. Now he knew Katie had seen him, and his mind raced to formulate a plan.

The silhouette was unmoving, standing and staring. As he watched, it seemed to him that the shape began to waver, not actually solid.

It's her.

The thing inside Cleve watched the window as well, hyper-aware of the being inside the house.

I'd recognize her anytime.

Without a doubt, he'd been seen. Truly seen. But it didn't matter because this one wasn't going to talk.

And if she did talk, nobody believed Katie. Cleve smiled. Sometimes, even Katie didn't believe what she was seeing and hearing, which worked out just fine for him.

But that thing in the window... he wasn't sure how he knew, but he definitely knew. That thing standing and staring at him was the very same thing that started all this.

If it wasn't for her, I wouldn't have died.

CHAPTER TWENTY-NINE

KATIE FELT A WHOLE NEW, wonderful world opening up before her. The house she wandered through was grand, richly furnished with a seemingly never-ending amount of rooms. A soft light was inside and out, warming the place with a love that graced everything. Even the air felt good to breathe. So many rooms, so many places to live in comfort. Here, she was safe. Here, she could be who she needed to be, with no fear and no worries about judgment from others.

She could live here forever, in this place of light.

"Katie-love, get up—quickly now!"

She didn't want to leave, she liked it where she was. Even the colors were more alive, infused with a healing energy that soothed her soul. This was a place of refuge, where no harm could enter.

"You've got to get up! You may be in danger—he's here!"

Her head hurt... why did her head hurt? The edges of darkness curled around her body, pulling her away from the dream world. A black stain spread across the world, obliterating everything.

"Are you awake yet? Good, you're starting to wake up. He was here, in the yard... oh dear, this is all my fault."

"What?" Katie's voice croaked, the word barely intelligible to her ears. Lord, it was dark outside. Why was she awake in the middle of the night?

Her throat burned. Reaching to the bedside table for the glass of water she always kept there, Katie felt nothing. *Damn.* Now she'd have to turn the light on to see where the hell her water was.

Fumbling for the lamp switch, fingers wrapped around Katie's hand—warm, solid fingers. Katie held her breath. This couldn't be happening.

"Don't turn the light on."

"Hannah?"

"Of course it's me, even though I don't exist. I'm going to let go of your hand now, but don't turn the light on or he'll see you. Promise?"

Katie nodded, despite the fact that it was dark and Hannah couldn't see her. Well, maybe she could; she was a ghost, after all. Even if she wasn't real, like Katie had said earlier, she certainly felt real enough tonight.

Damn. Now her head *really* hurt.

"What's going on?"

"So you've decided to talk to me now?"

Katie almost smiled at the petulant tone in Hannah's voice, but the pounding in her head prevented it. If she were going to be honest with herself, Hannah was her one true friend, the one who knew all her secrets and loved her despite everything. That kind of unconditional love was hard to find.

"Obviously, since you're the only one here with me. I need a drink."

"I think you've had quite enough of that for tonight." Hannah's voice was disapproving.

"Not that kind of drink. I need some water. I'm parched."

Katie sounded desperate to her own ears. It was no wonder, anyone would sound desperate after being woken up in the middle of the night by a woman who didn't exist but still managed to have a very solid feel to her.

Maybe I'm really losing it. Maybe this is from drinking too much. God, I really do have a problem.

"Here. Your water is right here," the unseen hand guided Katie's to the glass of water on the bedside table. "Take a sip and listen up, this is important. I know you don't want to acknowledge the fact that I'm here, but you can't get around it. I seem to have brought some sort of trouble upon the family, and it's time we fixed this. Perhaps this is why I've never been allowed to move on to the next life, maybe I need to make restitution here."

The water felt cool on Katie's throat as she tried not to drink too quickly. She thought for a moment about what Hannah had just said.

"Is this the story you were telling me earlier? When you went to jail?"

"Yes. I see it now, although I don't know why I didn't before. The man who was murdered, Titus? I think I told you he's here."

Katie sighed. Here it was again, the ghost-talk that made no sense to her at all. Or maybe there was something wrong with her head, making it impossible to figure things out. A distant portion of Katie's mind wondered if she was still drunk, but that thought didn't bear further review. She couldn't do anything about it right now anyway.

"Hannah, it's the middle of the night, my head is killing me, and you woke me out of a really awesome dream. You're going to have to be very specific if you want me to understand what you're talking about."

Katie's eyes started to adjust to the darkness, and she could see the hulking shapes of her bedroom furniture in the heavy grayness of her room. A soft glow moved around the space, as if agitated. Hannah was pacing.

"It was right before the war, the one where brother fought against brother. The Civil War, the one they've kept so alive in memory here in the South. I was working for a man named Titus Foote, like I told you. I believe Titus was hurting his family, his wife and children."

"What do you mean when you say 'hurting'? Do you mean he was beating them?" Katie was starting to wake now, although the headache clung to her like flypaper.

"I'm not entirely sure, but I do know he would raise a fist to them on a regular basis. There may have been more, but that's entirely suspicion on my part, not based on any fact. The thing is, after he was murdered, his family... well, they went a little crazy. Maybe they'd already been that way, but like I told you before, I got blamed for it all."

"I understand all that, Hannah, and I'm really sorry about it, but it happened so long ago. I still don't get what it has to do with me."

And why you had to wake me to tell me this. She didn't say it out loud, and she immediately felt a flash of guilt. If Hannah were alive, a flesh and blood friend or relative, Katie wouldn't have flinched at being woken up to help her. This wasn't any different, really, and she ought to be ashamed of herself for only thinking about going back to bed. Obviously, Hannah was distressed, and Katie needed to listen. It was the least she could do for the woman who had saved her so many years ago.

"It's not just you," Hannah told her. "It's your whole family. Titus is looking to destroy your entire family, and he's well on his way to making that happen."

"Hannah, the problem with this story is that if what you're telling me is true, Titus is already dead. How can he destroy my family?" It was a good point. The story Hannah was telling couldn't be real—it didn't make any sense.

"He's using another person as a vehicle for his spirit."

Katie was dumbfounded, headache forgotten as she thought about what

Hannah had just said.

"Do you mean he's in someone else's body?"

"Yes. This person would have to be a somewhat willing participant, which makes me think it's a descendant of the Foote family."

"Possession. You're talking about possession."

"Yes, I suppose I am. He's been here, Titus has, and the only way he can travel right now is by being inside someone else."

"Hannah…"

"Yes, Katie-love?"

"Do you think I'm an alcoholic?"

There was a brief silence. "Why do you ask a question like that now?"

Tears started rolling down Katie's face. "Because I can't help but wonder if I'm so far gone from drinking too much that I'm delusional. I am, aren't I? I have a problem, and it's too late, isn't it?"

A hand wrapped around Katie's arm, pulling her up and out of bed. "Come to the window, quickly, to see him. He's out there right now."

Katie swung her legs out of bed and walked with Hannah, who felt surprisingly solid. Looking down from her bedroom window, she discerned a shadowy figure walking out of her yard. It was too dark to see his face, but he strode quickly and with purpose.

Katie shook her head. "That doesn't mean anything. It's probably some kid cutting through my yard, late for his curfew."

"How about the fact that I knew he was there?" Hannah asked. "Besides, there's one more thing you need to know."

"What? Little blue smurfs are invading my attic?"

The tears were flowing freely now, which meant her eyes would be puffy in the morning. Walking back toward her bed, she felt around on the bedside table for her box of tissues.

"No, dear, you're not imagining this. You do drink too much, but you'll sort all that out later. Right now, you need to focus to keep everyone alive."

"Everyone?"

"I told you, Titus is looking for revenge against your whole family. I suspect he never realized it was Jenny who killed him. His spirit must have been hanging around, listening to her spread her lies about me. He blames me for his death, and now he wants his revenge… and he'll get it if you're not careful."

"So you think he's trying to kill my family?"

"He's already tried to kill your brother."

Katie felt as if a hammer had hit her chest. "How can you be sure?"

"I'm not," Hannah answered, "but the police are. Go downstairs and listen to the phone recorder."

"The phone what?"

"That thing that people talk on when you're not home. Anna Louise called while you were out tonight."

"You mean the answering machine?" She still had her parents' old technology to update. Another thought occurred to Katie. "Hannah, do you ever leave this house?"

"No, dear. For some reason, I can only leave if you're in extreme danger, and then I can only go where you are."

"Like that day..." Katie couldn't finish her sentence.

"Exactly. But I wouldn't want to be wandering around Yorktown anyway, would I? I don't think I'd know what to do out there. I died in this house, which may be the reason I stay here. Now, go downstairs."

Grabbing her robe off the door hook on her way out, Katie wrapped it around herself as she hurried down the stairs. Sure enough, the answering machine light in the kitchen blinked at her, indicating there was a message.

Katie's hands were shaking as she reached to push the "play" button. This was too bizarre, but whatever the message was would tell her whether or not it was all in her imagination. A moment later, the sound of Anna Louise's voice filled the kitchen.

"Katie, call me when you get this message. It's about Beau... he's okay, but..." Katie could hear her sister-in-law's voice start to quaver. "Katie, the police stopped by to talk to me. They've put a guard outside Beau's room. They think someone did this to him."

CHAPTER THIRTY

KATIE'S HEAD HURT, AND THIS time it wasn't just from being hung over. After hearing Anna Louise's message, there was no way she could get back to sleep. Unfortunately, Hannah disappeared around that time, too. If this ghost thing was real, Katie was going to have to help Hannah figure out how to make her spectral self available for a longer period of time. It wasn't right that she couldn't control that, and besides, Katie needed the company. Ghost or not, life was starting to get creepy, and Katie wasn't sure what to do about that.

She didn't even have Roland around to help her anymore. But that was probably her fault, too, like everything else.

After drifting into an uncomfortable doze around six in the morning, Katie woke with her alarm an hour later. There was no sleeping in. She had a class to teach that morning, and Ella was coming to pick her up. The plan was to drive to work together, as they both had that self-defense class later in the evening.

At least she'd be getting a workout—maybe that would help clear her head. Reuben didn't let them off easily. She'd have to make sure she was stone-cold sober, too. The deputies were looking at her funny at the last class, and she wasn't sure if they knew she'd been drinking or were simply stunned at her lack of coordination.

Maybe she'd have to work on that sobriety thing for more than just class. The thought made her nervous, though, so she pushed it away.

After a quick shower and change into work clothes, Katie stood in front of her bathroom mirror, trying to repair the damage a sleepless night had wrought. She didn't like using lots of makeup, but sometimes a little color on her face concealed whatever the previous night had etched. Brushing mascara on, she paused, hearing the sound of heavy knocking, followed by a voice.

"Katie! Katie, are you in here? Oh my God!"

Throwing the mascara wand on the sink, she ran out the bathroom door and down the stairs. The hall was foggy, making her disoriented.

"Who's here?"

Fear pulsed through her body, and a moment later, an ear-splitting shriek filled the air. It was the kitchen fire alarm.

Without thinking, Katie ran into the kitchen in time to see her neighbor, covered in powder, holding the kitchen faucet sprayer and dousing the wall behind the stove.

He turned toward her and yelled, "I think I've got it all. Are you okay?"

Katie was dumbfounded. "What the... what's going on?"

Her neighbor put the sprayer down and looked at her. "You must've forgotten about your breakfast. Looks like you won't be having any bacon this morning."

Her neighbor, Will, was in his mid-forties, a career military guy who was obviously getting ready for work, as he was dressed in fatigues.

"I was getting in my car when I saw the smoke coming out of your window. I wanted to make sure you were okay, but when you didn't answer, I panicked and came in. That's when I saw the fire." He paused, looking around. "I guess I made a mess, but I didn't know what else to do. I grabbed your flour from the canister on the counter to put out the grease fire and used the hose on the wall. You okay?"

Katie was dazed. "Flour? You knew where to find the flour?"

Will squinted at her. "Yeah, over in the canister on the counter. The one that says 'flour.' You sure you're okay?"

"No, I'm not okay. Why is there bacon on my stove?"

Will took a step backward. "Listen, Katie, I don't know about that. I just came in to help out. I saw the fire and did what I could... have you been... um... are you okay this morning?"

The mess in front of her didn't make any sense, and she was starting to feel like her life was a dream she couldn't wake up from.

"Will, I don't understand. I haven't even been downstairs yet. I didn't put any bacon on the stove."

Will shook his head. "I don't know what to tell you because someone sure as hell did—there's your blackened proof. I hate to ask, but were you drinking last night? Maybe you did something, or maybe you're still..."

Katie's frustration blossomed as tears started spilling down her cheeks.

Damn, she hated crying in front of people. It always made her feel so stupid.

"Aw, geez. I'm sorry. Listen, Katie, I didn't mean anything. I was just asking because it's kinda weird, you know?"

Katie nodded. "I know. It's not your fault. Yes, I was drinking last night, but I'm not still drunk."

"Okay."

Katie looked at Will sharply. She knew from the tone of his voice that "okay" didn't really mean "okay," it meant he was willing to go along with her, even though he knew otherwise.

Her neighbor thought she was drunk. How much lower could she sink? Despair settled in her heart.

"I... um... I've got to go to work, but I think the fire is out. Do you want me to call anyone?"

Katie shook her head. "No. Thanks for rushing in here. That was very nice of you. I'll be fine. I just have to clean this up."

"Yeah, from the looks of things, you had a really tough night. Hang in there, it's gonna get better. I know a good repair guy if you need him."

"I'll figure this out. Like you said, I'm sure it will get better."

Katie waved her arm at the charred mess in front of her, the pan resting crooked on the counter and flour strewn all over the stove and floor. How it would get better was a mystery, but she had to say something.

"Yeah, and from what I can see, you must've really tied one on."

Katie's brow wrinkled. "What are you talking about?"

Will shuffled his feet, clearly uncomfortable. "You know, the outside thing. Listen, I'm really sorry. I've got to go. Call me if you need help later, okay?"

Watching her neighbor's retreating back, Katie was hollow. Something was going on, and it didn't take a genius to know it wasn't good. For a moment, she wondered if perhaps she was simply going crazy.

Alcohol induced dementia. Maybe that's the explanation.

But then the message from Anna Louise flashed through her mind, along with Hannah's warning. Someone was trying to kill her family.

Dammit, she didn't have time to sort through it all right now. She had to get ready, Ella would be here in... checking her watch, she saw that she had just under an hour to clean up this mess and pull herself together.

But first, she'd better see what the hell her neighbor was talking about in the yard. She was willing to bet every last bottle she had that it wouldn't be good.

CHAPTER THIRTY-ONE

CLEVE FELT GOOD. THE MORNING'S work had given him a rush of
adrenaline—this was the kind of thing he enjoyed most. Mission accomplished,
and he hadn't been caught. He smiled, imagining Katie's response to the
morning events. Leaving the pan of bacon with the stove burner turned to
medium high was brilliant. It looked like she'd been cooking her breakfast and
had forgotten about it.

Was Katie confused, maybe fearful now? Or would she blame it all on
having too much to drink? So many possibilities. He thought about calling her
but decided to wait. He didn't want to push his luck with her, or worse, face
rejection.

Alcoholics were a funny sort of people… you didn't always know what to
expect. Kind of like his old man, who would go on a drinking rage for days at
a time, destroying things in his path. Cleve never wanted to be like that, never
wanted to be that out of control.

That would never happen to him. The voice guided him, comforted him.
The voice had been there since he was a child, the all-knowing being who
sometimes came in and took over his body, helped him do what he had to do.

Sometimes Cleve felt like surrendering to the voice, giving himself entirely
over to it and disappearing, letting the voice take over. That would be easiest,
really. But some thread of preservation had him holding on, some spark that
encouraged him to stay in this life a little longer.

The sharp knock interrupted his thoughts. Peering through the security
hole, Cleve saw a uniformed police officer looking back at him.

He opened the door a bit, leaving the chain on. Police officers made him nervous. "Yes?" Cleve asked, wondering if he should've even opened the door. What if someone had seen him at Katie's house? What if he was about to be arrested? Looking past the officer to the parking lot behind him, Cleve was relieved to see no other police or patrol cars.

"Hi, Cleve. I'm Kevin, a friend of Katie's."

"Is she okay? Has something happened?" Cleve hoped his voice held the right note of concern. He didn't want to overplay it.

Kevin avoided the question. "Can I come in?"

"Of course." Fumbling with the chain, Cleve slid it off and opened the door. "Has something happened to Katie?"

"No, she's fine. I just stopped by to say hi, welcome you to the area and all that. I heard you went out on a date with her. She told me you were new to the area."

A silence stretched between them to the point where it became obvious that Kevin wasn't going to offer anything more.

"We had a lovely time," Cleve said, knowing he was expected to fill in the silence. That was fine with him. Whatever game this guy was playing would be easy to go along with. "I took her to the beach for a picnic dinner. A lovely area, really. Do you spend much time there?"

"Usually only on patrol."

"Oh, that's too bad. All that history, gathered in one place... charming."

Kevin nodded. "Yes, it's a special place. Well, I just wanted to stop by and say hello, see how you're settling in here. Are you planning on staying in the area for long?"

Cleve had to suppress a smile. If Kevin was looking for a pissing contest, he'd picked the wrong guy. Cleve wasn't interested in asserting himself so much as blending in, being liked. He sat at the small round table in front of the room's only window and looked up at Kevin.

"I'd hoped to find a new place to live, and I'm starting to feel really at home here. After going to church and meeting so many nice people, then spending time with Katie, I'm seriously considering staying for a while. Have you been here long?"

"A few years." Kevin began to walk around the small motel room.

There wasn't much to see, and Cleve was glad he'd been careful with his belongings. Clothing and toiletries were carefully put away, and his papers were filed in neatly labeled folders in his backpack. The only thing he'd left out was his laptop, but the screen saver had come on and the screen was black;

nothing to see there.

Kevin stopped in front of the faux wood dresser and put his hands on his hips. "What do you do for a living? Are you looking for a job?"

Cleve smiled and leaned back in the chair. All the expected questions. "I do freelance IT work for a few large corporations. Most of it I can do from wherever I call home, and a couple of times a year I fly out to the corporate sites and do a visual check of everything."

"Must be nice."

Cleve shrugged. "It's good work, with the bonus of not having to go to the office. Sometimes I end up working more hours than I might have if I had to punch a clock, but there's always a price to pay, isn't there?"

Kevin nodded. "That's true. So, Cleve, where you from?"

"Up North. I lived in a few places here and there and finally got sick of the cold winters. I heard it was milder here, no snow or anything."

Cleve wondered how long he could drag this conversation on. Obviously, the nice police officer wanted to know more about him, so Cleve was going to have to figure out a way to muddy the waters a bit.

"New York?"

"Pardon?" Cleve put a look of mild confusion on his face.

"Are you from New York?" Kevin asked.

Cleve shook his head. "No. Great state, though. I used to go hiking through upstate New York for family vacations. Are you married?"

"No," Kevin answered. "So, where then? I've got some relatives up North. Where'd you come from?"

Cleve laughed. "Are you suggesting I might know them? It's a big area." Cleve knew the man was getting frustrated. He loved this sort of verbal sparring, especially when he knew he'd win. There was no doubt in his mind: Officer Kevin had a lot to learn.

"No. You just seem like you don't want to tell me where you came from for some reason. I'm not sure why, though." Kevin's stare was direct.

"Massachusetts." Cleve knew he'd told others Connecticut, but he couldn't have this guy going back and checking things out. "Danvers, Massachusetts." Besides, by the time good ol' Kevin here went back and tried to do a background check on Cleve Farrington from Danvers, Massachusetts, he'd be long gone.

"Well, Kevin, thanks for stopping by, but I've really got to get back to work. Maybe Katie and I can double date with you and your girlfriend next time. That'll give us a chance to know each other better."

With a smile, Cleve stood and offered his hand to Kevin and gave him a firm handshake. Yes, it was definitely time for Kevin to go.

Kevin stood outside Cleve's motel room door for a moment, feeling the skin on the back of his neck tingle. Something was off here, and this guy was probably the one Detective Burgess was looking for. He had no doubt Cleve was guilty of everything the detectives had told him about, and probably more. He'd have to go back and report this conversation, as much as he didn't want to. He shouldn't have been here, but he had to see for himself if Katie was in any danger. He was also going to have to figure out how he was going to keep both Katie and Ella safe, no easy task when it came to those two.

I'm probably going to get a reprimand, but I had to know who this guy was.

"Excuse me, sir?"

A woman in a maid's uniform stood in the alcove that housed the soda and ice machine, waving him over. Surveying the area as he approached her, he noticed she looked frightened.

"Ma'am, how can I help you?"

The maid looked around and lowered her voice to a whisper. "I saw you in that man's room, and I had to know." She stopped and looked at Kevin expectantly.

"Had to know what?" Kevin prompted.

"That guy, the one staying there, in the room you were just in... are you going to arrest him soon?"

CHAPTER THIRTY-TWO

KATIE LEANED HER HEAD AGAINST the headrest in Ella's car. The morning's events had exacted a toll on her already exhausted body, and she wondered how she would be able to get through an entire day of teaching. She closed her eyes, once again fighting unwanted tears.

"You okay?" Ella asked, concern lacing her voice.

"Mmmm. You know, they've assigned a police officer to guard my brother."

"What?"

"They think someone did this to him."

"I thought he had a heart attack. Were they wrong about that?"

"He did have a heart attack."

Katie took a deep breath, determined not to make a wisecrack about her brother's lack of healthy eating habits. She was no better, really, with her liquid lunches and hidden bottles. How could she say anything about him when she had so much dysfunction in her own life?

"They think he had a heart attack because of something that happened."

"How do they know this?" Ella was incredulous. "And why didn't Kevin tell me anything about it? Are you sure?"

Katie sighed. "I don't really know. I got a message from Anna Louise, and then my—"

She'd started to say "house ghost" but stopped. She knew Ella would believe her but she didn't want to talk about it.

"What about your protector, what's-her-name?"

Katie opened her eyes and sat up straight. "What are you talking about?"

"Anna Louise told me your parents' house has a resident ghost. We were talking about it one day when she asked how things worked out at my house. Is your ghost helping at all?"

"What did Anna Louise say?" Katie didn't mean to sound shrill, but she couldn't help it. "Has she ever seen Hannah?"

"That's right, Hannah. I forgot her name for a second. Yeah, she said she'd seen her not long after she started dating Beau. Didn't you know about this?"

Katie shook her head. "I had no idea Anna Louise knew this." But she should've known; her sister-in-law deserved a lot more credit than Katie ever gave her, which was starting to be clear.

"She said she'd told you, so I didn't think anything of it. I figured that's why you were so used to the whole ghost thing, you must've grown up with it. Are you okay? You don't look so good."

Katie blew out a breath she hadn't been aware she was holding. She needed to talk about some of this before she went completely crazy or ran out of alcohol, whichever came first.

"Thanks. I'm okay. I just don't know what's going on. How on Earth did that pan catch on fire in my kitchen this morning? Thank the Lord my neighbor saw the smoke—it could've been much worse."

Ella glanced sideways at her from the driver's seat with a look of concern. "Um... I'm guessing that you started to make breakfast and left it there too long..."

Katie was vehement. "No, I didn't. I wasn't going to eat breakfast this morning. My stomach was feeling a little queasy. I wouldn't cook bacon if my stomach was queasy."

She might be seeing ghosts at night, but she knew she hadn't cooked the bacon. Maybe Hannah knew what happened. The problem was that she didn't know how to call Hannah, the ghost just appeared.

"Maybe you forgot."

"How does someone forget putting bacon on the stove?"

Ella shot Katie another look, this one laced with the pity that Katie knew so well. It was the same look people gave her when they first started catching on and figuring out that maybe Katie Hollister had a drinking problem.

Katie was well and truly sick of that look.

Leaning her head back against the headrest, Katie closed her eyes. "El, listen, I don't think I can make it tonight. Don't worry, I'll get a ride home from work, but I really don't want to go to that self-defense class. I'm so tired, and I don't think I can make it through another of Reuben's grueling workouts."

Katie knew Ella was shaking her head, even though she couldn't see her.

"Sorry, Katie, but I think you need to go with us."

"Us?"

"My sister's going to be there, too."

Katie sighed. "No offense, sweetie, but I'm not sure I'm up to hanging out with your sister tonight either."

"When is anybody up to hanging out with my sister?" Ella asked with a smile in her voice. "I know she can be a real pain in the ass and a huge drama queen, but she needs to see you."

Katie opened her eyes and looked at Ella. "What do you mean, she needs to see me?" Suspicion laced her voice. "What's this about?"

"Whatever it is, we both need to hear it. I'm sorry I'm being so secretive, but I'm not sure what she's talking about either."

Katie stared out the car window as they drove down Fort Eustis Boulevard. The leaves on the trees were starting to show a tinge of color, and the sunlight spilling through gave the atmosphere a soft glow. Katie didn't like this time of year despite the milder temperatures and natural beauty of the season. For her, it signaled the march toward winter, a time of gray solitude that had the potential to blanket her in despair. She knew the key to getting through winters was to find a hobby and stay active. So, each year she struggled to keep busy and find positive things to do during the short, dark days.

Each year, she drank a little more.

Pulling herself back to the present, she looked at Ella. "What did Lisa say to convince you it was so important? Why can't she just conference call us or Skype or something?"

Ella laughed. "I know, I said the same thing. She told me that this was something we both needed to hear in person because then we'd have to decide what we're going to do about it."

Katie let her head fall back against the headrest again. "Well, that clears that up. Damn."

Ella nodded. "Yep, that's what I said: damn." There was a slight hesitation before Ella added, "And, Katie, one more thing. Reuben called and said that for tonight's class we should make sure we eat a small, healthy meal before we show up. And to make sure you knew not to have any alcohol before class."

"He really said that?"

"Sorry, sweetie, but yes, he really said that."

CHAPTER THIRTY-THREE

"THERE'S NOTHING QUITE LIKE THE sound of bone snapping!"

Reuben's enthusiasm was almost an affront to Katie's exhaustion, until she remembered the reason they were there. He was teaching them to defend themselves against the bad guys, a noble effort indeed—or it would be if Katie could remember any of those moves she'd learned.

At least some of her fear about the class had abated, mostly because she'd decided she was going to skip the last class. To heck with that whole "simulated attack" nonsense; there was no way she was going to let strange men lunge at her, pretend or not... now, if they were men who were unmarried that she'd picked out herself, that would be different.

"Hollister!" Reuben yelled across the school gymnasium.

Great. Now what?

"C'mon up here. Let's see how much you know."

Katie held back a sigh and eye roll, knowing it would only fuel the officer to greater heights of self-defense techniques. She could never remember when to bend a wrist and when to twist an arm.

Going to the middle of the gymnasium, she stood next to Reuben and faced him. The line of women in the class watched, expectant. Katie wasn't looking forward to this.

"All right, Hollister, I'm going to come at you by putting my arm around your shoulder. Show me what to do."

Standing perfectly still, Katie felt Reuben's arm drape across her shoulder.

Let's see, first I grab his hand... no, wait, his wrist... then I sort of duck, or maybe I should—

"Hollister!" Reuben yelled.

"What?" Katie asked, still fumbling with Reuben's arm.

Maybe I'm supposed to turn... that's it...

"Hollister, I would've had you abducted, robbed, and killed by now. Pay attention!"

Snap the fingers back. Isn't that what Reuben said? Or kick him in the shin?

Grabbing hold of his hand, Katie pulled his index finger out and pushed it backward at an unnatural angle while delivering a kick to the man's left shin.

"Hollister!" Reuben yelled, yanking his hand away from hers and sidestepping the kick. "Go back and stand in the line. I think we need to practice our kicks and punches. Ready, ladies? Defensive stance. I want to see a combination palm strike, block, straight kick, block. Twenty times. Ready? Go!"

By the end of the class, Katie was still tired but surprised to find herself more energized. The exercise had done her a world of good, even though she wasn't sure she'd ever be able to defend herself. She figured her best defense would be to run if it ever came to it.

"That was an interesting class," Lisa said as they gathered their things, getting ready to leave. "Let's talk about it more. Maybe we can go down to the Bay City Diner and get a milkshake or something."

"Or we can go to the Mexican restaurant and get a margarita," Katie added.

"Bay City Diner it is," Ella said. "C'mon, I'm driving. Dan's not picking you up, is he?"

Lisa shook her head. Her husband had dropped her off at the class earlier, waved to the women, and left.

"No, I told him I was going to be hanging out with you. He and the girls are home, working on homework and room cleaning."

"Probably more like pizza and video games," Ella said.

Lisa smiled. "Probably, but that's okay. Dan's such a good dad. I don't mind what they do while I'm out, as long as they're safe. They'll get their homework done eventually, no worries."

Katie looked over at Ella, concerned. It wasn't like Lisa to be so laid back and casual about things. Something was definitely up. She had no doubt Lisa would tell them exactly what it was, too.

Once they were seated and had ordered chocolate milkshakes, Lisa began. "I have to tell you something, Katie, and I don't want you to get mad at me."

Katie knew it had to be big, whatever it was. Lisa didn't usually apply tact of any sort to her beginning statements.

"I'm sure I won't be mad at you, so go ahead and just tell me. I can't stay too long. I've got to go see my brother tonight."

"Is everything okay? Have they taken him out of the coma yet?" Ella asked.

Katie shook her head. She briefly debated not mentioning the latest events but decided she needed to say something about the assault, especially since she already mentioned it to Ella this morning. They'd want to know what was going on, and it would be unsettling if they visited Beau and saw an armed guard at his bedside.

"No, and now something else really weird has happened. They've assigned a guard to his room. They think someone did something to him to cause his heart attack, and they want to make sure he's safe. I'm wondering if it has something to do with his work."

"I'm telling you, there are lots of weird things going on," Lisa said.

Katie didn't bother to suppress her sigh. Obviously, Lisa had something she needed to share, and they were sure to get the full dramatic impact of whatever it was.

"What's going on, Lisa?"

"It's about your new friend," Lisa answered slowly. Seeing the look on Katie's face, she added, "Remember, don't get mad at me. I just got curious, that's all."

"What do you mean by curious? What did you do?" Ella leaned forward in her seat, staring hard at Lisa.

"I thought that since Katie seemed interested in dating him, I should check him out. You know, you always hear about people claiming to be somebody, and they're lying or have a criminal record or something…" Lisa's voice trailed off as Ella and Katie stared at her.

"What did you do, hire an investigator?" Katie was genuinely curious. The funny thing was, Lisa was right. Katie should have thought of that before running off on a date with him alone, or better yet, before inviting him into her house and letting him know where she lived. She wasn't about to say that to Lisa, though. Telling her she was right was like giving a puppy your new pair of leather shoes. It was simply not done.

"I only did an internet background search," Lisa said, looking serious. "But the thing is, even though I didn't subscribe to any of those packages, I did find out some pretty creepy stuff." Digging through her purse on the bench next to her, Lisa pulled out several sheets of paper. Handing them to Katie, she said,

"Here, I printed everything out for you. It's kind of weird, and I thought you should know."

"What does it say?" Ella asked.

The waitress arrived then, and Lisa waited until everyone had their milkshake before answering. "Since this man claimed to be from Connecticut, I started my search there. After all, that's where our family is from. The state isn't big, and I know most of the major newspapers there, as well as news networks. First of all, he's not a registered sex offender, which is good."

"But?" Ella prompted.

"But he is dead, which is bad."

Katie looked up from the papers Lisa had handed her. "It says here that a man named Cleve Yodell died in a house fire last week, but there's a picture of someone that looks a little like my Cleve. This must be a weird coincidence."

Katie knew this couldn't be the man she was dating, despite the similar appearance. For one thing, the last names were different. Plus, there was no way a nice guy like Cleve Farrington would set out to deceive her. What reason would he have for that?

Looking at the picture, a thought niggled at the back of Katie's mind, along with the nagging sense that there was something she'd forgotten. The sound of Lisa's voice jerked her back to the table.

"Really?" Lisa asked. "How many people do you think are named Cleve who look like this?"

"I don't know." Ella sipped her milkshake. "Why don't you go Google it and find out?" Reaching across the table, she added, "Let me see that."

"This isn't funny," Lisa snapped. "Don't you get it? There's absolutely no reference to the guy Katie went out with—there's only this article stating that someone with that first name who looks like Katie's guy just died."

"It's not a very good picture," Ella said. "It might not be him."

"You didn't find any references to Cleve Farrington?" Katie asked. Despite the fact that she was certain this wasn't the same person, Katie was nervous.

"No, so don't you see what that means?"

"This probably isn't the guy Katie went out with?" Ella said.

"No, and this isn't something to joke about. This means something really bad." Lisa's face was creased with worry as she leaned forward, trying to make her point.

"Lisa, this picture is old and grainy. I don't think it's the same guy," Ella said.

"You've never seen him," Lisa snapped.

"No, but both of you told me about him. This picture doesn't match your descriptions, and don't you think this is a little far-fetched?"

"Why don't you go ahead and tell us what you think this is all about," Katie said, leaning back in the booth. Maybe Lisa had a good explanation for all this, something that would make Katie feel less anxious.

"It's obvious." Lisa's voice held a note of exasperation. "There's something wrong with the man Katie went out with. He's using the name Cleve Farrington, which is clearly an alias. I think the real question we need to ask is why would he assume someone else's identity, and who is he, really?"

CHAPTER THIRTY-FOUR

PEOPLE WITH ROUTINES WERE THE easiest to take advantage of. They went to work at the same time every day, they did their shopping on the same day every week, and if they deviated at all from their schedule, they told everyone about it.

On their date, Katie told Cleve all about her class with the police department. She even told him what nights she would be there.

Really, she should learn to be more careful.

Cleve smiled. *That's right, there's no time for learning anything. She's scheduled to die tomorrow. I'll bet that's not in her day planner.*

Avoiding the areas where Katie had left lights on, Cleve glided through her house. Getting in had been easy—the locks were old and flimsy, and it took him less than a minute to enter through the back door. He shook his head. It was a shame people were so trusting and didn't think things through. Those bushes in her front yard were perfect for hiding, and the locks were so predictably inadequate that it was a wonder nobody had taken advantage of this family yet. Maybe the next tenants would be more careful.

Stopping in the dining room, he placed a hand on the antique hutch that reflected a soft shine even in the dim light. The piece of furniture held an assortment of fine china and crystal glasses.

They were probably family heirlooms.

From a family that should not have existed, the voice whispered through his body. *All this, the lifetimes spent with finer things, should have been ours.*

Cleve's brow furrowed. This was a nice house, sure, but he didn't really see any evidence of finer things. This was a typical middle class house.

It's finer than what you grew up with.

That much was true.

I'll bet the Hollister family never had their heat turned off in September, just in time for a cold winter, the voice taunted.

Then again, whose fault was that anyway? Cleve's father spent so much time drinking his paycheck that he often forgot he had a family to take care of.

Your father would never have been a drunk if things had happened the way they were supposed to. I was killed, setting off a chain of events that proved devastating for us all. That death must be avenged to set us right, boy.

Cleve's hand lingered over a teacup in a saucer, white with a light blue fade at the top. The flowers on the cup were white, blue, and yellow, and both cup and saucer were rimmed with a fine blue line. Knowing his latex gloves would prevent fingerprints, he gave in to temptation. Turning on his penlight, he flipped it over to examine the bottom of the cup. It read: *Royal Albert, Bone China, England, 4471.*

The teacup looked like it belonged to somebody's grandmother. Cleve's hand caressed the fragile piece as a wave of longing swept through him. He'd never known a grandparent, never had a meal from a setting other than melamine plates. This very small thing set off a longing so strong, he thought he was having a heart attack as he found himself wanting more than he could put into words.

This would be one of those things he came back for after he killed Katie. The world would think it was a simple robbery, which fit in nicely with his plan.

That's right, take what's yours.

Cleve frowned, wanting the voice to stop. He could do very well on his own, and at times lately the voice was more of an annoyance than a help. It had no real vision, other than getting rid of a few people.

Cleve had vision, and knew he could go far in this world. After all, nobody had caught up with him yet, as they all assumed he was dead.

Putting the cup back in its exact spot, he moved on. Taking the stairs two at a time, a sense of urgency overtook him. Katie kept her computer in an upstairs bedroom, which he needed to access. He had a little message for her.

At the top of the stairs, he stopped, looking to his right. The bedroom with the computer was to the left, but as he glanced to the right, he froze, then blinked. At the end of the hallway was a light. And it moved. It shimmered and spread down the hall, coming toward him on a collision course.

It's her! It's the devil herself! You've got to stop her, or she'll kill you, too...

Cleve didn't know what to do. There was that strange light, standing in front of him now, almost appearing to dance. But the voice, the one that had guided him his whole life, now ripped through him, leaving jagged edges in his mind. Tonight it hurt to hear the voice, it hurt with a pain that left a wound on his soul, whatever might be left of it.

You must kill...

Shards of pain buzzed through his head, and he grabbed the stair railing as a wave of dizziness passed through him.

A female voice, soft, beguiling, echoed in his mind. *He has hurt you your entire life.*

This was new, this female voice. Nausea rolled his stomach as he wondered what she wanted. *Do not let him continue to destroy you.*

It was a gentle voice, but still, it clashed with the other and set off what felt like a series of explosions throughout his body. There seemed to be a battle of wills happening, and he was helpless to stop any of it.

Abruptly, both voices stopped. Taking great, gulping breaths, Cleve glanced around, nervous. Could they both have simply vanished?

It must be the house. This had never happened. He needed to get in and out quickly before something more serious happened.

Shaken and weak, he made his way to the office that held the computer at the end of the hall. Pushing the 'Power' button, he waited for the background to appear and opened a new document. Hands shaking, he typed a message onto the blank page, leaving it open on the screen for Katie to see:

I KNOW WHO YOU ARE.

YOU SHALL PAY FOR THE SINS OF YOUR ANCESTORS.

That should give her a fair enough warning. He doubted she'd even notice it if she came home drunk, which was highly likely.

When he finished typing, he looked around again, hoping that whatever had happened at the top of the stairs was over. Because seriously, if both voices decided to invade his head... he didn't know if he could survive that.

Chapter Thirty-Five

KATIE WALKED THROUGH HER FRONT door with a sense of unease and quietly made her way back into the kitchen.

Or what was left of it. Standing in the doorway to the kitchen, a bleak despair settled over her as she looked at the blackened ruins. She wouldn't call her parents, not yet. She'd handle this herself.

They've got enough on their minds right now, they don't need me adding to that. Again.

Sitting at the kitchen table, she could visually trace the pattern of the fire from the stove up the curtains. The walls were smudged with soot, and a charred scent still hung in the air. It was amazing the whole house hadn't burned to the ground, but the real wonder of it was after all the stupid things she'd done lately, she hadn't killed herself or someone else.

Walking to the cabinet to the left of the sink, she opened it to find her Mickey Mouse mug sitting on the shelf, waiting. That was a start. Pouring a healthy dose of vodka from the supply she kept under the sink, she went and sat back down at the table, hands wrapped around the cup.

The things Lisa said earlier floated through her mind, confusing her and fueling her thirst. But she didn't drink. Instead, she sat and stared into the liquid as if it were a crystal ball she could use to divine the future.

Frankly, she didn't have the energy to sort through Lisa's discovery. The strangeness of it all made her nervous, and right now she didn't want to feel nervous. She wanted to be a normal woman, a woman with a promising future who was starting to date a successful, handsome, normal man.

This is such a mess. I'm such a mess.

Things weren't right in her world, and it was time for a change. Her eyes filled with tears, which spilled down her face and onto her shirt as she sat, staring.

How did she get here? A cloak of loneliness settled around Katie, the feeling that she would never find her way in this world. Here she was, a grown woman, unable to pay her bills and living at her childhood home again. She did things when she drank that she should be ashamed of, but she continued to drink. She couldn't even begin to count the number of strangers she'd had sex with, all because she wanted company for a night or didn't want to drink alone.

And God knows, it was a miracle she hadn't killed anyone yet. Why her brother was in the hospital instead of her was another example of the unfairness of the Universe.

Staring morosely into her cup, the feather-light touch of what felt like arms wrapping around her produced a small smile. *Hannah.* Even after Katie had yelled at her and accused her of not being real, here she was, giving Katie a ghostly hug.

Maybe everything would somehow be all right.

Looking up, the curtains hung in blackened tatters at the window, a silent mockery to her moment of comfort.

Or maybe my drinking will be the death of me. I just don't know if I have the strength to stop. I don't know what I'm going to do.

The phone rang, jolting Katie out of her daze.

"Hey." The voice was soft, an old friend calling when she needed it most. The problem was that Katie wasn't sure if he was still her friend.

She was silent, not sure what to say to Roland. They'd been fighting so much, it made her head—and heart—hurt, but she didn't have the strength to fight anymore. Especially now.

"I just wanted to call and see how you're doing." Roland's voice was subdued. "I know you've had a rough time lately, and since our fight... I wanted to make sure you're okay."

"I don't know."

"You don't know if you're okay?"

Katie shook her head, then realized he couldn't see her. "No, I don't. Everything is wrong, and I know it's all my fault, but I don't know how to make it right again."

"Why don't you start at the beginning and tell me about it?"

It was an offering, an offering to renew their friendship. Katie breathed in through her nose, still staring at the cup in front of her.

"I think the beginning was a long time ago," she said, going back in time in her mind. She could still smell the scent of summer as a kid, that scent of cut grass and chlorine from the pool, the scent of freedom for kids who didn't have to go to school. Those scents still had the power to evoke fear in her.

"There was a man who lived in this neighborhood, quite a while ago. I don't remember his name, but he was always hanging out around the kids, down at the pool or at the playground. We didn't think anything of it at the time. We were just kids, you know?"

"How old were you?" Roland asked.

"I was ten years old, and I had a best friend named Liz who lived across the street from me. We were inseparable, used to hang out at each other's houses all the time and have sleepovers and stuff."

Katie remembered the sense of excitement she had whenever they were allowed to stay at each other's houses overnight, knowing they'd be up late. talking and giggling. Of course, sleepovers were not allowed on school nights for that very reason. Liz's house always smelled clean, like fresh laundry, and Liz said Katie's house always smelled like cookies baking. To this day, the scent of laundry or cookies signaled safety for her.

"Is Liz still alive?" Roland's voice was soothing, peaceful against the story that poured out of her.

"I guess she is, I'm not sure. She moved away a long time ago, and we never kept in touch. One day that guy, the creepy one who was always hanging around, he talked us into going in his house. He used a typical story: he said a kitten was in there that needed rescuing. Liz couldn't resist. She'd always loved animals and couldn't stand the thought of some poor little kitten dying."

"You went inside with her," Roland stated.

"Yes, and you can pretty much guess what happened. He got to Liz first, and I stood there and watched helplessly as he started to rape her. There wasn't anything I could do. He told me he would kill her if I ran... I think he would have, too." Katie wondered if the feeling of helplessness would ever leave, the feeling that she could have saved her friend if circumstances had been different.

"Did he rape you, too?"

Again, Katie shook her head, despite the fact that Roland couldn't see her. "No. My mother showed up with the police. Apparently, our house ghost, Hannah, alerted my mother to the danger I was in. My mother didn't hesitate. She called the police and told them they better get to that guy's house because he was hurting children, and she was on her way over to kill him."

"I'll bet that got them moving."

Katie laughed, despite herself. "Sure did. My mother can be ferocious when one of us is threatened." Belinda still displayed an intensity that was impressive when it came to protecting her children.

"It's a good thing your mom believed Hannah."

Katie sighed. "Which is more than I've been doing lately. Everything has spiraled so far out of control. I actually argued with Hannah the other day and told her she didn't exist. And this is the woman, or ghost, who saved my life when I was a kid." Waves of guilt washed over her, combined with a heart-pounding fear. She had the sinking feeling she'd done something very wrong.

"You know that you're not to blame; you were just a kid."

"It feels like it was my fault, though. I've always wondered if I'd tried a little harder that day to tell Liz we shouldn't go in there, maybe it would've turned out better. Maybe she wouldn't have gotten hurt, and then she wouldn't have moved away."

Her father had talked to her for a long time after that incident, counseling her that she was not to blame and sometimes bad things happened, no matter what. Her parents were steadfast in their love and support, and Katie wondered what was wrong with her that she had never been able to get past this particular incident in her life.

"There's nothing you could have done. He was bound to victimize someone. Unfortunately, emotions don't always understand logic, so I can see how you'd feel a certain way, even if you shouldn't."

"I always have feelings that don't make sense."

"So you numb them." Roland's statement wasn't accusatory, it was simply a statement of fact.

"Yes," Katie whispered. There was no point in hiding now. Her secret wasn't much of a secret.

"I never knew about that happening to you when you were a kid. That must've been rough," Roland said. "Is that the real reason why you drink as much as you do?"

There was only one choice. She'd come this far, and she had to grab hold of whatever help she could. The feeling was back, the sense of fear that made her wonder if she would survive.

Sooner or later, my drinking is going to kill me.

Katie closed her eyes. "I don't know."

CHAPTER THIRTY-SIX

KEVIN KNOCKED ON THE DOOR to Detective Winters' office, half-hoping nobody would be there. Then he could leave a note.

No, he couldn't leave a note. He'd get called into the office and asked for an explanation, and yelled at. Maybe he could leave a voicemail.

The simple fact was that Kevin had messed up. He let his emotions rule his actions and broke the rules. He never should have questioned Cleve, not even under the pretense of saying hello. Frankly, any six-year-old could tell that Kevin wasn't just saying hello, and that was a problem. If Cleve bolted before an arrest could be made, Kevin was in trouble.

He'd do it again, though, exactly the same way. He wasn't going to sit around and wait for some maniac to kill Katie or Ella. He'd just have to deal with whatever the consequences were to his career.

"Yeah?"

Detective Winters' voice was brusque. Kevin took a deep breath, opened the door, and stuck his head inside the office. Dani sat on the same side of the desk as Nick, leaning into him to see the stack of papers in front of them. Both Nick and Dani looked guilty.

Kevin cleared his throat before speaking. "I need to see you, sir. I had a conversation with the person you may be looking for, and I need to tell you about him."

Dani walked around the desk and gestured to a chair in the office. "Let's hear it, officer. What happened?"

"I saw Cleve at the motel out on Route 17—"

"What were you doing out there?" Nick interrupted.

This was where it was going to get tricky. Kevin needed to tell the truth, but he hoped he could mask it a little.

"Remember I told you my girlfriend is friends with Katie Hollister?" After both Dani and Nick nodded, Kevin continued. "Well, I asked Ella about the guy Katie is allegedly dating, and she didn't have a whole lot of information about him. So, I dropped by the place he's staying to give him a friendly hello, welcome to the area sort of thing." So much for masking the truth.

The silence expanded in the room, making it hard for Kevin to breathe. He continued anyway. "So, when I stopped in to say welcome to the area, heard you're going out with my friend, he let me in his room. For a minute."

Dani's jaw was set, her eyes steely. "So, I'm wondering, just out of curiosity, did you happen to show up in uniform?"

Kevin didn't want to answer. *You knew that going in; face up to it.* "Yes."

"You compromised my investigation because you wanted to go off on your own?" Dani's voice was low, and Kevin knew without being told that this meant she was beyond angry.

"I didn't want to go off on my own. I wanted to find out who Katie was dating." Seeing the look of disbelief on the faces of both Nick and Dani, he rushed to finish. "Listen, I spend lots of free time with Katie. My girlfriend is best friends with her. It made sense for me to go there."

"In uniform?" Nick asked. "What were you thinking?"

"I wasn't," Kevin admitted. "I was driving by the motel and decided to just do it. I know I shouldn't have gone in there like that, and I'm sorry. But I had to know who this guy was."

Kevin didn't blame Nick and Dani for being mad at him. In fact, they had every right to be furious. He might have cost them weeks of work, ruining the investigation. If Cleve decided to run, it would be because Kevin had tipped him off by showing up.

Ella and Katie come first. If I waited around and this guy's as bad as they say... Nick interrupted his thoughts. "So? What did you think?"

"I think he might be the guy you're looking for."

"What makes you say that? Are you that good of an investigator, Officer Drake?" It was obvious Dani was still mad. "Did you manage to beat a confession out of him, too?"

"Dani." Nick's voice was soft but somehow managed to stop Dani from saying anything more.

"Again, I'm sorry. But he said he came down here from up North, although he said Danvers, Massachusetts. He's evasive, doesn't want to answer any personal questions."

"Gee, imagine that: a police officer shows up at his door, and he doesn't want to answer any questions. Go figure," Dani said.

Kevin forced himself to remain still, not fidget. He knew he was in trouble, but there wasn't much he could do about that now. He'd probably be in more trouble if they knew he didn't regret it. There was no way Kevin was going to sit around and wait for Ella or Katie to get hurt.

My job is to protect, and that's what I'm doing. The rationalization worked fine until he saw the fire in Dani's eyes. She was pissed.

"What's this guy's name?" Nick asked.

"Cleve Farrington."

Dani and Nick looked at each other. "That works," Nick said, playing with the pencil in his hands. "He'd probably stick with the same first name, just change his last name."

"Wouldn't you think that would make him easier to find?" Kevin asked.

Dani shook her head. "No. These guys are really good at lying. Liars try to keep some strain of truth in everything they do, it makes it easier to lie. What else did you get from him?"

Kevin shook his head. "Not much. Like I said, I told him I wanted to stop by and introduce myself, I'd heard he started to date Katie, I asked him where he was from, did he like the area."

"Does he like the area?" Nick asked.

"He said he did. But the weird part happened when I left the room. The maid pulled me aside as I was walking to the car, asked me if I was going to arrest Cleve."

Dani's eyes sharpened. "What did he do to her?"

"What makes you think he did something to her?" Nick asked. "We never got any calls about that."

Dani gave Nick a look, which made him duck his head. "I know, I know," he admitted. "We don't always get calls about crimes. So, what did she say?"

"She said she had been cleaning the room one day and he came back, got really weird, and started yelling at her. She thought he was going to kill her, but when I asked if he specifically threatened her, she said no," Kevin said.

"Why did she think he was gonna kill her?" Dani asked.

"It was his attitude," Kevin answered. "He stood between her and the door, and for a few minutes she was positive her life was over, that he was going to rape her and kill her and dump her body in the river.”

“She said that?” Nick was surprised.

Kevin nodded. “In those exact words.”

Silence filled the office as Kevin stood, waiting. His jaw hurt from clenching it so tight, but he didn’t move. His eyes wandered over the sterile walls and haphazard stacks of paper. The faint smell of old, greasy food and burnt coffee reminded him that Dani and Nick had been working on this case almost nonstop.

“Let’s get a search warrant to go with the arrest warrant,” Dani said.

Kevin relaxed a little. Maybe this would turn out okay after all.

Picking up the phone, Nick nodded. “I’m calling the magistrate right now. Kevin, go with Dani and pick it up.”

“Me, sir?”

“Yeah, you. You put us on this path, don’t you think you should at least help us out a little more?”

“Okay.” *Not really, but I’ll do what I’m told. Something doesn’t feel right about any of this.*

“We’ll probably need to mobilize the SWAT team, too,” Dani said, grabbing her cell phone.

“They’re my next call,” Nick said.

“Good.” Dani nodded. She wadded up a piece of paper, throwing it in the wastebasket. “I don’t want to make any mistakes with this guy. He’s killed enough as it is.”

CHAPTER THIRTY-SEVEN

HOSPITALS ALL SMELLED THE SAME, like Clorox-covered death. It didn't bother Cleve much, but he wasn't sure he'd be able to work in a place like this. He only had to put up with the smell for a little while, he couldn't imagine dealing with it all the time.

This was his test run. Once he inserted himself into the family scene, it would be easy to finish the job. After all, he had a good reason to visit old Beau in the hospital: he was dating the guy's sister. And, since Beau was in a coma, there would be no spark of recognition, no finger pointing.

By tomorrow, it would all be over anyway. If he was lucky, he could eliminate the mother at the same time he got rid of Beau. Maybe he'd get rid of the father, too, just for fun. It would be a touching family moment, a time of togetherness.

He smiled, thinking of his father and the time he killed him. The voice had urged him on, told him he had to do it. The voice was right. His drunk-ass father had negotiated a deal with a trucker he'd met from God-knew-where, a deal involving an exchange of money for his son.

Like that was going to happen. Cleve snorted with derision, his father's voice ringing clear in his head as if the old man were standing right there. "It's time for you to make this family some money, boy. Now get your ass on over to that truck, get in, and do what the man says."

Cleve shot his father in the center of his forehead, a fairly quick kill. Striding outside, gun in hand, he raised and aimed for the trucker, who took off with a squeal of tires, never to be seen again.

He'd gone back inside, told his mother to clean up that mess, and went straight to the backyard to uncover the old well. Good thing they didn't have to drink well water anymore. It would've been rancid after he dumped his father's body down there.

Cleve's life was slightly better once his father was gone, although his mother relied on him for way too much. Eventually, he had to get rid of her, too, as she had become a burden he didn't want to deal with anymore.

The doors to the second floor whooshed open in front of him, allowing him access to the visitor's area. He was certain some family member or other would be there, someone he could sit and offer comfort to.

Turning left at the main nurse's station, he continued down the hallway to Room 232. Outside the door, a uniformed guard sat in a chair, thumbing through a magazine. Looking up, the guard said, "You here for a visit?"

Cleve nodded, amused. He could have saved them all money by letting them know that Beau wasn't in any danger tonight. He wondered what the guard would say if he told the man to go home, everything was okay for now.

"Your name?"

"Cleve Farrington. I'm a friend of the family."

The guard stood. "Wait here, please."

Turning, he entered the room, where Cleve could hear murmured voices. The guard came back, shaking his head when he saw Cleve. "Sorry, the family says they don't know you."

"Tell them I'm dating their daughter, Beau's sister Katie."

The guard, suspicious now, gave Cleve a hard stare. "When did you start dating her?"

"We had our first official date this week. I took her to the beach, and we had a picnic dinner." Cleve smiled at the guard. "It was very romantic."

"Really? Because it sounds very cheap to me. Stay right there."

He disappeared into the room and came back out again, followed by Belinda. "Hello, I'm Belinda, Katie's mother." She extended her hand to Cleve, looking him in the eyes as she did so. "I don't believe we've met."

"No, we haven't, and I'm sorry it has to be under such sad circumstances." Cleve grasped her hand with both of his, putting on his most sincere expression. "I met Katie at church last Sunday, and we really hit it off, so we've started dating. She told me about Beau, and I wanted to stop by to see how he's doing."

Belinda nodded. "Thank you. Is Katie with you?"

Cleve shook his head. "No. I actually thought she might be here, but that's okay. I wanted to stop by and see if you needed anything. Maybe I can run out and get some dinner for you or sit with Beau a while so you can take a break."

Belinda's voice was steely. "I don't need to take a break from sitting with my own son, Mr. Falloway."

Cleve cleared his throat. "Farrington."

"Mmmhmm. I think we're fine here. I'll let Katie know you stopped by. Thanks for coming. Goodbye."

Cleve stood still for a moment, perplexed. This had not gone at all how he had planned, and Belinda showed no sign of backing down or letting him into the room. He couldn't very well make a scene, or too many questions would be asked. He had no choice in the matter but to remain his usual charming self.

"It was lovely to meet you, Belinda. I do hope we cross paths again soon."

Belinda inclined her head toward him, watching as he turned to walk away. Seething, he kept his face impassive so nobody could see the rage that burrowed just beneath the surface.

How dare she treat me like that? Bitch. He was right: they all deserve to die.

"Who was that?"

"Nobody," Belinda told her husband as she settled on the chair next to him.

"Didn't seem like nobody to me."

"Someone who claims he's dating Katie."

"Katie's dating someone?" Surprise was evident on his face. "Why didn't she tell us?"

"Maybe she's not." Belinda's words were soft as her face darkened. "I didn't like him."

"What do you mean, you didn't like him? Did you chase him off?"

Belinda nodded. "Yes. Honestly, Katie hasn't mentioned dating anyone, and we have an armed guard sitting outside Beau's door because the police think someone tried to kill him. How do we know this wasn't the man who tried to kill our son?"

Belinda was surprised her husband didn't sigh when he answered. His opinion about his wife was clear: he loved her dearly but thought she was prone to dramatics. This time, however, he took what she said into consideration. "Why didn't you like him?"

Belinda didn't hesitate when she answered. "He reminded me of someone. He had the same eyes as that man who tried to hurt Katie and her friend all those years ago. His eyes were dead."

CHAPTER THIRTY-EIGHT

BELINDA ANSWERED ON THE SECOND ring. Katie felt stirrings of uncertainty but needed to talk to her mom, just for reassurance. Reassurance of what, she wasn't sure, but that didn't matter.

"Hi, Mom. I was just wondering how Beau is. Any changes?"

"Well, good morning to you, too. Isn't it a little early?" Belinda's voice held a faint note of surprise.

It was early for Katie, but she'd held her ground last night, determined not to drink. It wasn't her easiest night ever, nor was it her proudest. She felt stupid staring down a Mickey Mouse cup, but stare it down she did. She hadn't picked it up to take a sip, not once—but oh God, how she wanted to. With no alcohol in her system, she woke up that morning feeling more energy than normal.

It's from not drinking. I'm not hungover, like normal, although I guess being hungover isn't exactly normal for most people.

"I wanted to get an early start," she answered, evading any mention of alcohol. "So, any news?"

"He's doing really well, healing better than we thought he would. The doctors think he will be strong enough to bring out of the coma in a couple of days."

Katie breathed a sigh of relief. "That's awesome, Mom."

"It is," Belinda agreed. "Katie, I need to ask you something."

Katie's heart raced at the tone in her mother's voice. That tone usually meant trouble, the kind of trouble that Katie had caused.

"You don't have to answer if you don't want to."

"That's rather enigmatic." Katie wondered how bad this was going to be.

Maybe her mother had found out she'd almost killed the cat. Or maybe she found out about the roses. "Is this about the fire?" Katie asked.

"What fire?"

Crap. "I'll tell you about it later. What did you want to know?"

"Are you dating anyone right now?"

Katie was surprised, as this was the last thing she'd expected her mother to ask. "I've been out on one date with someone, but it's not serious or anything. He's not from around here, and I don't know how long he'll be in town. Why?" Thoughts of Lisa's dramatic announcement about Cleve's identity surfaced in her mind. She still didn't know what to think of all that and wasn't sure she had the energy to work it all out.

"A man came to the hospital last night to see your brother, told the security guard he was a friend of the family. His name was Cleve."

"Handsome guy, dark hair and blue eyes, kind of tall?"

"That sounds like him," Belinda agreed. "But I didn't let him in to see Beau."

"Why not?" Katie wondered what Cleve could possibly have done to arouse her mother's protective instincts. Maybe Lisa was right after all.

"I just... I didn't like him. He seemed... I don't know how to describe it, but I didn't trust him. Plus, we weren't sure who he was, and with the police saying what they did—"

"It's fine, Mom," Katie reassured her. "If he can't handle being kicked out of a hospital room by you, then he's not worth it."

"I'm so glad to hear you say that. I was worried you'd be upset with me."

Katie smiled. "Never."

"Will you be coming to the hospital today?"

"Yes. I'll come over after my classes are out. I've only got two classes to teach this afternoon, so I should be at the hospital by five."

"What will you do with yourself now that you're up so early?"

It was a typical Mom thing to ask, but Katie didn't know what to say. *Figure out my life? Call Alcoholics Anonymous? Throw away all the booze in the house? Hide in a closet?* "I'm not sure. It's been a while since I've had any free morning time."

"Why don't you go to the battlefields?" her mother suggested. "When you were a teenager, you used to love walking there, remember? You said it cleared your head and made you feel connected to the past."

"I remember," Katie mused.

Actually, until her mother had mentioned it, she'd forgotten how much she liked the silent stretch of land. She used to wander through, imagining what life was like for the colonials, wondering about the choices they'd been faced with and thinking about what she would have done had she lived at that time. For some reason, walking through the redoubts and cannons relaxed her, probably because the fields were usually empty of people.

"That's a good idea. I'll have my phone with me, so if anything changes, call me."

"I will. You be careful. I love you."

"Love you too, Mom."

The September morning was mild, without a cloud in the sky. The peacefulness of the day was a stark contrast to the chaos of her mind.

Last night, Katie had gone online and looked up the website for Alcoholics Anonymous. It was informative, but it was scary. There was a quiz she'd taken that was supposed to gauge whether or not she was an alcoholic. All she had to do was answer yes or no to the twelve questions.

According to the site, answering yes to four or more of the questions signified a problem with alcohol. Katie answered yes to nine of the questions.

It was time to face the truth, and to do this she needed help. Maybe Roland would be there to help her—he had hinted as much last night. But ultimately, this was something she had to do on her own.

Please, God, give me strength. I want my life, I want... more. I don't want to be messed up anymore.

Most of her current problems could be traced to drinking. All her financial troubles were the result of spending at least three hundred dollars every week on booze. That was twelve hundred dollars every month, as good as thrown away. That was her entire mortgage payment.

Katie's shoulders slumped. *I'm such an idiot. Normal people do not live like this. I'll probably end up living in my parents' house for the rest of my life.*

She thought about the other issues she had from drinking: the days she'd missed work, the conversations she couldn't remember, the sex with strangers. *Holy crow, the way I've been living, I'm lucky to be alive.*

She had to join a group like AA. Katie wasn't sure how she felt about that. She'd never seen herself as someone who needed to go to meetings and tell everyone her problems. Then again, the information sheet she'd read last night said the only requirement for membership was a desire to stop drinking.

She wanted to stop drinking, but she didn't want the membership. Maybe there was some other way. Maybe she could do this alone.

The beginnings of a dull ache started behind her left eye as she realized the dichotomy of her thoughts.

Her phone buzzed in her pocket, signaling a text message. Pulling the phone out, she held her breath. Maybe something happened with her brother... maybe her mother was texting to tell her to come to the hospital immediately... maybe it was Roland...

Her life was full of *maybes*.

Squinting at her phone, Katie smiled. The message was short:

WHERE R U?

CHAPTER THIRTY-NINE

CLEVE KNEW VERY WELL WHERE Katie was. He'd followed her that morning, surprised she was up so early. *Good thing I was watching. Gotta be ready for last-minute changes to the plan.*

His text message asking her location was a ruse. When she texted back *battlefields*, he smirked, sending another message:

AM AT CHURCH. COME ON OVER.

It all came from him, the voice, the idea to lure her to the church.

Kill her in the House of God, expose her for the sinner that she is. Do it.

Cleve could feel his body start to fill with the Other, a feeling that was not entirely uncomfortable. It was like taking a backseat and watching the scenery flash by. While he wasn't exactly in control, he still knew what was going on. The Other felt strong today, stronger than before.

The voice pounded through his head. *You know who I am. Say it.*

Titus. The one who was unjustly murdered.

Titus edged further into his mind, filling his body. Cleve's control began to slip as Titus grew stronger.

Sitting in a front pew, Cleve/Titus waited, tools at his feet. *I'll take over from here, boy.* The clanging of a metal door closing reverberated through Cleve as he fell into the abyss, losing control.

This body is mine, and I'm not leaving. I have strength now, strength from all that has been done, and I shall live within this flesh and use it as my own.

Cleve watched from inside his head, unable to speak or move. He'd been pushed into a locked room in his mind. The smell of rotting flesh was all around, but that couldn't be possible. This was his mind, Cleve's—how could

Titus take over so completely? It was not supposed to be this way. Usually, they shared his body and Titus only came out once in a while. He wasn't supposed to take over. That wasn't part of the plan.

Focusing his energy, Cleve threw himself against the steel bars that held him in place.

We've created a fortress in there, you and I, Titus laughed. *Through our words, actions, and deeds. There's no escape.*

Horror flooded Cleve, the horror borne of knowing his fate was worse than death. In this jail, there was no appeal. Into his own mind he'd been cast, left to suffer until the end—and the end, Cleve realized, only came with death. The release he struggled for might not happen for a very long time. Cleve was a healthy young man.

"Can I help you?"

Still able to see everything around him, Cleve looked out at a man standing in the front of the church. Dressed casually in jeans and a button down denim shirt, Cleve recognized him as the pastor who had given Sunday's sermon.

"Delightful," Titus said, forcing Cleve's face into a smile.

"Excuse me?" The pastor looked confused, understandably. Cleve was confused, too, and it was his body.

"This is going to be a delightful day," Titus said.

"Do I know you? I think you were here this Sunday, right?" The pastor moved to take a seat in the pew, but Titus stood and blocked him.

"Yes, it was me. Sort of." Titus giggled then, a high-pitched sound that made Cleve's head hurt… if he even had a head anymore.

The pastor nodded, examining Titus. "So, tell me about yourself."

"There's nothing to tell. So many think they know me, but you cannot truly know another, can you?"

"Maybe not." The pastor paused, searching Titus' eyes. "Tell me, what is it you're seeking? What do you really want?"

Cleve could feel the disdain Titus had for the man. "You would not understand what I seek."

"Try me." The pastor looked comfortable, standing in front of Titus with his hands clasped behind his back, non-threatening, the picture of patience. "You know, the soul can be both powerful and shy."

"Do. Not. Talk. To. Me." Spittle flew from his mouth as Titus glared at the pastor. "You know nothing of the soul, nothing of everlasting life. You know nothing of a death that reaches far beyond the grave, a death without end."

Cleve knew what would happen to the pastor and watched with small interest to see if there would be a struggle. Perhaps the man was stronger than he looked. Perhaps this man of God really could overpower Titus.

Titus walked around the man and strode to the altar. Grabbing a chalice, he faced the pastor. "Do you drink from this every week, hoping to attain a pathway to God? Don't you know your soul is blackened by the sins of those who came into this place of worship?"

The pastor's face turned gray, and he slowly reached his arm out. "I can help you, but you've got to let me help. Hand me the chalice, and tell me why you're here."

Purposefully walking toward the pastor, Titus raised the chalice in front of him, as if in supplication. When he got close to the pastor, he swung the chalice up, striking the man on the chin, then swung it back down again, striking him on top of the head. "Felled by a tool of God." Titus laughed as the pastor crumpled to the ground.

A loud gasp echoed through the church. Titus swung around, spying Katie standing in the middle of the aisle.

"Cleve?" Uncertainty filled her voice.

"Almost," Titus giggled.

Katie looked at the pastor's still form at the head of the church. "Why did you do that?"

Cleve walked closer to her, moving slowly, as if she were a frightened animal. "Come here," he commanded. "There's much work to be done to right the wrongs of so long ago. Come, help me."

Katie's face reflected her confusion as she backed up. "What?"

"Katie-love, don't listen to him! Get out now, while you still can!"

CHAPTER FORTY

"HANNAH?"

A mixture of surprise and fear ran through Katie. Either she was going crazy or something was very, very wrong. Hannah only appeared outside the house during extreme circumstances.

Katie's head hurt, and her hands started to shake. This was definitely not the best time to stop drinking, but apparently there was *never* going to be a good time to stop drinking. She shook her head a little, trying to figure out what was happening in front of her.

"You..." Cleve's lips twisted into a sneer. "Have you come to watch your ancestors pay the price for your devilry?" Moving quickly, he lunged and grabbed Katie's arm, creating immediate bruises under her sleeve.

"Release her! She's done nothing!" Hannah cried.

"I know no such thing, witch."

Katie tried to pull her arm out of Cleve's grip, but he held on and dragged her to the front of the church, where the pastor lay prone.

"I don't know what's going on here, but Hannah's right: you need to let go of me."

"Shut up," Cleve replied in a surprisingly amiable tone.

Katie tried to take a deep breath, hoping to push her fear away. This was no time to be afraid.

"I did not kill you," Hannah said, appearing in front of them. Katie jumped a little at the sudden change of location the spirit made.

You'd think I'd be used to her moving around like this. Oh God, I think maybe I'm going crazy. This can't be happening.

"Of course you did. I was there, remember?" Cleve didn't bother looking at Hannah, instead picking up a gasoline container.

"Were you awake to see it happen?" Hannah demanded. "Because from what I remember, all indications were that you were killed in your sleep."

"Okay, hate to interrupt this happy reunion, but can somebody please tell me what the hell is going on here?" Katie was desperate. She didn't understand any of this—maybe it was from some kind of alcohol withdrawal. Or maybe she'd finally lost her mind.

"It's simple, really," Cleve answered. "That woman killed me. Now her family must pay the price."

"It was a long time ago and has nothing to do with her," Hannah argued.

"How long?" Katie asked.

"Let me at least tell her," Hannah pleaded as Cleve began splashing gasoline on the pews and altar rails.

Cleve paused, looking at Hannah, then gave her a slow nod. "Fine. Do try to tell us your version of events that day."

Hannah inclined her head toward him before turning to Katie and speaking. "It was early May, the year 1861. Spring had just gotten a foothold on Connecticut, and the smell of lilacs blooming and fresh turned earth was everywhere. Of course, it was hard to focus on some of that as there was talk of a war about to begin."

"The Civil War," Katie said. "This was right before it started." Katie knew Hannah was stalling for time, trying to tell the story in the longest way possible. Would anyone arrive soon to help, or was she on her own?

"Exactly," Hannah continued. "I had just come to this country from Ireland and gotten a job cleaning house and cooking for Titus Foote in the small town of Watertown, in Connecticut. It was a lovely area, full of rolling hills and peaceful people. But there was a dark stain living with us all at that time, a stain that would forever alter the course of events." Turning to Cleve, Hannah pointed a finger. "That stain I speak of came directly from you."

"Liar," Cleve spat. "You try to create a different picture of the events that day, but I know what happened."

"No, you don't, because I am telling you I did not kill you. What reason do I have to lie to you now?"

"Excuse me, but there's one really huge thing here that doesn't make any sense," Katie said. "If Hannah killed you, why are you holding onto my arm so tight? I know for a fact that ghosts don't have that kind of grip."

Maybe I can distract him somehow. I've got to keep him talking so I can figure a way out.

"It's not the man you know who's holding your arm. It's Titus, and he's taken over Cleve's body," Hannah answered.

"Oh." Katie didn't know what else to say because this day really couldn't have gotten any weirder.

"That day you speak of, I was out by the creek, doing the wash. I did not know you were dead until I finally came upstairs to wake you. I didn't want to disturb you, but I knew it was getting late and you would be very angry with me for letting you stay in bed all day."

"Then why did you run?" Cleve asked.

"How do you know what she did? You were already dead," Katie said, still struggling with his grip on her arm. He was stronger than he looked, though, and his grip didn't lessen.

"I was witness to the jury of inquest held after they discovered me. Since my murder, I have been unable to rest, waiting for the day when I could avenge my death."

"I'm sorry you died so young—" Katie said, then tried to kick Cleve's shin. He sidestepped her easily.

"He was no longer a young man," Hannah said, with a distinct sneer on her ghostly face. Katie stared, amazed to see Hannah solidify as she spoke. "He was 79 years old, not young and probably destined to die soon anyway."

"Liar!" Cleve roared.

"How old do you remember being?" Katie asked, trying to keep him talking. The more she kept him occupied, the better chance she had of getting out of there. Looking over at the pastor lying on the floor, she amended that thought—the better chance she had of getting them *both* out of there. *This time, I'm not going to let someone else get hurt.*

"I was not close to death," Cleve continued, glaring at Hannah. "You pushed me into it. I had at least another decade left."

"The one thing I admit to is that I should not have left," Hannah told Katie. "I went into the room and saw him lying there. It was as gruesome a thing as I'd ever seen in my young life. I got scared and ran, leaving his body in the bed where he had been murdered." Turning to Cleve, she addressed him. "It was disrespectful and wrong of me to leave you, but I was afraid the murderer would come after me next."

Exasperated, Katie yelled, "Can someone please explain why my ghost keeps talking to the guy I went on a date with as if he was someone from the 1800s?"

"Your ghost?" An amused smile played at Hannah's lips. "I believe I am here for the entire family, but you certainly do seem to need me more than the others. As far as the man you went on a date with, he's gone now. That's why I was so confused, I couldn't see it at first."

"See what?" Katie said.

"Titus Foote, the man who was murdered, has taken over the body of your friend Cleve."

Katie's brow wrinkled in confusion. "That's what you said, but I don't understand. Do you mean that Titus is... that he possessed Cleve? How could that happen?"

"Cleve is my direct descendent, therefore, I am entitled to enter his body at will and use it for my own purposes," Titus/Cleve said.

"Not exactly for your own purposes," Hannah corrected. "You've taken advantage of a situation and twisted things around a bit."

Katie lunged at the man, determined to at least jab him in the eyes. Swinging a gasoline can, he smacked her arm down before she could reach him.

"Does it really matter?" Titus/Cleve sneered.

"Yes," Katie told him. "Everything matters. Hannah, is this why you went to jail?"

Hannah nodded. "I was convicted of a crime I did not commit and spent the next six years in jail. I had to admit a guilt I did not have in order to be let out. The prison wardens told me to leave Connecticut and never return. That's exactly what I did. I came to Virginia and started a whole new life."

"It was his daughter, wasn't it?" Katie asked. "I remember you talking about this. I may have been drunk a lot, but I do remember some of what you said."

Cleve/Titus snorted. "All my children loved me." Twisting Katie's arm behind her back, he yelled, "Stop struggling! You'll only make it worse."

Hannah was gentle this time when she spoke. "Yes, they did. But you lost so many of them, didn't you? The first two wives died, and then you lost five more children. But you had Jenny."

Cleve/Titus smiled, remembering. "Yes, sweet Jenny."

"She wasn't so sweet," Hannah told him.

"You were jealous. You were always jealous of her. She was everything you wanted to be."

"She was crazy." Hannah's words were blunt, enraging Cleve/Titus. "I'm sorry, but I've had lots of time to consider this, and I know she killed you."

"How could you know such a thing?" Cleve/Titus bellowed.

"Because it makes sense," Hannah argued. "She had access to your room, she had her own axe that she used to slaughter the animals for food—and don't forget, she was kind of crazy. I watched her dissect a bird once, taking it apart piece by piece while the bird was still alive."

"She was probably dressing it, preparing it for cooking," Cleve/Titus said.

"She tossed the parts into a hole in the ground when she was done," Hannah told them.

Katie was uncomfortable and scared. This situation was beyond anything she could've ever imagined, and Cleve/Titus was hurting her arm. She looked to Hannah for help, realizing the irony of seeking help from a ghost but desperate enough to try.

Looking at her, Hannah said one word. "Reuben."

CHAPTER FORTY-ONE

FOR A MOMENT, KATIE HAD no idea what Hannah was talking about. Why would she mention a sandwich at a time like this? Then it clicked: the self-defense classes. Maybe she could use something she learned there.

Isn't this the exact reason I took the class?

Remembering her last experience with Reuben, her hopes plummeted. She was going to die today, but she wasn't going to die without a fight.

Wrapping an arm around her neck, Cleve/Titus dragged her forward and splashed more gasoline around the altar. Katie tried to ignore the stench as the fumes clung to her eyes and nostrils.

"It's lovely that the good Reverend decided to join us," Cleve/Titus said. "I'm certain once authorities find the bodies within this building, they'll be able to tell that he attacked you but could not escape his own treachery." Shaking his head, he added, "It's a shame, really, a man of the cloth and all that, committing such a heinous crime."

Reaching into his pocket, he pulled out matches, at the same time tightening his grip on Katie's neck. Suddenly, instinct took over—or maybe it was all that practice Reuben had insisted on in class. Quickly bending her knees and dropping her weight, Katie threw Cleve/Titus off balance. Using her elbow, she jabbed backwards and caught him in the ribs while stomping her foot on top of his. She barely heard his cries of rage as she continued to stomp, kick, and punch him the way she'd been taught.

Reuben's voice echoed in her head: *Do what you need to do, and don't stop. When you can, run for the exit.*

That couldn't happen without helping the pastor first. Bringing her arm up, Katie elbowed Cleve/Titus while at the same time kicking his right shin. Losing her balance, she started to fall as his grip tightened on her.

Get mad! Reuben's voice yelled in her head.

She could do that. After all, she was trying to figure out her life, and here was this weirdo trying to end it.

Not today.

Pulling herself out of the fall, she twisted around to face him. Ignoring the pain as Cleve/Titus wrapped her hair around his hand and pulled, Katie brought a fist down hard onto his nose. Not stopping, she jabbed him in the eye with her other hand. Cleve/Titus let go of Katie, giving her a push as he did so, catching her off balance and causing her to land on her side on the floor. She could see the pastor stirring, as if he were waking. She had to get to him before that monster knocked him out again and killed him.

"You shall burn for your sins, as well as the sins of your family. I will take what is rightfully mine and resume my place in this world," Cleve/Titus' voice rang out through the church.

"You cannot become human again, not in this manner!" Hannah cried, standing next to Katie.

Cleve/Titus looked at her and smiled. "I already have."

Before Katie could react, he struck a match and tossed it onto the gasoline-soaked floor. A wall of flame burst in front of Katie, stunning her. The fire burned hot and strong, and she squinted against the smoke and fumes that assailed her. Through the flames, she could see the man she knew as Cleve slipping out the side door.

"I'm with you, Katie-love," Hannah's soft voice surrounded her. "Go quickly."

Holding an arm across her face, Katie dropped to the floor and crawled around the flames to get to the pastor. Trying to raise himself up on one elbow, he wore a dazed expression on his face.

"I'm going to help you," Katie told him, "so wrap your arm around my shoulders and lean on me."

For a moment, Katie thought he didn't understand her. His face was blank, as if nothing registered. Finally, he nodded and threw an arm across her. Standing to a half-crouch, they began to make their way through the rolling smoke toward the door. The weight of the pastor, combined with her injuries, slowed them. After a full minute, they'd only moved a couple of feet.

"Stop," the pastor gasped. "We're going the wrong way."

By this time, the smoke was so thick, Katie couldn't see anything. The fire had quickly consumed the altar and front of the church, and Katie was certain the rest of the building was not far behind. Usually, old buildings like this church were made of materials that were highly flammable, and she had no doubt she was losing precious seconds standing there trying to orient herself.

"The heat," she cried. "He started the fire at the altar, so let's move away from the heat toward the doors at the front."

The pastor nodded. "Okay."

Trying to move quickly, they stumbled down the center aisle, Katie's legs bent under his weight as he leaned on her even more. A moment later, he collapsed on top of her.

Sinking to the floor with the pastor, Katie tried to figure out what to do. Leaving the man to burn inside the church was not an option, so her only choice was to try to drag him to safety. Grabbing his torso and pulling, her heart sank. He was dead weight, and she didn't think she had the strength to get them both out of there.

"I'm with you. You're going to be fine," Hannah called through the smoke.

Hysteria bubbled within Katie as she struggled to maintain her grip on the pastor while sweat dripped down her face. She had to make it through this, she couldn't die now.

Why not? The insidious voice snaked inside her, the voice that argued and railed against the world, the voice that championed her need for self-destruction.

This was the piece of herself that helped her drink, the part that encouraged her to live her life without feeling or caring what happened next. This was the voice that sometimes told her it didn't matter whether she lived or died and sometimes suggested that death might be a nice alternative.

Except she did care. She cared more than she wanted to admit. She knew she drank to tamp down those thoughts and feelings, she drank to forget the pain that came from nowhere and cut her inside. She drank to feel better about herself because so often she felt like nobody, empty and worthless. Everyone else was so normal, so able to live the way they were supposed to live, while Katie's life was always slightly... off.

Different.

Oddball.

Screw-up.

She couldn't save her best friend when she was younger, and she probably wouldn't be able to save herself now.

Except now she wanted everything, every moment. In this space in time, Katie knew how precious each second was, and she didn't want to give any away.

What do you really want? She'd heard the pastor ask Cleve, or whoever he was, that very question. She knew now, without a doubt, what her answer was.

I want to stop drinking.

I want a normal life.

I don't want to hide anymore.

Time was running out, and she'd only managed to move the pastor a few feet.

I don't know if I can survive this.

But she had to, there was so much she still had to do. She hadn't known how much she wanted to live until death was such a real possibility. She still had to tell Roland how much she loved him, even if he had moved on and started dating someone else. Nothing was more important in this world than letting people know how you felt, especially when it came to love.

"Katie!"

Katie wasn't sure if she was hallucinating or not. The smoke had grown so thick she'd dropped to the floor, still struggling to drag the pastor to the front. She'd barely moved closer to her escape, and the flames were inching closer.

"Katie, where are you?"

If she was hallucinating, it didn't really matter, did it? "Here," she screamed despite a sore throat, hoping she could be heard. "In the center aisle."

"Keep talking..."

"I'm right here...I'm with the pastor...we're on the floor..."

Katie didn't care if she was babbling. She couldn't control the hysteria that rose in her or the tears that streamed down her face.

"Please... I'm right here..."

He materialized, grabbing hold of her. Katie gave a short sob as she pulled herself halfway up. As the darkness closed in, she collapsed onto Roland.

CHAPTER FORTY-TWO

THE MOTEL ROOM WAS EMPTY. She should've expected that much, but Dani had been so certain they were going to get Cleve, she was already imagining her flight home. Her hands still had a tremor from the adrenaline high that kicked through her body when they stormed the place.

"I hope we're not too late," Nick muttered, running a hand through his hair and surveying the cheap room.

Dani wondered the same thing but refused to give voice to those thoughts. Saying it out loud wouldn't make it true, but she didn't want to tempt fate. They needed all the luck they could get at this point.

"Where do you think he'd go?" Nick asked.

Dani shook her head. "Who knows? His stuff is still here, so for all we know he's out having lunch somewhere. But everything is packed up nice and neat, so I'm pretty sure he's not planning on being here much longer."

After showing the search and arrest warrants to the motel manager, a young kid barely into his twenties, he'd readily given them a key to the room. It was obvious from the combination of excitement and fear reflected in the kid's eyes that this was the first time an arrest had happened since he'd worked there. Dani took one look at his pimply face and clamped her hand over his.

"Don't call anyone about this," she warned. "If I see any mention of this on social media, I'm coming to find you." He shook his head, unable to talk.

Wearing a bullet-proof vest and followed by the SWAT team, Dani was ready. She led the way into the room, prepared for anything.

Unlocking the door and swinging it open, she yelled "Police! Don't move!" to an empty space. After a quick survey of the room, she ran into the bathroom to find nobody was there. "Clear!" Dani couldn't help wondering if Cleve knew they were coming. He was smart and ruthless, he must have known his time was almost up.

Crime scene technicians were now going through potential evidence, hopefully finding and bagging items that would make this guy's trial an afterthought. Dani tried to put herself in Cleve's place to figure out where he would go. He was a stranger in a strange town, so he'd most likely gravitate to what he knew.

The Hollister family.

"Call the hospital and call Kevin," Dani said to Nick.

"Already on it." With his cell phone plastered to one ear, Nick covered his other ear with his right hand as he spoke. "The suspect that may be responsible for the attack on Beau Hollister is missing. If you need extra help, call for back up. This guy is extremely dangerous and probably armed, so if something feels off, don't wait to call for help. We'll let you know if there are any updates."

As he ended the call, his phone immediately rang. "Winters." Nick caught Dani's eye, signaling to her that the call was important. "Right, thanks. We're on our way."

Without looking at Dani, he said, "Let's go. They can finish without us."

"Where are we going?" Dani asked as they sprinted to the car.

"Katie Hollister is hanging out at the battlefields. Alone."

"How do you know this?"

Throwing the car into reverse, Nick gave her an impish grin. God, she loved working with this man.

"That was Kevin. Roland called to let him know."

"Who?"

"Another friend of theirs. Anyway, Roland is on his way to find Katie."

Nick flipped the light and siren on, clearing traffic as they turned onto Route 17. Despite the fact that they didn't talk about it, both of them knew the significance of Katie Hollister spending time alone at the battlefields. It meant she was a walking target, exactly the sort of thing Cleve Yodell would be watching and waiting for. They needed to find her, now.

Taking a right at Cook Road, Nick turned the light and siren off again. His voice was grim. "Don't want to let him know we're coming."

"We think alike."

Dani leaned forward in her seat, as if by doing so she could get them there faster. This was it, she could feel it. Was it wrong to be excited at the prospect of finally catching a killer? No, she decided. Ultimately, it was about helping people and making the world a little better place. There was no way she could ever get rid of all the scumbags, but right now Dani was only focused on getting rid of one. Just this one.

"You smell that?" Nick asked. Without stopping, he swung left onto Ballard Street at the end of Cook Road, his speed well above the posted limit. "Something's on fire," he added.

Dani strained as she scanned the empty fields. She didn't see anybody, which was worrisome. Shouldn't the Hollister girl be out there with that Roland guy? There were acres and acres of battlefields, they could be anywhere.

Nick pulled the car to a stop in the middle of the street and sat with the motor idling. "What are you doing?" Dani asked.

"Something's burning."

Dani knew it was too much of a coincidence that there was a fire in the exact spot they were looking for Cleve.

Unbuckling her seat belt, she pushed the car door open and stepped halfway out. Standing with one foot still in the car, she inhaled, noting the breeze, and got back in.

"Over there," she said, climbing in and pointing to a street on the right.

Nick accelerated, turning onto Church Street. Cresting a small hill, they saw it. Smoke was pouring out of a church.

"Shit," Nick said. "That thing's so old, it's gonna go up like a box of matches."

Dani didn't wait to hear Nick call the fire in over the radio. Bolting from the car, she ran toward the burning building. When she saw the dark figure run from the back of the church, Dani didn't hesitate. She drew her weapon and ran after him. "Stop! Police!"

To her surprise, he stopped. Raising his arms in the air, he turned and faced her, smiling. She recognized him immediately from the picture they'd been circulating, the one they'd gotten from motor vehicle. Cleve Yodell stood in front of her.

His voice was gritty, and the cadence was slightly off. "Ms. Burgess, how nice of you to come. You have perfect timing."

Nick, standing next to her with his weapon aimed, began to circle around to Dani's right, trying to move closer to Cleve.

"Keep your hands where I can see them," Dani ordered.

"You're just in time to get Cleve," he said, smiling. Before she could figure out what he meant, Cleve Yodell collapsed in front of them.

CHAPTER FORTY-THREE

GREEN, BLUE, AND RED LIGHTS *hung above the stage, flashing colors onto the dance floor. The combination of the thumping music, decorations, and excited energy created a magical feeling in the school cafeteria. Somehow, the PTA had even managed to eliminate the smell of the Salisbury Steak lunch from earlier that day.*

Liz grabbed her arm. "We have got to request 'Tennessee,'" she squealed. "I love that song."

Katie nodded, experiencing a curious blend of happiness and grief. She was in the fifth grade, and this would be the last year for her to be at the elementary school dance. It was her favorite event of the year. She loved coming here with her friends, dancing, whispering, giggling... even having her parents standing on the sidelines was sort of nice, though she'd never admit that to anyone.

"C'mon, aren't you gonna dance?" Liz asked while pulling at Katie.

Katie frowned. "Liz, I..."

"What's wrong?"

Katie shook her head. "I don't know, but I don't feel quite right. I'm sorry."

Everything around them slowed, a moment frozen in the dreamtime. Katie and her best friend were alone in the darkened and silent cafeteria.

"I'm sorry."

"You couldn't stop it," Liz told her. "And I'm okay now."

"How can you be okay after what he did to you?"

Liz shrugged. "Therapy. My family. Lots of support. Just because we moved away doesn't mean it turned out bad. I miss you, though."

"But you never kept in touch... you left," Katie cried. "I thought you blamed me."

Liz enfolded Katie in a warm embrace. "How could I blame someone who was just as young as me?" Shaking her head, Liz stepped away. "You were the one who said we shouldn't go in there, you were the one with common sense. It was my own fault, really. I should've known he was a creep."

Katie stared at her friend, surprised. "Liz, it wasn't our fault. Like you said, we were kids. He's the one to blame, not us."

"Why are you surprised by this?"

"I'm surprised I didn't realize it until now. It's not my fault."

Liz smiled. "I guess you could even say we're heroes."

"What do you mean?"

"He's still in jail, you know."

Katie looked down. She hadn't known. She hadn't wanted to know. She was afraid he would get out and come back and finish what he started. Her mother had reassured her this wouldn't happen, but it never helped.

"I thought he'd be out by now."

"Katie, don't you remember? They found evidence all over his house. We weren't the first kids he did this to, and he probably would have gone on to hurt more. Plus, they tied him to that kidnapped kid down in Alabama."

"What? What kid in Alabama?"

Liz sighed. "It was some runaway that he trapped. I think the kid tried to get away but didn't make it. Anyway, he's still in jail because he took that kid, so those charges got added to the other charges. He's not getting out, ever."

Katie let out a breath she hadn't known she was holding and looked closely at her friend. Liz was somehow older but with faint traces of a young girl still.

"You know, Katie, you can call me anytime you want."

"I don't know how to reach you. We haven't talked in years."

"Yes, we have," Liz corrected. "I call you every now and then, but I don't expect you to remember talking to me."

Katie's confusion turned to embarrassment. "Every time you call, I'm drunk, aren't I?"

Liz nodded. "You should do something about that."

"Yeah, I think I'm gonna have to." Katie paused, uncertain. "Now what?"

Liz put her arms around Katie and whispered in her ear. "Now you start your life."

CHAPTER FORTY-FOUR

SOMETHING COVERED HER FACE, SUFFOCATING her. Katie struggled up through the darkness, trying to rip the thing off.

"Hey, easy. You don't want to do that," Roland's gentle voice reached out to her. "It's only oxygen. It's helping you breathe."

Squinting against the assault of light, a nameless fear rose in Katie.

"Sweetheart, I'm right here. You're going to be okay." Her mother leaned over, brushing the hair away from Katie's face. "You're in the hospital, but you're going to be okay. There was a fire, but you and the pastor are fine. You saved his life."

Katie shook her head, terrified. They didn't know about Cleve, how he'd tried to kill them and he was going to kill her whole family. She clawed at the mask covering her mouth and nose. It didn't matter why it was there—she couldn't talk with that thing on her face.

"Calm down. It's okay. They got him," Roland said, grabbing hold of her hand. "I know that's what you're worried about, but the police are here to talk to you."

Leaning back against the pillow, Katie took a breath, trying to get her breathing back to normal. If Roland said everything was okay, then it must be. He wouldn't lie to her.

Tears streamed down her mother's face. "He's in jail. That son of a bitch tried to hurt my children, both of you..."

Roland shot Belinda a wary look and put a hand on her arm. Even in her weakened state, Katie was sure that Roland was trying to protect them, both her and her mother. But if what they said was true, it was over.

Almost. The real battle is about to begin. Katie closed her eyes, tired. She had a lot of work to do.

"The police want to talk to you, but if you're not up for it, you don't have to." Roland's voice was soothing. "They've been here the whole time, waiting for you to wake up." After a moment's pause, he added, "We all have."

Katie opened her eyes and nodded. She wanted to get this over with, but she also wanted information. Information about who that man was, and why he tried to kill her. The whole thing was surreal, and she still didn't fully understand what had happened in the church.

"I'll let them know you're awake."

Roland left the room, and Belinda grasped Katie's hand tighter. "I'm so sorry... I knew something was off about that man..."

Katie gently covered her mother's hand with her own. When Belinda looked at her, Katie pointed to the oxygen mask.

Smiling through her tears, Belinda said, "Let's go ahead and take it off, but just for a little bit. You'll need to take it off anyway to talk to the police." She reached over and gently removed the mask from her daughter's face.

"Mom." Katie's throat was sore, and her voice was a whisper. "It's not your fault. Besides, everything turned out fine, I'm okay."

Belinda brushed Katie's forehead with her hand again, as if she couldn't get enough of her daughter. "Your father is waiting outside, too. Lots of people are. We've been taking turns coming in to see you. The hospital staff only allows two of us in at one time."

Taking turns? Katie's forehead wrinkled as she tried to figure out the time. "What time is it?"

"Around noon."

Noon? That wasn't possible because when she went into the church...

"You've been here since yesterday."

Closing her eyes for a moment, Katie experienced a rush of emotion. She'd been out of it for a whole day, lying in this hospital bed. Someone really and truly tried to kill her. She'd survived. Holy crap, Reuben was right: she had *definitely* needed his class.

"Ms. Hollister?"

Opening her eyes, Katie saw that her mother had moved to the corner chair and a man and woman were standing over her bed.

"I think I know you." She squinted, trying to remember.

The man nodded once. "Detective Nick Winters, ma'am. And this is

Detective Dani Burgess, here from the Watertown, Connecticut, police department."

"You can just call me Dani," the woman in front of her said. Katie wondered why Dani wore her hair tied back like that. She would look so much prettier if she let it down.

"Nick Winters... yeah, I think I know your sister..."

Katie's thoughts drifted as a wave of exhaustion swept through her. She didn't understand how she could be tired after sleeping a whole day.

"Ma'am, we need to ask you a few questions about what happened yesterday." The voice belonged to the female detective. "How are you feeling?"

Katie looked at her and nodded. "I'm okay, but I'm tired."

"You can ask questions, but you'll have to be quick about it," Belinda's voice commanded from the corner of the room. Katie smiled at her mother, loving how she took charge of the situation.

"Why did you go to the church yesterday?" Dani asked.

"He texted me," Katie answered. The two detectives looked at each other.

"We'll get a subpoena for those phone records," Nick said.

"Why did he want to kill me?" Katie asked.

"Did he try to hurt you as soon as you got there?" Dani asked, avoiding Katie's question.

Katie thought for a moment. The images from yesterday were still jumbled in her mind, and she tried to sort through them. Haltingly, and in a whispered voice, she began to tell them about walking through the battlefield and receiving the text message from Cleve. Stopping by the church to see him, she'd stood in the doorway as he railed at the pastor.

"He didn't make any sense," Katie admitted. "I couldn't figure out why he was so upset. It was like he was talking another language. He's a stranger here, but he was acting like he knew us."

Katie knew the story Hannah had told was probably the truth, but she wasn't going to share that with the police. A tale of ghostly revenge was not likely to make its way into a police report. It was best if she just acted like she didn't know what was going on.

Belinda's sharp look told Katie that her mother knew she was fabricating at least a little. She'd have to talk to Belinda later, explain what she knew. Belinda would believe her because Belinda knew Hannah. Unfortunately, Katie wasn't able to introduce Hannah to the police.

"When he attacked the pastor and knocked him out, I got so upset, I went right in there. I remember asking him what he was doing, and then he grabbed me." She went on to tell them about the struggle, the fire, and Roland's rescue. The last part was the clearest in her mind. "If Roland hadn't come in when he did, I don't think…" She tried to blink back the tears, but they spilled out anyway.

"Okay, I think we have enough for now." Nick nodded at her. "I know you've been through a lot, but we can wait and ask more questions later."

Dani moved closer to the bed, leaning over Katie. "You did good. You did really good. I'm proud of you."

Katie didn't know this woman, but Dani's words of praise meant the world to her, probably because they were heartfelt.

"Thank you. But, what do you know about him?"

Dani and Nick exchanged another look before Dani answered. "I came here to track him down. He's wanted on suspicion of homicide in Connecticut. We think he killed his wife and her lover, then tried to burn the house to cover the evidence."

"How did you know he'd be here?" Belinda asked.

"There was a journal in a safe in the house," Dani said. "It was all about your family, dating back to the 1800s. Apparently, one of your ancestors was accused of killing one of this guy's ancestors, and he wanted revenge."

Katie looked at her mother, trying to will Belinda not to ask any more questions.

"That's the craziest thing I've ever heard of," Belinda sputtered. Obviously, Katie's psychic thought-giving techniques weren't working.

"You're right, it is crazy. From what we could piece together, you had a relative who came to Yorktown in the 1800s by the name of Hannah Donovan. She'd worked for a man named Titus Foote back in Connecticut and was accused of murdering him in his bed. The family held onto this story, and Cleve wanted revenge for what happened." Dani looked from Belinda to Katie. "Did you know about this story?"

Belinda shook her head, but Katie couldn't tell if her mother was covering up what she knew or not. You never knew with Belinda.

"From what we can tell, 'crazy' runs in his family," Nick added. "The evidence that Dani and her team gathered suggests that Cleve was abused as a child, but the abuse was generational."

"Isn't it always?" Katie murmured.

"We also know that he tried to kill your brother, but thankfully that didn't work," Nick said.

"Is Beau okay?" Katie's anxiety rose at hearing the detective's statement.

"He's fine. He's supposed to be released from here soon," Belinda said with a half-laugh, half-sob.

"Your brother had a heart attack, which was probably what saved his life," Dani said. "When Cleve tried to kill your brother, he started to torture him first. We think that triggered the heart attack in Beau, but when he passed out, Cleve thought your brother was dead and left him there."

"He was probably more focused on getting away than checking to make sure your brother was dead," Nick said.

Katie's heart dropped. She'd gone out on a date with the man who tried to kill her own brother. Boy, she sure knew how to pick 'em.

"My daughter is getting tired. You'll have to leave," Belinda announced, standing. "Plus, she needs to get that oxygen mask back on."

Katie could barely feel her mother's hands as she fastened the oxygen mask back on her face. Moments later, she drifted back into sleep.

Katie opened her eyes slowly to a semi-darkened room. Lying in the hospital bed, she marveled that she'd been able to sleep at all. A hospital is a noisy place, and it was surprising that anyone could get any rest.

"Katie-love, I'm so glad you're doing better."

A distant corner of her mind realized there was no longer an oxygen mask on her face, but she didn't stop to wonder about that. Hannah was standing in front of her.

"How did you get here?"

Hannah shrugged. "I willed it, I suppose. I'm still not entirely sure how this whole thing works."

"Hannah, do you know..." Katie had trouble forming the words. "Do you understand what happened back at the church? I'm having a little trouble with it."

Hannah looked sad. "I'm so sorry for all this, Katie-love. I'd hoped to avoid it, but that wasn't meant to be."

"You did try to warn me," Katie said. "I didn't want to listen."

"It all goes back to Titus, the man who was murdered. Like I said, I'm fairly certain his daughter did it."

"Except there's no proof, no way to clear your name." Katie was upset. After everything Hannah had done for her, it only seemed right that Katie clear the woman's name.

Hannah laughed. "That doesn't matter to me, not at all. It's not like I'm alive, you know."

"But—"

"Shhh, don't worry about all that. What happened was terrible, but maybe inevitable. Titus could never accept his own death, much less the way it happened. I think he's been waiting for years to take over just the right person."

"Do you mean 'take over' as in possess?" Katie wasn't sure about this part—those memories were still vague.

"I think Titus has been planning this since Cleve was a boy," Hannah answered. "It was probably easy for him because Cleve was already not quite right."

"Mentally ill? Insane? Crazy?"

Katie knew she sounded bitter, but she couldn't help it. This was the man who had set out to kill her and her family.

"Yes, crazy is a good word. When the opportunity came, Titus took it and fully entered Cleve's body."

"So what happened to Cleve?" This was the part that confused Katie.

"I think in situations like this, the person gets locked into their own mind, unable to control the body's words and actions. It would be like being in prison in your head and you can't reach anyone to get out."

Katie shivered. "How do you know all this?"

A frown appeared on Hannah's face. "I don't know. Maybe being dead gives me special insight or something."

"Something to look forward to," Katie said.

"Katie-love, we need to talk."

Katie closed her eyes, knowing what was coming.

"It's time, Katie. You know it's time."

Katie nodded as the weariness once again descended. "I know. I'm ready." Looking at Hannah, something occurred to Katie. "I've never called you 'Grandma', but that's what you are, isn't it? You're my great... however many greats grandmother." Even in death, Hannah proved her devotion and love to the family, so Katie decided to get to know her better. "Now that this ordeal is over, will I still see you?"

Hannah's smile was sad. "I don't know, Katie-love."

CHAPTER FORTY-FIVE

EVERYONE WAS THERE. KATIE'S PARENTS, her brother and sister-in-law, even Roland and Ella had shown up for this event. "Help yourself to the food in the kitchen," Belinda announced. "There's plenty for everyone."

"Thanks for bringing all this food, Mom," Katie said.

"I'm sure you'll have plenty of leftovers, dear, to get you through the next week or so."

"Always a mom, aren't you?" Katie teased. When Belinda didn't reply, Katie hesitated. She knew what was really going on, and she knew it was time to face the music. "Why don't we get everyone in the living room?" she suggested to her mother.

Silence descended in the house as everyone gathered in the living room. Katie stood in front of the large bow window that faced the front yard, looking at her friends and family with a profound sense of gratitude.

"I know why you're all here," she began.

"Really?" Beau asked. He sat next to his wife, Anna Louise, looking slightly uncomfortable. Katie was glad to see that she couldn't tell he'd just spent the last week in the hospital, part of that in a coma.

"Yes, Beau, I do." Katie's voice was gentle. She'd faced her own demons, and nothing her family said could be worse than anything she'd already said to herself.

"Do you know what it's been like living with you, watching you destroy yourself? Watching Mom and Dad die a little bit every time they thought you were dead, only to have it turn out you were just drunk?"

Okay, so maybe this was going to be worse than she thought. Apparently coming to terms with her alcoholism was easier than listening to a catalog of her sins.

Belinda shot Beau a warning look. "Sweetheart, we love you very much, and we want what's best for you."

"We want you to straighten up," Beau said.

"I will if you will," Katie shot back.

"What the hell is that supposed to mean?" Beau's face turned red, the anger obvious in his posture.

"Beau, calm down," Anna Louise muttered, covering his hand with her own. "It's not good for you to get worked up like this."

"She's right," Katie said. "It's not good for you. You're still recovering from what that freak did to you, plus having a heart attack. But let's be honest here, okay? Because this day is really about all of us being well, our whole family."

"Oh, so now we're all about being healthy?" Beau snorted. "That's just great. This from a woman who spends most of her life drunk, forgetting to be places and letting others down. How many times have you gotten behind the wheel of the car and driven when you shouldn't have? Do you know how lucky you are you haven't killed anyone yet?"

"I don't think this sort of talk is going to help," Roland interjected. "We're here to help Katie, not yell at her."

"Well, speak for yourself," Beau said, looking around the room. "I don't know about the rest of you, but I'm plenty ticked off."

Katie decided to sit and gingerly lowered herself to the edge of the wingback chair near the window. This was nothing new, of course. Beau had been telling her this sort of thing for years. The difference now was that she forced herself to listen.

"You're right," she told her brother.

Beau's eyes widened as he was momentarily speechless.

Katie's smile held more than a touch of sadness. "I've been doing this... I've been drinking for a long time, and I know I've hurt lots of people by doing it."

"It sounds like you've given this some thought," Anna Louise said. "I imagine recent events have changed your outlook on life."

"True." Katie took a deep breath. "But I don't know if it even matters why. I just know I have to face this. I've got to find a way to stop drinking."

Roland's voice was gentle. "When was the last time you had a drink?"

Katie shook her head. "I was so nervous about this lunch today. I knew why y'all were coming here. I knew it was going to be an intervention, and I woke up thinking it would be my last chance to have a drink. I knew if I took just a few sips to get me through this, I'd be okay and I'd be able to do it. I figured if I was going to quit, I might as well have one last farewell drink before it happened."

"You had a drink this morning?" Ella's voice reflected the incredulous look on her face. "Really? You thought it would be okay to have a drink before you quit? Isn't that like eating the entire container of ice cream before going on a diet?"

Katie smiled. "You're right, it is. But no, I didn't have that drink. I wanted to. I wanted it so badly, I could taste it, but I didn't. God knows, I don't know how I managed, but I didn't touch the stuff."

"Is it still hidden?" Roland asked.

Katie nodded. "There's bottles hidden all over this house. I've been afraid to get rid of them because I'm afraid I won't be able to. What if I pull the bottles out, and instead of pouring it down the sink, I pour it down my throat?"

Nobody spoke. The only sound that could be heard was the clock ticking in the kitchen.

Finally, Katie's father cleared his throat. "Katie, sweetheart, we love you. I love you. I'll do whatever you need me to do, and if that means holding you down while you try to get to the bottle, then that's what I'll do. Anything, whatever it takes." His voice trailed off as he wiped the tears that flowed down his face.

Her mother nodded. "Your father and I, we were never sure how to help you. We thought maybe you'd grow out of it... but that wasn't going to happen, was it? Tell us what you need right now."

Everyone was staring at her, making Katie uncomfortable. She'd thought this would be easy because she was doing what everyone wanted, but she didn't take into account the discomfort she would feel in revealing herself to the world.

"I need to stop drinking," Katie whispered. "It's a little embarrassing, I'm not sure I can do it. I've tried before, you know, but it never worked."

"What's going to work? Do you want to go to a rehab center? Your father and I will pay for that." Belinda's voice reflected anxiety and concern.

"I don't want to go away," Katie said.

Across from her, Beau shook his head. "Of course you don't want to go away, something like that might work. Do you really want to sober up, or are you just saying something you think we all want to hear?"

"I want to try this here. I don't blame you for feeling the way you do. I know I've let you all down before, but I don't want to go to rehab."

Katie shook her head as she spoke, trying to make her point. The last thing she wanted was to go sit in some strange place for a month while she came to terms with her drinking. It would probably mean the loss of her job, one more thing she wasn't prepared to accept.

Her voice was small. "Please, I want to try to do it here."

"Katie, I'm sure you're drinking for the same reason most people drink: to cover up how you're really feeling," Beau said. "But I've got to tell you something, and don't you ever forget this. If you let me down, it was only because I let you down when you were a kid."

Katie's brow creased. "What are you talking about? How did you let me down?"

"What happened to you with that guy, it shouldn't have happened. I'm your big brother, it was my job to protect you."

"That's a load of crap, and you know it."

Beau sat back on the couch, not speaking for a moment. "No, it's not a load of crap. Don't you think I know that's why you drink? If I'd been with you that day, you wouldn't have—"

Anger flashed through Katie's body, and she spoke without thinking. "I wasn't some delicate flower who needed protecting. That's not how it worked. I was a kid, but so were you. It wasn't anyone's fault, it was just one of those awful things that happen. Besides, with that kind of logic, it would be my fault that you got attacked by that crazy guy, right?"

"No, I'm the big brother—"

"And I'm the sister that Hannah talked to," Katie spat the words, anger filling her body. "I'm the one Hannah warned. I'm the one who should have been sober and listening to her when she told me this guy was in town and wanted to hurt us. But no, what do I do? I go out on a date with the guy, that's what. So whose fault is it that we almost got killed by crazy Cleve, huh?"

Beau smiled, then laughed. "Geez, are you serious? Hannah's been here? I haven't heard about her in years. Do you mean she saved us again?"

Katie nodded, puzzled at her brother's reaction. Why was he laughing?

"I don't know why I'm laughing," Beau said, "But all of a sudden, this whole thing seems so weird, it's funny."

"Delayed reaction," Belinda announced.

"I thought she was always here," Ella said.

"Can we focus on talking about what we came here to talk about?" Roland asked.

"Hannah is a collective figment of this family's imagination," Katie's father answered Ella.

"She is not," Katie exclaimed. "She's real."

"You know, if it wasn't for her, I don't know what would've happened when you were a kid," Belinda added.

"Um... can we focus on sobriety?" Roland said.

Katie looked at Roland. "Yes, I'm going to go to AA meetings."

"What do you mean 'collective figment of your family's imagination'?" Ella asked. "That sounds kind of weird. Is Hannah the ghost that Katie told me about?"

Katie's father sighed. "There's no such thing as ghosts."

"Yes, there is," Beau argued. "And you'd better start believing because it looks like once again Hannah has saved this family's—"

"I'm pregnant." Anna Louise's announcement effectively stopped all conversation. "So, having said that, I'm also tired and hormonal. Can we get on with this so I can eat?"

Belinda's face was white, and her mouth opened and closed for a moment, but no words came out.

"Mom? Are you okay?" Beau looked over at Anna Louise. "We were going to tell you later, but apparently my wife thought now was a good time."

"Now is a perfect time," Anna Louise declared. "So, Katie, will you go to Alcoholics Anonymous meetings?"

Katie nodded. "Every day. I've got the schedule and plan on going to my second meeting tonight."

Anna Louise was like a general prepared to finish the battle. "Good, you've already been to one. Do you have a sponsor?"

Katie shook her head. "Not yet."

"Okay. Well, be sure to get one tonight. Are you going to meetings alone?"

"Yes, but if anyone wants to come with me, tonight's an open meeting."

"What's an open meeting?" Beau asked.

"It means that you don't have to be a member of AA to go to the meeting. Anyone can go," Roland answered.

Anna Louise nodded. "Fine, either Ella or Roland will go with you. Now, does anyone have anything else they'd like to say to Katie before we begin lunch?"

Chastened, everyone shook their head, even Katie. They knew better than to mess with a pregnant, hormonal, and hungry woman.

Anna Louise stood. "Great. Let's eat."

Katie wasn't hungry. Her stomach felt unsettled, almost as if she'd been out drinking the night before. She wondered if she'd ever feel normal again, not that she was sure she knew what normal was anyway.

"How are you holding up?" Roland said from behind her. Handing her a plate piled with cold cuts and pasta salad, he told her, "Eat. You need to keep your strength up. You just got out of the hospital, and there's a long road ahead of you."

Katie nodded. "Thanks. I'm not hungry right now, though."

They stood next to each other, not talking. For the first time in a very long time, Katie was uncomfortable with the silence between her and Roland. In the past, they'd been able to hang out as friends, and it didn't matter if they talked about anything or not. Now, everything was different.

Roland cleared his throat. "I hope you know, it's not that I didn't care…"

Katie looked at the floor. "I was a mess—I still am. I know you care, and you weren't sure what to do with me. You tried to help."

"You're not the first or only person I know who is an alcoholic," Roland told her. "If you really want it, you can stay sober. Some of the wisest elders I know are going into their second or third decade of sobriety."

"So I have to wait until I'm an elder for wisdom?" Katie gave a half-laugh, not sure if she should be joking or not.

Roland put a finger under her chin and tilted her face up to look at him. "No, but you do have to take it one day at a time for the sobriety to stick. You're not going to get better tomorrow, or next month, or next year, but that doesn't matter. All that matters is right now, so don't think about anything else."

"I don't understand," Katie said.

"Just focus on not drinking today and let tomorrow take care of itself," Roland told her.

Katie took a deep breath. "Sounds good to me. I don't think I'd make it if I had to think about next week or next year anyway. But there are some things I need to think about, and there are some things I need to say."

Roland put his plate down and grabbed Katie's arm. "C'mon, let's go outside for the rest of this talk. I have a feeling your mother would love to hear what we're saying."

Katie laughed. "She's my mother, of course she wants to hear it."

"No, I don't," Belinda cried. "I'm not listening at all."

"We'll be outside, Mom."

The warm sunshine felt good as they walked into the backyard. There was a summer lounge chair in the yard that Katie had left out, so they sat side by side on the blue mesh.

"Roland, I've got to tell you something." Taking another deep breath, Katie braced herself to say the words that should have been said long ago. "When I thought I was going to die in that church, I thought of you."

"And there I was," Roland teased.

"Yes, and there you were, but that's not why I thought of you." This was more difficult than she thought it would be, but she couldn't stop now. She'd come too far for that.

"Katie, you don't have to—"

"I know, but I want to tell you this. I know you've moved on with your life, and I know you're dating someone else right now, but you need to know how I feel about you. Roland, I love you. I've always loved you, but I didn't think you would ever look at me that way."

Roland stared at the ground in front of him. "Why didn't you think I was interested in you?"

"Because it was like you could see into my soul, and I knew that you knew my secret. And I knew you didn't want any part of that." There, she said it. *I don't know if I'm relieved or horrified.*

Turning his head to look at her, Roland said, "I might not want any part of the drinking, but I most certainly do want to have some part in your life."

Katie nodded. "Friends, right?"

"No. I mean, yes." Roland ran a hand through his hair, a sure sign of frustration. "You've been through a lot, lately, and I don't want to add to that... but Katie, I've had feelings for you for a long time, too."

"Really?"

Roland nodded. "Yes, really. But we can't act on that... not right now."

"I know. You have a girlfriend, and it wouldn't be fair to her."

It was time to put everything on the table, but she wasn't going to beg him to dump this woman or wait for her to sober up. Roland needed to get on with his life.

He shook his head. "I don't have a girlfriend. I went on a couple of dates, but it didn't work out. She kept trying to change me."

"After only a couple of dates?"

"Yeah, can you believe that? She didn't like the way I dressed, she didn't like my motorcycle, she didn't think I should be friends with you—"

"You told her about me?"

"I might have mentioned you," he said. "I mentioned Ella, too, but it was mostly you she objected to."

Katie's mood brightened. The day was looking better already. "So, what are you saying?"

Roland's voice was serious. "I'm saying that if we start a relationship now, it could interfere with you getting sober. I can't do that to you, not when you've come this far."

Katie was confused. "So, we'll still be friends?"

Roland put his arm around her, pulling her close. "Of course we'll still be friends. And I'm here to help you get through this. I know you can do it." Looking into her eyes, he added, "I'll wait for you, Kate. I'll wait until you're ready, until your sponsor says you're ready—"

"What does a sponsor have to do with you and me?" Katie interrupted.

Roland laughed. "You'll see. Your sponsor is going to be your lifeline and the one to help you through the worst of it. But I'll be there, too."

"So, you're saying someday?" It was more than she could hope for, and she didn't know if she had the right to take what he was offering. She didn't think she had it in her to refuse, though.

Roland nodded. "Someday sounds about right. We don't have to be in a rush, Kate. We've got lots of time, and I want to make sure we get this right. But make no mistake about this, I'm not going anywhere. I've waited this long for you, I can wait a little longer."

Katie snuggled into his arm, wondering how and if this could ever work. But maybe it didn't matter. Maybe Roland was right, and all she needed to think about was this moment.

CHAPTER FORTY-SIX

WRAPPED IN HER FUZZY WHITE bathrobe, Dani walked onto the deck outside her room. As she relaxed in an Adirondack chair, the sky lightened from gray to dusty pink. It was her last morning in Yorktown, and she wanted to spend as much time as possible in her room at the bed and breakfast. She'd started to think of the place as her little haven of peace, with its soothing colors and beautiful antiques. The history steeped throughout the house rooted her to the area, as if she could reach out and touch those who had lived here before, becoming part of their past.

Looking behind her, she thought about the room's namesake: Pocahontas.

I wonder if Pocahontas would be surprised to know her story has survived for so many years or that we made a cartoon movie about her with a character who doesn't look anything like her.

The silence of the morning wrapped around her, and she was surprised to feel a slight chill in the air. She'd have to get out of this chair for some coffee, but first she wanted to sit back and enjoy a quiet moment.

The moment didn't last long, though. The dull vibration of the cell phone she'd left on the bureau intruded, forcing her to her feet.

Who the heck is calling at this hour? Must be work.

Moving quickly, she went inside and grabbed the phone. "Burgess."

"Good morning. I hope I didn't wake you."

Dani was stunned. She wasn't expecting this call. "Nick, is everything okay?"

"Everything's fine. Sorry about the early call. I figured you might be getting on the road when the sun came up, and I wanted to catch you before you left."

"What's up?"

"I was wondering if you wanted to have breakfast with me before you left." Nick paused for a moment, then cleared his throat. "You know, as a kind of goodbye. A goodbye breakfast."

Dani wasn't used to sharing her feelings with others and was grateful Nick couldn't see her smile.

"Breakfast sounds good. I don't have to be at the airport until this afternoon."

"Great. I'll pick you up in ten."

"Minutes?"

"Um... okay, fifteen?"

"No, ten minutes is fine. I'll see you then."

Ending the call, she ran to her suitcase to pull out her most flattering jeans, the ones that made her look skinny—or at least didn't make her look fat. Not that she was fat, but she wanted to look good. It was one thing to work a case together and share meals, it was another to just share meals.

Whatever his reasons might be for asking her to breakfast, Dani was damn sure she was going to look her best.

They decided to eat in the downstairs dining room, as the scents drifting out of the kitchen were almost too much to walk past. Sitting at a private table, Nick looked around at the deep burgundy walls and cream-colored fireplace mantle, taking in the historic map prints housed in ornate frames.

"Nice," he breathed.

"You've never been here?" Dani was surprised.

Nick shook his head. "No, never really thought about it. But it's elegant in here, and the food smells great."

The innkeeper came out at that moment, beaming at them. "Ms. Burgess, I'm so glad you're going to eat with us this morning. You need a good, hearty breakfast." Lowering his voice, he leaned in to speak to them. "I heard all about that horrible incident with the church... I'm so glad everyone made it out alive. That was the reason for you being here, wasn't it?"

Dani nodded. "Hi, Cam. I'm afraid so, but like you said, everything worked out okay in the end."

Cam turned to Nick. "And are you a detective, too?"

Nick nodded, extending his hand. "Nick Winters. Nice to meet you."

"Hi, Nick. I'm Cam, the innkeeper here. For today's breakfast, you'll be having homemade waffles, poached pears with cranberries, and a side of bacon.

Here's your coffee. Any questions?"

Nick shook his head, looking delirious. "Sounds great to me."

"And breakfast for you, young man, is on the house," Cam told him.

"What?" Dani asked. "Wait a minute, we didn't expect—"

"Ms. Burgess, since you've been staying here, I haven't seen much of you at all. You've been busy working on that case, and obviously you did a good job because a very bad man is now in jail. I know that Nick was part of that, too, and since you have not once had my breakfast, I insist that both of you accept this. I won't take no for an answer."

"Okay," Nick said.

Cam smiled and walked away. Dani looked at Nick.

"Okay? You cave, just like that?"

Nick nodded. "Sure do. Did you catch a whiff of what's coming out of that kitchen? I'm not saying no to any of that."

Dani took the cloth napkin off the table and placed it in her lap. "I suppose that's as good a reason as any. Anyway, thanks for meeting me for breakfast. Is everything in order, ready to go?"

Nick nodded. "Mr. Yodell, or Farrington, as he called himself, will be ready for transport with your officers tomorrow. I understand your chief is sending someone down for that."

"They try not to take any chances with prisoner transport. I know the guys who will be hauling Cleve back. They're experienced and know what they're doing."

The silence that fell between them was not uncomfortable, it was the silence of two people content to be in each other's company.

Nick cleared his throat. "So what happens for you next?"

"I go home and finish Arson Investigation School. Then, who knows?"

Nick fiddled with his coffee cup. "Do you think you'll stay with the Watertown PD?"

Dani hesitated. She'd grown up in Watertown, her family was there, her history was there. But there were lots of other places that she might be comfortable living, and Yorktown was a good example of that.

Half-teasing, she asked, "Why, do you guys have an opening here?"

Nick shrugged. "You never know. Did I ever tell you about my father?"

Dani shook her head, not surprised by the abrupt change in conversation. Nick would get to the point when he needed to.

"No, you never mentioned him. Is he still alive?"

"No, he died a while ago. The thing is, he was a real jerk. He wasn't nice to anyone, ever. When I was a kid... well, let's just say I don't think he really wanted kids and would've been happier without me around."

"I'm sorry."

There wasn't much else Dani could say to that since she couldn't rewrite history. She'd seen enough depravity to know that it existed, and she'd also seen enough to know that not everyone was beaten by it. Circumstances didn't always dictate who you became in life; sometimes determination had something to do with it, too.

"My point is, I've never really had a relationship, never really saw myself as someone who could settle down, much less have a girlfriend. But with you, it's different. With you I feel like we have this connection, like maybe we could have something if we tried." Nick looked into Dani's eyes. "Is this too much for you?"

Dani smiled. "No. I know what you mean, but I was trying to stay focused on the case and not think of anything else while I was here. And now..."

"...you're getting ready to fly home," Nick finished for her. "So what do you think? Would you like to try a long distance relationship?"

Dani couldn't speak for a moment. She'd known he would ask something like this, but she didn't expect him to be so abrupt about it. She should've seen it coming, though. People in law enforcement weren't always known for subtlety. Or, at least the people she knew in law enforcement weren't.

She was horrified to find her vocal cords frozen. Finally, she answered. "How would this work?"

"We'd rack up lots of airline miles, probably get a free flight or two out of it."

"Or train miles."

"Or we could meet in the middle," Nick suggested.

Dani made a face. "Where are we going to get the money to do something like that on a regular basis?"

"Maybe we can freelance in other towns, earn our room and board." Nick covered her hand with his. "If there's one thing I've learned, it's that if you want something you've got to reach out and grab it, otherwise, it goes away. I could've just let you go home, never said anything to you, but then we'd both be wondering about this thing between us. However we do it, let's give it a try. What do we have to lose?"

Looking at his hand on hers, Dani hesitated. Like he said, what did she have to lose? Probably nothing, and she wouldn't know if this would work if she didn't try. Hadn't she been lusting after this guy the whole time she was here anyway?

"Let's give it a try, but on one condition," Dani said.

"What's that?"

"I won't stay in a chain hotel."

Nick smiled and squeezed her hand.

"Deal."

CHAPTER FORTY-SEVEN

"KATIE-LOVE, YOU BETTER GET up. Your mother is coming to visit."

The familiar lilting voice made Katie smile even before she opened her eyes.

"How do you know these things? You must have some sort of pipeline to unlimited knowledge. Maybe you can tell me about chaos theory or the nature of God or something."

Rolling onto her back, she saw the sky outside her window was gray, overhung with low clouds. Katie tended to sleep late when the sun wasn't shining through to wake her.

She squinted at the figure hovering near the end of the bed. "Is something wrong?"

A moment's fear jolted her upright before she saw Hannah smile. Katie relaxed; Hannah wouldn't smile if someone was in trouble—or would she?

"No. I'm here because..." The voice faded, but the ghostly figure remained.

Katie experienced a flash of guilt and didn't know what to say. She owed Hannah so much, but how do you repay a ghost? It wasn't like she could go out and get her a card or candy to say thank you.

"I wasn't sure I would see you again. I assumed you'd be... home." She knew it was lame, but she wasn't sure if she should say "heaven" or "other world" or anything at all.

"I thought I'd be moving on as well," Hannah said, her voice coming through again. "But apparently, it's not my time."

Katie's guilt grew. It was her fault Hannah couldn't move on and be with her own husband and children. Obviously, Katie needed a lot of protecting, and while it was wonderful to have a spirit to guide and watch over her, she was dismayed that it came at an emotional cost to Hannah. The job of watching over the Hollister family had to be tiring.

"Hannah, I'm so sorry. I can say a prayer or something, ask for you to go home…"

Hannah smiled. "It's fine, dear. I'm exactly where I'm supposed to be, and I don't need to know when I'll leave. It would be difficult to exist at all if we always knew what was going to happen next, don't you think? I'm sure I'll go home when it's time."

Putting a pillow in her lap, Katie leaned forward. "I went to my meeting last night."

"I hope you're planning to go every night," Hannah said. Her abrupt words were softened by her kind tone, words that Katie already knew but still needed to hear.

"It's hard, you know? It's been a few weeks, and I'm already catching myself thinking, 'Oh, I don't need to go today—I went yesterday, I'll be fine,' but it doesn't work like that."

No, that would be too easy. Katie knew from talking with others that complacency could kill her. She'd heard stories of people who started going to Alcoholics Anonymous and decided they could do it on their own, only to get caught back into a life of drinking and pain. The one phrase she heard from her sponsor every day was, "stay sober and go to meetings." So far, she'd been able to do that for an entire three weeks. Like Roland suggested, she was taking things one day at a time, including her relationship with him.

"I see that you and Roland went out again last night," Hannah said.

Katie swung her legs out of bed and pulled a bathrobe around her. A slight chill was settling in the air, and the morning temperatures had been dipping lower. "We're just friends."

"Be careful, Katie. Don't let yourself get distracted from what's important."

Katie knew Hannah meant well, but she couldn't help feeling a surge of annoyance at the advice. One mother was enough.

Then again, if Selena, her sponsor from AA, knew what she was thinking, she'd probably tell Katie not to get so cocky about her recovery that she couldn't hear truth when it was spoken. The whole concept of having a sponsor was still somewhat bizarre to Katie. This was a woman who acted like a cross between a friend, mother, and counselor. The premise of the Alcoholics Anonymous group she went to was that each person, once they had made some progress in the program, helped others by 'sponsoring' them. Being a sponsor was a big deal, it meant that you were available to people 24/7, on call should any of your sponsees need help. Having another alcoholic to talk with was a key foundation to the program, and the general consensus was that it helped everyone to be able to talk freely with each other.

After her second meeting, Katie had been urged to seek sponsorship immediately. As others told her, this was vital to the success of staying sober, as her sponsor would assume continuing responsibility for helping her live a life without alcohol.

The woman Katie asked to be her sponsor was an older woman who resembled an aging hippie, with long gray hair falling in a braid down her back. Selena had ten years of sobriety and exuded an air of peace and warmth. Katie was drawn to her immediately, and at her third meeting asked Selena to be her sponsor.

So far it was going well, but some days were easier than others. *That's the nature of recovery. There are layers of emotions and pain riding through my life. I'm just grateful to have gotten this far.*

The ghost followed Katie down the stairs and into the kitchen, watching as Katie measured coffee into the automatic coffeemaker. Katie's silence stretched across the room.

"Katie-love, you know how easy it would be to wrap yourself up in a relationship and ignore the real work you have to do. If you don't take care of yourself—"

"You're right," Katie admitted. "I was just thinking about all of it. I've been thinking a lot lately about reality and illusion and what that's meant in my life."

"You mean the reality of having your dead relatives telling you what to do?"

Katie laughed. "That's part of it. But there's more. I've been thinking about the illusion that I've lived with all these years, that I'm less of a person because of what happened, that the grief I've lived with is who I am instead of something I experienced."

This was a topic she'd thought about for the past few weeks and had discussed with her new friends at Alcoholics Anonymous meetings. The subject also came up during late night phone calls with Roland. For years, Katie had believed that there was something wrong with her and she wasn't as good, smart, or worthy as anyone else. This idea that she was somehow less of a person fed her alcoholism, creating a cycle she was just beginning to break away from.

Some days were easier than others.

"I'm working on trying to understand how my beliefs in illusions have hurt me, like my belief that I don't deserve anything good has created a reality where good things can't happen to me," Katie said.

Hannah gave her great-granddaughter a ghostly smile. "Sounds like you've got some serious thinking to do. Just keep at it, and keep talking to people about your drinking. I'm on your side, Katie-love. Always have been."

"I wish I could hug you, Hannah."

"Not to worry, I can feel your love easily enough."

"Now what? You're still here, so does that mean that we have more killers headed our way?" Katie was only half-joking, as a jolt of fear snaked down her spine.

"I don't know, my dear, but if I were a betting sort of woman, I might lay odds on this family needing me once or twice more. I know I'm not done yet, so I'll be around until I'm called home."

"What do you think's going to happen?" Katie asked.

"I'm afraid I can't say, Katie-love, but don't worry about it. I'm sure whatever happens, you'll be just fine."

Katie sighed. If there was one thing she was learning from her friends at AA, it was that she couldn't control everything. Heck, she couldn't really control anything except maybe her own self. There was no point in obsessing about things that might or might not happen, despite her tendency to want to do so. For now, she'd focus on her recovery and her own one day at a time. And perhaps someday, in the distant future, she'd find her way into that place of healing inside herself, the place where her soul lodged, endless and whole.

For now, she'd focus on trying not to drink.

CHAPTER FORTY-EIGHT

THE ROOM WAS MOSTLY DARK, except for the weak light that sometimes struggled its way through the window set high on the wall. Even at that height, the window had bars, as if he'd turn into an insect and crawl his way up and through the opening.

Frankly, he didn't have the time for that sort of thing, nor did he have the energy. Cleve was a very busy man.

The sound of someone screaming echoed down the halls and mingled with laughter. The inmate population in here was crazy, legally and medically. This was the place they'd sent him to determine if he was fit for trial, to figure out if he was what they called "competent."

He wasn't crazy, but there was no way he could tell them that. He was just as normal as the rest of them in here, the people locked in the confines of their minds. The way he saw it, everyone around him had just taken a wrong turn in their consciousness and had a little trouble setting themselves straight again.

Or maybe, like him, they were fighting for their soul.

Cleve knew the moment Titus left it would create a hole in his being, tearing apart his consciousness and shredding whatever was left of him. Because of Titus, he had been able to grow, both physically and spiritually, but now Titus couldn't leave until Cleve figured out a way to survive without him.

Like a fabric made from more than one fiber, once Titus left his body, he would become a shell of what he used to be, torn and ragged. It was like taking the cotton out of a weave of cotton and linen; it wouldn't work. Once something was woven together, it usually couldn't be undone. Not without serious damage.

Besides, there was no way he was going to shoulder the entire blame for all this. Titus thought he'd be able to sneak away and avoid serving time in prison—Cleve wasn't going to let that happen.

When Titus had taken over his mind and body, Cleve thought he was helpless to do anything about it. Pushed into the recesses of his own mind, he watched with a combination of fascination and fear as Titus set about destroying Katie Hollister in the church. It wasn't until he was outside and standing in front of the police that Cleve realized what was going to happen.

Titus would go away, and Cleve would go to jail and face execution. Not only that, Cleve would never be whole again.

The voice that had been with him his entire life, his friend, guide, and mentor, was leaving. In desperation, Cleve had tried to lock his mind to hold onto Titus. Using every bit of willpower and imagination he had, he imagined a gate of reinforced steel wrapping around the edges of his consciousness that kept Titus secure.

Whether it was determination, imagination, or magic, Cleve never knew, but he was somehow able to hold the spirit of Titus Foote within his own body.

Every day, Cleve sat in his cell, focused on reinforcing the barriers that held Titus in place. Every day, he imagined putting more steel girders in his head, with heavier locks and keys that didn't exist. When he finished, he rested, only to begin again the following day.

Maintaining a prison was hard work.

Titus tried to get Cleve to let go, to set Titus free.

You can't keep me here forever, boy. You've got to let me go sooner or later.

I don't want you to leave yet. We have more work to do.

No, our work is finished. I'm tired; it's time to let go.

Why, so I can sit in a jail cell and rot away the rest of my life?

That won't happen, boy.

How do you know?

But it didn't matter how Titus knew—Cleve had a feeling what Titus said was true. He wasn't destined to be locked up forever, and sooner or later his time for freedom would come.

In the meantime, Cleve would keep his old friend with him by reinforcing the barriers that held him every day. He would do this until he knew what the rest of his soul's purpose was, until Cleve could continue to do the work he was meant to do.

Cleve looked forward to that, to a future that would surely come.

AUTHOR'S NOTE

Watertown, Connecticut is a small, peaceful town located in the western portion of the state, approximately 97 miles from New York City, with a population of around 22,000 people. Incorporated in 1780, Watertown had always been a relatively low-crime area. The spring of 1861 brought Watertown's second murder, that of farmer Titus Foote. It was believed his housekeeper, a young Irish immigrant, murdered him with an axe. Although she served some jail time, she was released rather quickly and disappeared after that.

This story is intriguing on many levels, which is why I decided to write about it. *Revenge of the Past* is a completely fictionalized account of what could have happened, as we have no way of knowing what truly did happen.

You can find more information on the history of Watertown or the story of the Titus Foote murder in the book *Watertown, CT, Images of America* by Florence T. Crowell.

ACKNOWLEDGEMENTS

Books are not written by one person alone, as there are many others that offer information, support, and love. In saying that, I would like to express my most sincere thanks to the following people:

Darlene DeRosa, Silvana LaPorta Moffa, Gail Murphy, Patty Smith, Cindy Wilson, Zita Fisher, Kathy Fisher, and Carrie Pagels, my friends and support system. I am so blessed and lucky to have friends that have been with me through the years, and that will always be there when I need them, especially when I call and ask if my ideas are crazy.

The York-Poquoson Sheriff's Office instructors for the Rape Aggression Defense RAD program, Sgt. Reginald Simms, Sgt. Elizabeth Simmons, Captain James Richardson, Deputy Mike Russell, and Deputy Shawn Kekoa-Dearhart. Your patience with my questions is unparalleled, and I thank you for allowing me to constantly pester you. The RAD program is a genuine asset to the community, and I strongly encourage all women to check with their local law enforcement to see if it is offered.

Captain Paul Long of the York County Department of Fire and Life Safety, for information about fires and procedures. You are a very patient and knowledgeable man, and any mistakes related to fires and firefighting in this book are entirely my own.

Mr. Terry T. Dillon, for sharing your considerable wealth of knowledge on fires and investigative techniques. Thank you for letting me simply call and ask the really gruesome questions.

Detective Mark Raimo of the Watertown Police Department, thank you for answering my local law enforcement questions.

Lt. Dennis Ivey of the York-Poquoson Sheriff's Office, for allowing me to ask questions about multi-jurisdictional investigations. Your insight was incredibly helpful.

Rev. Carleton Bakkum, for allowing me to pester him with the 'what-if' questions about Grace Church.

Steve Fisher, for reading the first draft and offering insight and comments.

Mr. Hunter, for allowing me to corner him at a birthday party and ask medical opinions. Again, any mistakes in medicine are my own.

My fellow writers at the James-York critique group, as well as Chesapeake Bay Writers, for their support and encouragement.

A big, huge thank you to Florence Crowell and her son, Charles Crowell, for their Facebook posts on Watertown History. If you haven't already done so, check out Florence T. Crowell's Historic Watertown Connecticut Photo Gallery on Facebook.

My brother, Louis, for always telling me to write. Thank you for believing in me.

And as always, to my husband and son, I thank you. You are both incredible, special people, and you make my world a brighter place. I love you.

ABOUT THE AUTHOR

Narielle Living is a freelance writer based out of the tidewater area of Virginia. In addition, she is the editor and publisher of *Fiddler Magazine,* editor of the Williamsburg magazine *Next Door Neighbors* and has written hundreds of do-it-yourself articles for online magazines. Her mysteries include *Signs of the South, Revenge of the Past, Madness in Brewster Square, Birding in Brewster Square, Searching in Brewster Square, Christmas in Virginia,* and she co-authored *Chesapeake Bay Karma—The Amulet.* Her fiction also appears in the anthology *Harboring Secrets.* She edits both fiction and non-fiction, and loves helping other writers achieve their goals. Narielle is currently working on the next books in the Brewster Square series as well as other fun writing projects. For information about her books or workshops, visit blue-fortune.com or find her on Facebook, Instagram, and Twitter.